KISSED BY HER

CHELSEA M. CAMERON

Get Free Books and Stories!

Tropetastic romance with a twist, Happily Ever Afters guaranteed! You can expect humor and heart in every Chelsea M. Cameron romance.

Get access to a free book, free stories, and free bonus chapters! Join Chelsea's Newsletter to get a bonus story about Layne and Honor, receive a free ebook, get access to future exclusive bonus material, news, and discounts.

And now, back to Kissed By Her…

About Kissed By Her

I was so looking forward to this summer. My job as a nanny for eleven-year-old twins means never a dull moment, and I'm excited about hanging out with my best friend, Joy, and reading all the books we can get our hands on next to my employer's fabulous pool.

Then my boss goes and hires a new assistant who is clearly gunning to be his second wife. Honor Conroy could not be more obvious in her motives and I can't understand how he doesn't see it.

She keeps getting under my skin, and even the twins are pulling pranks to try and get her out of their lives. I deny any involvement when their father finds out about their hijinks.

Then Honor decides to invade my book club—my sanctuary. I've had it, so I decide to confront her and, somehow, in the heat of the moment, her lips end up on mine in the fiercest kiss I've ever had in my life.

Turns out the gold-digger I imagined isn't the real Honor, and my heart may never recover from finding out who she really is under that ice-queen facade.

Chapter One

"She's here," my best friend Joy whispered in my ear as I browsed the shelves of Mainely Books, my favorite place in the entire world.

Of course, she was.

No matter where I went, I couldn't escape Honor Conroy. Not only was she invading the sanctity of my bookstore, she'd also invaded my workplace, as well.

"Do you want me to go drop a book on her head? Or maybe throw one of the fake spiders at her?" Joy asked.

"No, I don't want you to get fired," I said. Working as a bookseller was Joy's full-time gig and I didn't want her to jeopardize that.

"Kendra will think it's funny," Joy said, speaking of her boss, who was actually younger than me. She'd opened the bookstore early this year after getting a massive inheritance from her grandmother. Wish I'd had a rich grandmother.

"The best way to deal with Honor is to ignore her," I said. Not easy to do.

The day we'd first met, we'd had an interaction that was… charged, for lack of a better word. Ever since then, she'd been under my skin. Things got worse when she had started chasing my boss, a divorced father of two who was rich as fuck. That had sunk her even lower in my opinion.

"If you say so," Joy said, leaving me to go ring up a customer. I continued my exploration of the romance shelves, looking for something new. Joy always put things aside for me she knew I'd like, but I still found a gem on the shelves sometimes. I loved the thrill of the hunt for just the right book.

I skipped over the signed Skylar Alyssa sapphic romances because I'd already read the ones that were out. Twice. I closed my eyes and ran my fingers along the shelves and then stopped when it felt right.

Opening my eyes, I pulled the book down from the shelf. Well now. Judging from the cover, it was a romance between a human and a sexy alien woman. Score. This wasn't one I'd read before. I hadn't read a sci-fi book in a while and for some reason, this called to me. Holding the book to my chest, I skipped up to the counter and slapped it down so Joy could check me out.

"Interesting," Joy said. "I haven't read that one. You absolutely have to tell me how it is."

"You know I will," I said as Joy and I chatted while she finished the sale and added a bookmark and receipt to the inside cover of the book.

I felt someone standing behind me and I could feel the irritation radiating off them. Without even turning around, I knew who it was. I swore I could smell her expensive perfume. Or maybe it was her leather bag that cost more than my car. The special bag you had to make an appointment to even get into the store to look at. What utter bullshit.

Her impatience made me want to talk to Joy for a thousand years, like when someone honked at you to pull out of the parking spot.

Joy gave me a look finally and I turned around to stare into a pair of designer sunglasses. Her perfectly highlighted blonde hair was pulled back, showcasing her high cheekbones and plump lips. She might only be twenty-four, but I wondered if she'd had work done. Faces like that just didn't happen in nature without a little help from science.

"Excuse me," she said. "I'm in a hurry." Her voice was ice cold.

"In a hurry to go sit by the pool in a bikini and hope that Mark notices you?" I asked, keeping my voice sickly sweet.

I couldn't see her eyes, but I imagined that they narrowed behind her sunglasses. Her delicate nostrils flared, just the tiniest bit, which was the only outward sign that I had pushed her buttons.

Pushing Honor's buttons was one of my favorite hobbies. Hey, there wasn't a whole lot to do in Arrowbridge, Maine, that didn't involve getting wasted with your friends for the millionth time or setting things on fire in an abandoned field.

Honor stood there, not saying a word. She knew by now that I disliked silence and would do almost anything to fill it.

She scored a point when I decided to bail first, saying goodbye to Joy over my shoulder.

"See you later, Honor," I said, keeping my tone cheerful.

I watched her flinch and laughed as I pushed through the door of the bookshop.

ELEVEN-YEAR-OLD GIRLS ARE children who think they're adults. The two I was in charge of were giving me a headache.

"What did your dad say?" I asked the girls standing in front of me. Their brown eyes blinked in unison.

"We haven't asked him yet," Riley said, twisting her fingers together. I'd been taking care of the girls since they were babies, so I could always tell them apart, even if they dressed identically, which they never did.

"What do you think he's going to say?" I asked Zoey. Today she'd wanted to be different than Riley, so I'd braided her auburn hair back from her face and left Riley's in a ponytail.

Riley and Zoey shared what I called a "twin look."

"Yeah, that's what I thought. Now, go do your homework," I said, pointing up the stairs.

They both groaned. I gently tugged on Riley's ponytail.

"If you do your homework, maybe I'll make you some brownie sundaes," I said. Being a nanny for eleven years meant I wasn't above bribery to get desired results.

The twin's faces lit up at the same time and they dashed up the stairs as I laughed.

Those girls.

I walked back into the massive kitchen and started cleaning up from dinner. In addition to my nanny duties, I also helped clean and manage the large home. Mark Jewel traveled a lot for his work as a business consultant, so on his weeks with the kids, I was the stability in their life. Their mom, Sadie, also lived in Arrowbridge in another nice home and shared custody with Mark, and I would go back and forth with them to each house. It might be confusing to others, but over the years we'd honed our system.

By the time I finished in the kitchen and walked around the rest of the house to clean things up for the night, I was exhausted. In another week, the girls would be out of school and I'd have them with me full time. I was prepared with activities for both inside the house and outside. When they were little, it was so much easier to throw water wings on them and toss them in the pool all day or set up a sprinkler for them to run through. Now our summers were more labor intensive for me. Mark had given me raises as the girls had gotten older, though, so I wasn't complaining.

It was almost time for me to be off the clock, and I'd head across the property to the guest house, where I'd lived these past eleven years.

In the not-so-distant future, the girls were going to be old enough that they could watch themselves most of the time, and I was going to be out of a job. I tried not to think about it, because if I did, I'd have a massive fucking breakdown about my complete lack of a career backup plan.

The girls did their homework, which wasn't much considering it was almost the end of the school year, and then I treated them to brownie sundaes before shooing them into the shower before bed.

I walked down to Mark's office and knocked on the door. There was no answer, but I pushed it open anyway. If he was on a call, then I would just come back later.

Mark wasn't in his office, but Honor was, looking very cozy at his desk, sitting in his chair. She had her own freaking desk and chair, but she just had to sit in his. Gross.

I rolled my eyes.

"Where is he?" I asked.

"Bathroom," she said, without looking up from the computer.

"Can you tell him I'm heading out for the night?" I asked her.

Honor ignored me and squinted just barely at the screen. I had to admit, it was kind of cute seeing someone who looked like her squinting. Maybe she needed glasses. I bet she'd be too vain to wear them, but there were always contacts.

"Hello? Did you hear me?" I asked, waving my arms.

"What?" Honor asked, her voice snapping.

Mark came up behind me, saving me from having to speak any more to Honor.

"Heading out?" he asked, sliding around me and into the office.

"Yeah, the girls are upstairs, homework is done for the night, and they've had ice cream," I said.

Mark rolled his eyes. "Thanks for that."

"Hey, I wouldn't be able to feed it to them if you didn't pay for it," I pointed out.

Mark smiled. He was in his late-thirties and incredibly handsome. If I had any attraction to men at all, I probably would have fallen in love with him years ago. That man was swoon-worthy in every sense of the word.

"Yes, but if I didn't buy ice cream for them, I would never hear the end of it," he said, and we both laughed.

"Good night," he said, leaning over Honor's shoulder to look at something on the screen.

"Good night," I said, waving.

Honor never acknowledged me.

Bitch.

Chapter Two

THERE WERE many perks to my job, and living in the guest house was a huge one. Not only was it larger than anything I could have afforded on my own, it was impeccably decorated. When the girls were younger I'd had my own room in the main house, but once Mark had been sure they weren't going to drown in the toilet if they went to the bathroom in the middle of the night by themselves, he handed me the keys and said it was all mine. Even hired a fancy decorator to make it beautiful and asked my opinion on some of the furniture.

I luxuriated under the rainfall showerhead before stepping out of the enormous shower and sitting down on the bathroom bench to moisturize and then brush the tangles out of my light-brown hair. I'd gotten it highlighted in preparation for the summer and even though I couldn't tan to save my life, I at least wanted my hair to look like I'd spent some time in the sun.

My phone buzzed with a message from Joy. She and Sydney, my other best friend, shared an apartment in downtown Arrowbridge, but they still texted each other when they were sitting in the same room.

Sydney was always creating her own memes and they were always really silly, but they never failed to make me laugh.

This one was of her cat, Clementine, passed out on her back with her tongue out and the caption "me when someone cancels plans."

Excuse me, you don't like hanging out with us? I sent.

I don't like hanging out with other people. You don't count in this scenario she responded.

Good, because I was about to be upset Joy said.

The three of us had been tight for at least five years now. Sydney grew up in Arrowbridge and came back after college to manage her mother's pottery studio, Rocky Lake Pottery. Unfortunately, Sydney hadn't inherited her mother's gift for throwing pottery, but she could do everything else when it came to running a business. Joy came here six years ago for an ex and had ended up falling in love with the little town and stayed. She now worked at Mainely Books and helped feed my reading habit.

They'd been by my side through so many things, including the death of my grandfather, my anxiety about my job, and all the other ups and downs of life. Joy and Sydney were more than ride-or-die. Apart from my brother Liam, the twins, Mark, and Sadie, they were my favorite people.

I threw my pajamas on and flopped on my huge bed. Mark had said it was absolutely fine to order a California King, so I had. I was trying to enjoy it because I didn't think I'd be able to afford a place that would be big enough for a bed this size.

My days as Mary Poppins were numbered, and trying not to completely flip out about it was a daily battle.

I grabbed a pillow to scream into for a few seconds before grabbing my journal and writing down a few things I was grateful for today. Joy had gotten me into the practice, and it was nice at the end of the day to remember that I did have a good life. People who loved me. An amazing job that I adored doing every day. Thousands of books at my fingertips on my ereader. Cake.

Maybe I should start a journal for all my annoyances, but number one on that list would probably always be Honor. She was a daily thorn in my side, and I couldn't wait for her to fuck something up so Mark would fire her.

Worst case scenario was she'd finally convince him to marry her and then I'd be stuck with her as my boss and that would ruin everything.

Mark had dated here and there over the years, but never seriously. He had a rule about not introducing anyone to the girls until they were serious, and he'd never gotten that far. Sadie was notorious for her bad dating luck that it was almost a joke at this point.

It was obvious to anyone that Mark was still in love with his ex-wife and someday, somehow, my romance-loving heart knew that they were going to find their way back to each other.

That would also conveniently solve my Honor problem.

Obviously, I would never interfere in my employer's love life, but it was so, so tempting.

I went out to the kitchen to make a cup of chamomile tea to help me sleep and glanced over at the main house and saw that Honor's car was gone. Good. One of these days I was afraid she was just going to show up and move all her shit in and declare herself Mark's wife and he'd be too much of a nice guy to throw her out once she got her claws into him.

Mark was surprisingly dense when it came to women coming after him. Honor wasn't the first, and she wouldn't be the last, either.

I rolled my eyes as I poured hot water into my cup, adding some local wildflower honey for sweetness.

I drank my tea in bed with my current read, a sapphic romance set at a boarding school with one of the sexiest love interests I'd read in a long time. Joy had recommended it to me, and I was absolutely floored at how good the writing was. In spite of the calming tea, I ended up staying up way too late with the book and only stopped reading when I dropped my ereader on my face because my hand went numb.

Time for bed.

"YOU READY FOR ICE CREAM?" I asked when I picked up the twins on their last day of school.

They hopped in the backseat of my car with their bags after long drawn-out goodbyes with their friends they were literally going to see this weekend.

Mark paid me extra for sleepover chaperoning and honestly, I had a great time and didn't mind doing it that much. This weekend we were having a pool party and movie night. Riley and Zoey had gotten a huge inflatable projector screen for their last birthday from both their parents, and we'd put it to good use many times.

The girls and I went to the local ice cream stand in town, which was packed. Everyone else had the same idea as we did, and the three of us got in line to wait to order cones.

"What are you getting, Zo-go?" I asked, stroking her braid. Both girls had the most beautiful hair, so I had hours and hours of braiding practice under my belt by this point.

"Vanilla soft serve in a waffle cone," Zoey said.

"You always get the same thing," Riley said. "I'm getting peanut butter cup with rainbow sprinkles and marshmallow and caramel and cherries."

Zoey made a face. "Gross."

For as alike as the girls looked, their tastes were night and day.

"What are you going to get?" Riley asked me.

"I'm not sure yet," I said. I had a few favorites and it was all about figuring out what I was in the mood for.

The girls chatted with the people in line, and I ended up not having a second to think as more and more people got in line.

Then it was my turn and the frazzled teenager at the window was asking me what I wanted.

I ended up with a milkshake because it was easier to drink while I drove.

As soon as they got their ice cream, the twins abandoned me to go sit with their friends and I chatted with some of the other parents who had also been abandoned by their kids.

By the time I was able to drag the girls away, it was nearly time for dinner.

"Come on, you're going to see everyone tomorrow," I said as they whined and I handed them wipes for their hands before they got in the car.

The complaining continued until we got back to the house.

"Okay, backpacks upstairs, and pick out nice outfits. Your dad is taking us out to dinner." Every year, Mark and Sadie switched off who took the kids out for a celebratory dinner at the end of the school year. They aced co-parenting in a way I'd never seen before.

More grumbling as they took their things upstairs and I walked around the house, picking things up here and there. I also double-checked that I had everything for the party. Food, drinks, extra towels, blankets, pillows, the works. There were enough rooms for all the girls coming to sleep in beds, but they were all still young enough that sleeping in a pile in the living room had greater appeal.

Plus, the living room was nearer to the kitchen so they could sneak into the fridge for snacks in the middle of the night and I'd pretend not to notice from where I slept in the first-floor guest room. A bunch of tween girls was a lot of things, but subtle and quiet weren't any of them.

I ran the vacuum through the downstairs and cleaned the powder room because I'd forgotten to earlier in the day. I was just tossing the gloves I'd used when I heard someone clearing their throat.

I turned around to see Honor, waiting impatiently.

"Can I help you?" I asked, turning on the sink to wash the smell of the gloves off my hands.

"Just waiting," she said.

"There are like fifteen bathrooms in this house. Go use a different one," I said. There weren't fifteen, there were seven, but seven was still a lot.

Honor huffed as if I'd asked her to go use an outhouse and walked away.

"You want me to wipe your ass too?" I called out.

"What?" Mark stuck his head out of his office.

I put a cheery smile on my face. "Nothing. I'll just make sure the girls are ready for dinner."

I shoved my cleaning supplies in the closet and walked into Mark's office.

"I'm almost ready," he said, his eyes flicking from his computer screen to his phone screen and back.

"Great," I said. "I'm going to change too and then I'll make sure the monsters are dressed appropriately."

Riley liked to experiment with fashion and sometimes her choices weren't right for a semi-nice dinner with one of her parents.

I stopped over at the guest house to throw on a pair of my nicer pants and a button-down shirt.

When I got back, I headed upstairs and had to fight Riley so she wouldn't wear one of her favorite t-shirts that had a farting unicorn on it.

"Can we please not do this now?" I asked. "You can wear it tomorrow. All your friends will love it."

She pouted and stomped her feet, but I got her to put on another shirt (without a farting unicorn) and shoved them downstairs.

Honor was perched on the couch in the family room off the kitchen.

"You still here?" I asked.

She gave me a tight smile but didn't answer.

"Ready to go?" Mark asked as he came down the hall from the master bedroom in a fresh shirt and tie.

"Yup," I said, stealing a glance at Honor, who wasn't moving.

"Look at you two," Mark said, going to the twins and kissing both of them on the head. "My girls are so grown up." They'd gotten their red hair and height from Mark, and their sweet smiles and more of their personalities from Sadie.

They both beamed and gave him hugs. In a few years they would probably hate his guts and not want to be seen with him in public, so I knew he was cherishing these last few times before that happened.

"Oh, Honor is going to join us," Mark said, ushering the girls out to his car.

I turned to look at Honor, who smirked at me with a smile that could only be described as the cat who ate the canary.

I kept all my cursing internal as I smiled back at her and said, "The more the merrier."

SOMEHOW HONOR ENDED up in the front seat and I was in back with the kids. I chatted with them and kept my eye on Honor as we drove outside of Arrowbridge to the twin's favorite restaurant. They got to pick where they went, and every year we ended up at a medium quality chain steakhouse, much to their father's chagrin. Mark was more of a linens and expensive wine list and menu mostly in French kind of person, but he would lower his standards for his kids.

I did have a little bit of satisfaction that Honor was probably going to lose her shit eating at a place like this. She was a fancy pants, through and through. I bet she wouldn't even know what to do in a fast-food drive through.

Mark had reserved us a booth, which was good since the wait would have been awful. I guess every other local family had the same idea of bringing their kids out tonight. Riley and Zoey waved to their friends as I sat down.

Even though I'd tried to maneuver myself in between the twins, I ended up with Zoey on my right and Honor on my left. She made sure to get a seat next to Mark.

I could smell her perfume, which probably cost more per bottle than my car. It's got to be some expensive fancy shit. It's actually lighter than I would have expected. Like…fresh-cut flowers or fresh laundry or something. It wasn't overpowering. I'd just get little whiffs of it every now and then as she moved.

The smell was messing with my brain as I stared at my menu and tried to decide what I wanted.

Much to my surprise, Honor didn't order wine. She got a blended lemonade which was what the girls ended up ordering as well. It was strange to see her getting something like that.

And then she ordered the steak and lobster, the most expensive thing on the menu and I couldn't help but roll my eyes. Of course, she did. Mark was paying and she was going to take advantage.

I got my usual of a cheeseburger topped with onion rings and the bacon cheese fries.

Both girls ordered way more than they could eat, as usual, so I was already calculating how many to-go boxes we'd need to take everything they didn't eat home.

Mark ordered a steak, and you could tell he was not excited about eating it, but he sucked it up.

Our appetizers arrived and I watched as Honor daintily ate chips and spinach artichoke dip, using a spoon to put the dip on her chips. I tried not to stare too much.

Mark asked the twins about their day and what they were doing for their sleepover and I was only half paying attention. Honor hadn't bothered to engage them in conversation at all. She only had eyes and ears for Mark.

"Having fun?" I asked Honor in a low voice.

"Time of my life," she said, spooning a dollop of spinach and artichoke dip onto a chip and then eating it as carefully as possible. I'd never seen anyone do that. It made me want to eat my chips as messily as possible purely for spite.

When our entrées arrived, I kept glancing at Honor as she carefully cut her steak into precise bites. Was she trying to eat, or perform eating in the classiest possible way? Who could tell.

"I would pay good money to see you eat a lobster right out of the shell," I said.

There was no way to eat a lobster daintily when you had to crack it open. I had sliced my hand open on bits of shell more than one time. You got water everywhere and then you had to dig the meat out. That was part of the fun, though. You weren't supposed to look cute eating lobster. It was a meal of delicious carnage.

People like Honor weren't cut out for that kind of thing. She'd probably send the lobster back to the kitchen and make some minimum wage earner crack it and arrange it all pretty on the plate for her.

I shoved my burger in my mouth and made sure the twins ate enough and tried to keep food from staining my shirt at the same time. It was a lot of work while I also watched Honor try to draw Mark into conversation. She kept drifting closer and closer to him, like she was going to crawl into his lap or something.

If I didn't know better, I would have said she was running her foot up and down his leg under the table.

The twins claimed they were "full" after a few bites, but then they begged and pleaded for dessert.

"Didn't you already have ice cream today?" Mark asked, narrowing his eyes.

"Yes," Riley said slowly. "But that was *hours* and *hours* ago. And it's our last day of school."

Mark sighed the sigh of a thousand suffering dads and flagged down a server for a dessert menu.

Not one to ever say no to dessert, I got a slice of coconut cake while the twins ordered the mega chocolate chip cookie skillet, which was large enough to feed a family of eight, but which they devoured themselves.

Honor ordered the flourless chocolate cake with raspberry sauce and ate it with those perfect little bites, not getting anything on her clothes. She patted her mouth with her napkin and didn't even scrape the plate to get the last of the crumbs.

The twins licked their spoons and begged Mark to let them go say hi to their friends. He waved them off and then the server brought us the check.

Honor didn't even try to pay. She left her wallet in her designer purse. Sure, Mark was her employer, but still. This wasn't a working dinner. She'd just invited herself to be part of this family like they were already married. Sinking her hooks deeper and deeper.

Riley and Zoey were still wired from the cookie, so they jabbered all the way back to the house.

"Come on, time for showers and bed," I said, shoving them toward the front door.

Honor lingered behind, like she was going to have a private tête-à-tête with Mark.

"It's getting cold out here," I said loudly, rubbing my arms. It really wasn't, but I wanted to throw a wrench in her plans if I could. It was the least I could do to save Mark from a gold-digger who wanted his money and nothing else.

"Thank you for a lovely evening," Honor said, leaning close to Mark. He was looking at something on my phone and not even paying attention to her. I was a little proud of him.

"Oh, you're welcome. I hope you have some fun plans this weekend," Mark said, glancing up from his phone and then heading toward the front door. "See you on Monday, Honor."

His phone rang and he lifted it to his ear.

Honor opened her mouth to say something to him, but then closed it.

"See you on Monday," I said, making my voice sweet. "You have a fantastic evening."

Her eyes narrowed and I could tell she wanted to curse or flip me off so much, but she just gave me a little wave and headed to her car.

Chapter Three

SADIE CAME over the next morning to help with the sleepover. She'd had to work late the previous evening at her boutique, so she hadn't seen the girls until today.

She also brought even more snacks and drinks than the kids could possibly ever consume, but at least I could take advantage and sneak a few over to the guest house.

"I'm so glad you're here," I said as we worked on getting the trays of food ready for lunch.

"I wouldn't miss it," she said, adding little rolls of turkey and ham and pepperoni to one of the trays so the girls could pick what they wanted and make their own sandwiches.

The twins were already in the pool doing handstands and chicken fighting and making tons of noise while Mark tried to make sure no one drowned and that they all applied sunscreen periodically.

"How's everything?" I asked her.

"Another tragic date in the books," she said, rolling her eyes. She looked so much like the twins it was unnerving sometimes. I would see one or both of them make an expression or say something a certain way that was a carbon copy of their mother.

"Oh, do tell," I said, popping a strawberry slice into my mouth.

Sadie sighed and told me how the guy she'd been talking to for weeks didn't seem to remember their conversations, and definitely thought she was someone else. He'd even gotten her name wrong.

"And then he claimed his wallet was stolen, so I didn't even get a free dinner out of it. Can you believe that?" Sadie asked.

"You are just cursed when it comes to online dating, I swear."

"Mom? Layne?" Riley called, sticking her head through the glass door that separated the house from the backyard with the pool.

"We're coming," I yelled back and picked up one of the trays. Sadie grabbed two others and followed me to feed the monsters.

I ONLY ENDED up having to break up one fight before dinner, and only a few tears were shed. When you were a tween, everything felt like too much, and I could remember that feeling well, so I gave as much grace as I could.

Honestly, I'd wanted to confiscate their phones when they arrived, since so much of their drama took place online and was fueled by the ability to post fast and think later.

The most I could do was monitor them as much as possible. Eleven-year-olds weren't as sneaky as they thought they were, and when things got quiet, that was usually a sign something was going down.

Mark spent a lot of his afternoon blowing up floats so the

girls could stay in the pool for their movie. I ran out to get the pizza and when I came back Sadie was on her way out.

She laughed as she accepted wet hugs from her girls and kissed them on their chlorine-scented heads.

"I'll see you on Monday," she said.

I also watched Mark walk her out and damn, there was some tension there.

I was smiling to myself at their chemistry when a familiar car pulled into the back of the house right next to Mark's SUV.

"Shit," I said under my breath. Couldn't she leave us alone?

Honor got out of her car, her blonde hair falling perfectly on her shoulders in styled waves. She looked like she traveled everywhere with a glam squad. She'd probably put that in her wedding vows if she could. In sickness and in glam…

I was surprised to see her wearing a flowing black dress instead of her usual work attire.

She was dressed for an evening near the pool.

Sadie drove off and Honor approached Mark, a smile on her face. He nodded and jogged back to the house.

Had she come over here dressed like that, pretending she needed some paperwork, hoping that Mark would just invite her to stay?

She had guts, I'd give her that.

If only Mark could see what the hell she was doing.

He came back out and handed her a folder, which she took from his hand.

I watched as he gestured toward the party and she nodded and followed him toward the pool.

"What are we looking at?" Riley said, pushing at my arm. Zoey was on my other side.

"Nothing," I said.

"She's here now, too?" Riley asked. "She was at dinner last night."

"I don't like her," Zoey said. I wanted to hug both of them.

"Now girls, if we don't have anything nice to say, don't say anything at all," I said, trying to be a good nanny.

"She's mean and she's here all the time," Riley said.

None of these were lies, but I zipped my lips and shoved them back toward the pool.

"Go, the pizza is getting cold."

They skipped off to join their friends, who had put all the floats together to form a mega float and had blankets and towels to make beds.

Mark put the movie on, and I went around to make sure everyone had what they needed.

Honor had taken one of the deck chairs and appeared to be trying to draw Mark into conversation, but he got a phone call and went back inside to take it.

"Crashing the twin's dinner and now their party? Could you be any more transparent?" I asked, sliding into the seat next to her.

She sipped at a glass of lemonade and turned her eyes to the movie screen. I knew she wasn't watching this.

"I had to pick something up from Mark and he invited me to stay," she said.

"Right, sure," I said, getting up and snagging a few pieces of semi-cold pizza and throwing them on a plate. I'd been so busy with the party I'd barely eaten all day and I was famished.

"You know, Mark is absolutely and completely in love with Sadie," I said, pulling a pepperoni off the pizza and munching on it before folding the slice in half and taking a huge bite.

I hoped it made Honor uncomfortable.

"I don't know why you're telling me this," she said, her voice cool.

"Whatever. You didn't come here for the kids or the movie

or the pizza, so that must mean you're here for Mark. I know he doesn't see it, but I do. I've got my eyes on you."

I took two fingers, pointed at my eyes and then pointed at her to show I was watching.

Honor rolled her eyes. "You're a very dramatic person."

"A dramatic person that sees through your little plan."

I munched on my pizza and she flinched. Ha.

"Want some pizza? I'll share." I held out my half-eaten slice.

"No, thank you," Honor said, not taking her eyes off the screen.

"You're no fun," I said just as Mark came back.

"Are you hungry? We've got tons of pizza," he said to Honor.

She beamed up at him and I almost choked on another bite. "I'd love some, thank you."

Mark got her a piece as well as some napkins. She took it from him with a grateful smile.

"Why don't you sit down? You look like you've been running around all day," she said, and I was shocked she didn't stroke his arm and bat her eyelashes as she did it.

"Sit down and I'll grab you a drink," Honor said, setting the plate down and getting up in one smooth motion. Her dress was deceptively loose, but when she moved, it clung to her every curve. I would say this for Honor, she had an incredible body. Shocking that she hadn't pulled off the dress and revealed a string bikini that would show even more of her assets.

Mark sat down in the chair on the other side of Honor with a heavy sigh.

"Tired yet?" I asked him and he huffed out a laugh. Honor came back with more pizza and a beer that she must have gotten from the kitchen. Awfully comfortable in his house already.

"Here you go," Honor said with a sultry voice as she slunk down in her chair again.

"I thought when they started sleeping through the night that things would calm down, but it seems like the parenting just never ends."

As if he'd spoken it into existence, Zoey got out of the pool too fast and took a tumble, scraping her knee. We kept a first aid kit with the pool supplies and I went to grab it as Mark assessed the damage and patched her up.

After the initial shock of the fall wore off, Zoey wanted to get away from her dad and back to her friends as quickly as possible.

"Go on," he said, laughing and touching her shoulder. "And remember not to run."

She nodded and was back crashing on the floats with her friends again.

"It never ends," I said, packing up the first aid kit again.

"Never," Mark said.

I glanced over to the chair where Honor was sitting, but she was gone. Maybe she ran away. One could dream.

Mark and I sat back down and worked on our pizza.

"Where's Honor?" I asked when she'd been gone for at least ten minutes.

Mark looked up as if he'd just remembered she exited. "I'm not sure. Is she in the house?"

"I don't know," I said. Why was he asking me? I wasn't her keeper. He was supposed to be hers, someday.

"Can you go see if she's inside? I'll stay out here."

Why couldn't he go? I opened my mouth to argue, but then I shut it.

"Sure," I said, pretending it was fine.

I got up and shoved another piece of pizza in my mouth, walking as I chewed.

The house was much quieter than it would be when the

girls finished the movie and came back inside. If they had their way, the twins would have convinced their dad to get a massive pool cover they could sleep on. He and their mother had both vetoed that idea, mostly for safety reasons.

I wandered through the kitchen and then hit the powder room. The door was closed, so I knocked.

"Hey, Honor? Are you okay?" I hated that my voice actually sounded concerned. I didn't care if she was puking her guts out.

There was a beat of silence. "I'm fine." Her voice was tight.

"Okay, just checking. Mark asked me to."

"He did?" Her voice changed.

"Remember to wash your hands when you're done," I said and then left before she could make a biting response.

The credits were rolling on the movie and the girls were ready for something sweet, so I set up the sundae station so everyone could have what they wanted.

I completely forgot about Honor, but then I glanced out to see Mark cleaning up and saw her talking to him, one hand twirling some of her hair.

Please. That was one of the oldest tricks in the book. I pictured Honor reading a "How to Seduce a Rich Man" book and practicing her hair twirling and smiling in a mirror.

Once the girls were full of ice cream, I sent some of them off to wash the chlorine out of their hair and get their pajamas on.

Mark came back in and helped me move the family room furniture to set everything out for the girls to sleep.

"Honor gone?" I asked.

"Yeah, she headed home," he said as we pushed one of the couches out of the way.

"Seems strange for her to come over here for a file on a Saturday. I thought you scanned everything?" Mark's business was digital. They had paper copies of some things, but everything else was online.

"We have a deal going through on Monday and she just wanted to make sure she had a backup," he said. I stared at him for a second.

How could a grown man with a successful business be this clueless?

I was just about to say something about Honor when Riley and Zoey bounced down the stairs from their showers and asked me if I could braid their hair.

"Absolutely my loves. Sit down at Layne's Salon," I said. They fought over who got to go first, but Zoey won Rock, Paper, Scissors, so she sat down on the floor while I was in a chair behind her.

"I wish my hair was purple," Zoey said with a sigh.

"Ask your parents," I said. I'd witnessed this tactic dozens of times before. They seemed to think if they asked me, I might let them get away with something without checking with their parents first.

"What if they say no?" Zoey asked as I combed through the tangles in her hair. A few of the other girls had returned from their showers and were snuggling into the little nest we'd made.

"I don't think they will," I said. Mark and Sadie were super supportive parents.

"But Riley doesn't want purple hair," Zoey said.

"So? You don't dress alike." Their mom had always hated the assumption that they should dress alike, as if they were one person and not two, so she'd never put them in the same outfit at the same time.

"I know," Zoey said, and then she sighed. Oh, the stress of being eleven.

"I think you'd look awesome with purple hair," I said. "You know what? We could get some temporary color and try it out if you want. I bet your parents would want you to do that before you did anything with bleach. Now, what kind of braid do you want?"

Zoey wanted a Rapunzel braid and Riley asked for bubble braids, and then a line formed, and my fingers started to ache after a while, but I didn't stop until the last girl was satisfied.

"There you go, my lovely," I said, patting the head of the last girl, who'd wanted a braid crown.

Things were winding down, and most of the girls were under the blankets with their phones and whispering to each other and then giggling.

I checked the time and then went to find Mark. He was in his office.

"Hey, I'm going to say goodnight to the girls and head to my room. I'll check on the even hours and you on the odd hours?" I asked. We'd done this routine before. It meant not a lot of sleep for me, but I could take a big, long nap tomorrow. I was already looking forward to it.

Mark nodded and then picked up his phone to send a message. One of these days that man was going to cut back on work, but that wasn't today.

"Okay, time for bed. That doesn't mean you have to go to sleep, but let's keep the volume down. Bathroom is down the hall, and I'm staying in the guest room. If something happens, I do not want you to hesitate to get me. You won't get in trouble, I promise." I made sure to make eye contact with each of them. I would absolutely much rather have them come to me because some girl snuck in booze stolen from her parents and someone was sick than have them hide it from me, and I knew Mark was the same way. Not two minutes after my speech, he came out and gave the same one.

He joined me in the kitchen as I made myself a cup of tea for the long night ahead.

"Was that good? Do you think they got it?" he asked me in

a low voice as one girl was telling a story and the group broke out in giggles. They were so damn cute.

"I think you did a great job," I said, patting his arm. "They're going to be fine. This isn't either of our first rodeo."

"No, but it gets harder as they get older. And then I remember all the stuff I used to do as a kid and think of my girls doing that, and it scares me."

"But look at how you turned out. And you're not alone. They have a wonderful mother leading them, and I'm not scared to lay down the law."

Mark nodded. "You're right. You're right. I'm just stressed with this upcoming deal and all the work that's ahead of me." He rubbed his face and yawned. "I'm going to grab a nap before my first check," he said.

"You got it, boss," I said, and he waved before he headed down the hall to his room.

I took my tea into the guest room and made myself comfortable. I had a book I was going to finish and then had already downloaded the next one in the series, so I barely even had to pause before diving in.

The kids thought they were being quiet, but they kept getting progressively louder as they gained their second wind. They'd probably sleep a few hours max, wake up, and be raring to go for another full day. Oh, to be young again. I was going to need at least two days to recover from this sleepover.

I heard Mark go out for the first check and all the girls pretended to be asleep. It really was cute. The next time I went out, they did the same, but I caught some of them giggling.

The rest of the night passed pretty smoothly, with the exception of one poor girl sleepwalking and getting lost in the kitchen.

Mark helped me with breakfast, and we got everyone fed and back to their parents in one piece.

The twins were ecstatic and even begged Mark to let

everyone stay longer, but their parents had all kinds of plans and the twins were left bereft.

"You're going to see your friends all the time. You have a whole beautiful summer ahead of you," I said. "It's going to be awesome."

They still pouted and fussed until I sent them upstairs to put their bathing suits on so they could chill in the pool while I took a nap.

Mark was making them lunch when I got up and looking pretty tired himself, so I sent him off for his own siesta while I picked up from the chaos of the sleepover. That took most of the day and I had to bribe the girls to help.

"We're tired," Riley whined, and Zoey gave me her best pathetic look.

"Yeah, yeah, you weren't tired when you were staying up all night with your friends. Go deflate the floats and put them in the storage shed," I said, and they did it, but took their sweet time.

The rest of the day was lowkey and I was released from my duties to go back to the guest house.

I'd just woken up from my second nap when I saw I had some missed messages from Joy and Sydney.

Pool free? Joy asked. Mark let me have my friends over to enjoy the pool (within reason) anytime I wanted.

Yeah, kids are gone and it's all cleaned up. Mark ran the pool bot earlier. I sent.

We will be there in a half an hour with dinner. Sydney replied.

I loved my friends.

I hit the shower and put on my one-piece and a pretty dress with a banana leaf print on it.

I stopped over to the house to tell Mark I was having my friends over.

"Can we hang out too?" Riley said, overhearing the conversation.

"Just for a little while, okay?" I said. Joy and Sydney were very accommodating when it came to the twins and they were happy to hang out with my charges when they came over, but they had their limits.

Joy and Sydney arrived in Joy's car since they were coming from the same place.

"Thank god, I'm ready for adult conversation," I said, giving them both hugs and helping them unload stuff from the car. They'd stopped and gotten tacos from a local place, as well as Cokes and churros for dessert with a special caramel sauce that I would inject into my veins if I could.

"You are both my angels and I love you," I said as we set everything up by the pool. "Do you want drinks?"

"Yes, please," Joy said, and Sydney nodded.

I went inside as the twins ran out and attacked Joy and Sydney. I made some quick mojitos and yelled at the twins to come in and help me carry them out.

"Can we have some?" Riley asked.

"Absolutely not, kid. Absolutely not."

Riley rolled her eyes. "Not those. The ones without alcohol in them."

"Still no," I said. "But I can mix you up something fun and put lots of cherries in it."

That seemed to appease them, so I made some Shirley Temples with lime in them and handed those off while Mark called them inside for dinner. He didn't get as much time to cook as he liked, but making Sunday dinner was a ritual for him. Tonight it was pulled pork sandwiches with fresh slaw and creamy curry potato salad. He was putting a plate aside for me to have tomorrow.

"Cheers," I said, and we all tapped our glasses together and lounged on the deck chairs and stuffed our faces with tacos and talked about books and Arrowbridge gossip and nothing at all.

I, of course, had to vent my Honor frustrations. My friends had heard it all before, but they listened to me bitch because they were the two best friends that anyone could have.

"It's just so obvious. I'm considering telling Mark. He doesn't seem to be able to see it," I said, going for my third taco.

"Don't say anything," Joy said, shaking her head and squeezing lime juice onto her taco. "You shouldn't get involved with your boss's love life. That is just a recipe for disaster. Please back me up on this." The last comment was directed at Sydney, who was busy trying to shove an entire taco into her mouth in one go and failing.

"Don't do it," Sydney said and then took a more reasonable bite.

"So, what am I going to do when he shows up and she's wearing a wedding dress and has somehow gotten his signature on a wedding license and is going to marry him at gunpoint?"

Both of them stared at me. "You've really thought about this, haven't you?" Joy said.

"I mean, she's been escalating in the past few weeks. I think she's going to use this summer to try and lock things down."

I shivered, imagining her showing up again and again. Was she going to offer to drive the kids to camp with Mark?

"I'm afraid she's going to kidnap him and take him to Vegas," I said, but they both laughed. "What? These are real concerns."

Joy and Sydney shared a look. "I think you're reading too much into this," Sydney said. "Do you really think Mark is that clueless?"

"I mean, judging on how he's been ignoring her behavior up until now, yes?" I said.

"Maybe he does see it, and he's trying to figure out how to

address it. She's his employee. Things could get weird for him, legally, if he doesn't handle it the right way," Joy said. "Have you ever considered that?"

Honestly, I hadn't. I should have.

"Okay, fine," I said. "It's still shady as fuck."

"Yes, it is," Sydney said. "But it's not your problem to solve, Layne."

I narrowed my eyes. "I know you think I'm going above and beyond my paygrade, but I care about what happens to this family. I love those kids and I won't let some gold-digging hussy become their stepmom."

Joy started laughing. "Did you just call her a hussy?"

"It was a kinder word than what I wanted to call her," I said.

Sydney snorted. "Mark is smart. He'll figure it out."

I sincerely hoped so.

Chapter Four

We hung out until it got late, and I slumped into bed, completely exhausted.

My alarm the next morning came way too early, and I had to make the girls breakfast and supervise them until it was time to go over to their mom's house for the week. I'd be with them during the day, but Sadie got done with work in the early evening so she could be with Riley and Zoey, make them dinner and spend the evenings with them. I took that time to get ahead on cleaning and organizing the house and just doing my own shit.

It would have been ideal, if not for the fact that I had to keep seeing Honor. She kept randomly popping out of Mark's office for whatever reason. I was organizing the fridge and making a list to go shopping for the week when she pushed beside me to get some water from the fridge. She couldn't just fill up her water bottle from the sink like a normal person.

"Excuse me," I said, but she ignored me. "You're a really rude person, you know."

I turned to face her as she filled a glass with water and sipped it.

"You don't know anything about me," she said.

"I know you're trying to be wife number two. It's not going to work," I said.

She drained the rest of her water and set the glass in the sink. "Like I said, you know nothing about me."

Okay, fine. "Let me guess, your rich parents gave you everything, and you probably owned a horse and went to the country club on the weekends. You don't have any student loan debt because your parents paid for you to go to some legacy school where you didn't study because you're one of those people who doesn't have to. The worst thing that's ever happened to you is that your coffee was made with whole milk instead of oak milk. How did I do?"

I didn't know what had come over me. I guess I'd been repressing some shit for a while, and it all came tumbling out.

Honor gave me a bored look. "Are you done? Did that feel good?"

I took a breath. "Yeah, actually it did. What's your response?"

Honor turned to walk away, but then faced me again. "That you have no fucking clue."

I'd never heard her curse before, but the word seemed to come easily to her.

She didn't see me staring after her in shock. Well. I guess Honor had more fire under her chilly exterior than I'd thought. Honestly, I was kind of impressed. Who knew she had that in her?

I grabbed the reusable grocery bags and headed out to the store. As much as I tried to stop thinking about my little encounter with Honor, I couldn't. It kept running through my mind as I tried to remember everything on the grocery list, get it into the bags, get the bags back to the house, and then take the girls to their mom's house before getting back to make dinner for Mark. I had the leftovers from the previous evening for myself.

Liam ended up calling me just as I was finishing heating up my dinner in the guest house.

"Hey, what's up?" I said as I put the phone on speaker so I could rinse my dishes and put them in the dishwasher.

"Not a whole lot. How's life at the mansion?" he asked.

"You know I don't live there, right? I'm in the guest house?" I said, wiping my hands off.

"Classy, classy," he said, but I knew he was joking. Liam and I hadn't grown up with much and we had both worked our asses off to get where we were. He lived a few miles away in Hartford and managed a coffee shop. He'd busted his ass when he graduated high school and had taken community college classes at night to get his Associate's degree in business management and he had his shit together, all in the midst of transitioning. I was so fucking proud of everything he'd done. Now we just had to find him a nice girl to settle down with.

"You been on any dates lately?" I asked.

I could hear him rolling his eyes. "No. I'm busy, Layne. With work, with life. Maybe I'll get a pet or something."

Well, a pet wasn't as great as a girlfriend, but it was something. I worried about him being lonely even though he had a ton of friends. It was my job as his big sister to worry, though.

"You should get something low-maintenance," I said.

"That's a good point, I'll think about it. How's the family?" he asked.

When I'd become part of Mark's family, they'd also scooped up my brother along with me. Mark had given him business advice, written him a letter of recommendation, and included him in any and all holiday plans, since we were basically estranged from our parents.

"The kids are out of school and I'm hoping I can keep

them from killing each other from boredom this summer, and Honor is really going for it with Mark."

Liam laughed. "One of these days she's going to drug him and drag him to Vegas."

"That's what I said!"

We laughed together and I vented about Honor and he vented about work and it was really good to talk to him.

We hung up and I decided to grab a popsicle from the freezer and sit outside for a few minutes looking at the stars.

The lights in the pool made everything look a little eerie, but I liked it.

When the girls were with their mom, I really did miss them. I mean, I was literally going to pick them up tomorrow morning to go to the beach for the day. I was going to be sick of them in no time, but right now, I wished they were begging me to let them stay up later.

I went inside and made some tea and put on a sheet mask while I selected a new book to read. I'd just finished a series, so I was in need of something new.

I was feeling some historical romance, so I selected a book that had been on my TBR for a while, but I'd been saving. Now seemed like a good time to open it up. Plus, the ladies in gowns on the cover were hot.

I settled into bed and went ahead and lost myself in someone else's love story.

~

ON TUESDAY, the girls had their dance class, so I dropped them off and then headed to the bookstore to bug Joy and see if there was anything new. I arrived just in time to see her and Kendra, the owner, along with Kendra's girlfriend, Theo, working on the window display.

I waved to them and then pushed the door open, smiling instantly at the ding of the bell over the door.

I inhaled the scent of the books and closed my eyes for just a moment.

This was my happy place.

"You look like a weirdo when you do that," Joy's voice said behind me.

"Shhh, I'm having a moment."

"Can you have your moment not blocking the front door?" Kendra asked, so I opened my eyes and turned around.

"Re-doing the display?" I asked as Theo wiped sweat from her forehead. I let myself respectfully stare at her arms for a second. Theo made furniture, including all the bookshelves in the shop, and all of the chairs and even the ladders that slid from one shelf to another. Theo was a woman of many talents. And she was hot as fuck. In addition to the arms, she had curly red hair that fell rakishly on her forehead.

"And now you're being a creep," Joy said in my ear.

"Sorry," I said, shaking my head at myself. "I'm back."

"There was something not quite right," Kendra said as she got down from the window. "Now I have to go see it from the front."

Theo had made a giant wooden heart with little shelves on it, where Kendra and Joy had arranged books with different covers to make a rainbow.

Kendra went out and Theo got down and leaned against one of the shelves. I did my best not to ogle her.

"She's been rearranging for hours," Joy said.

"Don't worry. I'll stage an intervention soon," Theo said with a grin.

There was a loud knock at the window and Kendra motioned to Theo.

Theo pushed off the shelf and hopped back up into the window to mess with the books until Kendra was happy.

"They're so cute," I said.

"Jealous?" Joy asked.

"I mean, aren't you?"

Joy went back behind the counter in case a customer came over. "I don't know. I have too much other crap going on. My mom and my sisters are up my ass about dating, though, which makes me want to stay single even more just to annoy them." Joy flipped her dark ponytail over her shoulder. She had the straightest, silkiest hair I'd ever seen, and I was jealous of it all the time.

"For real, if I don't bring a date to my sister's wedding in a few months, I think my mom's going to take matters into her own hands." Joy shuddered and then a customer with a few books came up and I gave her a little wave so I could let her get back to work while I browsed.

The romance section had been updated a little since I'd been here, so I scanned to look for something new.

I was reading the back of one when Joy came back.

"You ready for book club?" she asked.

"Pft, I'm always ready for book club." The book in my hands didn't appeal to me, so I slid it back on the shelf for some other reader.

The first Thursday of every month was my absolute favorite day at my favorite place. Our Mainely Books Club hadn't meant to end up as an all-queer romance club, but every month when we voted on books, we kept ended up voting for queer romances. This month's book was one of my absolute favorite books. I'd already read it three times. I'd even considered buying a silky green dress like the woman wore on the cover, but that might seem like too much. Joy and I had at least agreed to wear green shirts.

"I'm going to need it," I said. "I feel like everything is annoying me lately."

"You need to get laid," Joy said casually, frowning at a book that was in the wrong place.

"Joy!" I said, looking around to make sure no one overheard her. "Don't be so loud about my sex life."

Joy rolled her eyes. "Don't be so dramatic. It's not like you even *have* a sex life right now."

"What the hell!" I smacked her arm and she laughed. "Thanks a lot. I guess I'll ask Sydney to be my best friend now since you don't want to be anymore."

Joy laughed. "I'm sorry, but you know it's true. We gotta find you someone. I just want someone to appreciate how awesome you are."

I made a face. "I'm good."

I liked the idea of dating. Getting pretty and going out to dinner with a hot girl. Flirting. Maybe getting laid. But then my life would change, and I might not get to read as much as I wanted to. I'd have to share my California King. And what if they wanted me to move? What if they got a job in Alaska and I had to decide if I wanted to leave everything behind?

Just considering all that gave me stress hives.

"You know, one of these days love is going to bite you in the ass and you're going to change your tune," Joy said, and then headed back to the counter. I decided not to buy anything and followed her.

"Yeah, I very much doubt that," I said.

∼

I COUNTED DOWN the hours until book club on Thursday night. The twins were being especially ornery for some reason. I was chalking it up to them adjusting to being out of school and not having their normal structure. I had talked with both Mark and Sadie to figure out what we could all do to make sure they didn't spiral into chaos demons. Lots of activities, keeping bedtimes and mornings regular, and making sure they saw their friends. It was a full-time job, and Mark and Sadie paid me good money for it.

By the time I was heading to the bookstore, I was ready to have a few drinks and think about nothing but books for a few hours. Oh, and gush about how much I loved this month's book.

I'd worn my green silk shirt and was feeling pretty fancy.

I pushed through the door and smiled at the people who were already here.

"Look at you, all on theme," Kendra said, doing a little shimmy in her green silk dress. It was short and really pretty. "I tried to get Theo to join me, and all I could get was a green silk tie, but that works. It really works."

She let out a happy little sigh and then Theo walked by. Kendra let out a whistle and Theo glared at her.

"You've got to stop doing that," Theo said. "It's getting out of hand."

Kendra skipped over and gave Theo a kiss on her cheek. "You love my hands. You love what I can do with them."

I looked away, trying not to blush. Kendra and Theo were definitely in love. I'd even caught them about to hook up in the bathroom once. That had been extremely embarrassing for all parties involved.

"I'm going to get a glass of wine," I said loudly, but Kendra and Theo didn't hear me. Theo was now whispering something in Kendra's ear, and she was giggling.

I grabbed onto Joy, who was setting up the drinks table in the back of the store. The other employee, Erin, was setting up chairs (also made by Theo).

"Rosé?" Joy asked me.

"All day," I said, accepting the little plastic cup of wine from her. Kendra had been smart to get a liquor license so she could serve alcohol during book club if she wanted to.

"Thank you, my dear," I said and went to greet some of the other members. Sydney had saved me and Joy a spot.

"I'm loving this," Sydney said, touching the sleeve of my blouse. She'd gone a more subtle route with emerald earrings and necklace, but she still looked amazing. Sydney was gorgeous, and I wasn't just saying that because she was one of my best friends. People on the streets of Arrowbridge literally stopped and stared at her when she walked by. Her hair fell in dark ringlets down her back, and her shape was the most perfect hourglass. Seriously, she should be studied by science.

We were just about ready to start, and I'd gotten up to replenish my plate of snacks when someone else pushed through the door and walked between the shelves and joined us in the back.

I was just putting another piece of cheese on my plate when I looked up to see who else was joining us. When I registered who it was, I almost dropped my plate.

"Fuck," I said as Honor Conroy sashayed her way over and took the last empty chair, which happened to be on my right.

Fuck again.

Kendra announced that we were going to start, and I had to go sit down.

Right next to Honor.

"What are you doing here?" I hissed at her as she crossed her ankles. "Did you even read the book?"

She pulled a worn paperback out of her designer leather bag and held it up. The spine was cracked and the pages were curling a little bit. This was a book that had been read more than a few times.

"Yes, I did," she said, and then looked at Kendra, who was having everyone go around and introduce themselves. When the group first started, there were a lot more people. They had fallen off, but some new people would come every time.

This week, Honor was the only new person.

"Okay, so who wants to start and share your impressions of the book?" Kendra said, looking around.

Joy went first, and I was distracted by Honor just…sitting next to me. As if this was completely normal. I pulled out my phone and did something I never thought I would do.

I texted Honor.

The only reason I had her number was for emergencies. I kept it for the girl's safety only and I'd never used it until now.

Are you trying to make me miserable? Why are you here?

I tried to listen to the rest of the group as I waited for Honor to answer the message. Her phone buzzed in her purse and I watched her pull it out. She read the message and then glanced at me before typing out a response.

Not everything is about you, Layne.

I snorted and Sydney nudged me. "What are you doing?"

I leaned over and whispered in her ear. "Honor is here, and the only reason has to be to piss me off."

Sydney leaned back in her chair to get a look at Honor.

"Maybe she just loves this book," she whispered back.

Okay, I wasn't getting anywhere with Sydney. Joy would have understood, but she was on Syd's other side, so I couldn't talk to her. I was stuck.

I sat there and tried to participate but it wasn't easy with Honor right there. She didn't even participate. It wasn't like that was mandatory, because this was a very lowkey book club, but the point of coming was to talk about the book and she wasn't talking. That further cemented my belief that she was here to piss me off. Things were going to be interesting at the Jewel house tomorrow. I was absolutely going to ask her about this. Until then, I just seethed until it was time to get a second round of snacks. Since Joy and Sydney lived right upstairs, we'd always grab the leftovers and I'd go up and hang out with them until late. Tonight I had a lot to talk about.

Honor didn't stick around when Kendra called for the end of the discussion. She just put her book in her bag, flipped her hair, and walked out without another word.

"So that was weird as fuck," I said, turning to Joy and Syd.

"Did you know she was coming?" Joy asked.

"No, not at all. I didn't know that she even knew about it." I mean, I had seen her in here before, but it was just…weird.

She'd infiltrated my job and now my book club. What was next? The guest house?

"Very weird," Sydney agreed as we cleaned up and put away the chairs and grabbed the rest of the food and the dregs of the wine to take upstairs.

"I just don't know what her angle is," I said as we walked up the narrow stairs and into the apartment. I dropped the bottles in the kitchen and grabbed a glass. Another glass of wine was definitely needed right now, in addition to some more cheese.

"Maybe she thinks getting in good with you will help her with Mark?" Joy said, popping an olive into her mouth.

"Maybe?" I said. "But I don't know why. It's more likely she knew this would annoy the shit out of me. It seems to be her main hobby."

We all stood around the kitchen and speculated while Clementine the cat begged for attention.

"I don't know," I said when none of us could figure out any definitive answers.

"Oh my god, did I tell you about the lady who wanted my mom to make her a pottery dildo, but she was pretending it was supposed to be a vase?" Sydney said and that distracted me from thinking about Honor for a while.

∼

FRIDAY AT SADIE'S house started with hula hooping and trampoline until lunch, and then the afternoon was spent making and decorating cupcakes. My rule with Riley and Zoey was at least one indoor activity per day and one outdoor activity (weather permitting).

"You're the best kids," I said, hugging them when they showed me the cupcakes they'd decorated for their parents. "I hope I have kids half as awesome as you are."

"When are you going to have kids?" Riley asked, and Zoey elbowed her.

"You're not supposed to ask people that," Zoey said.

"Why not?" Riley asked.

I picked up a handful of rainbow sprinkles to add to my cupcake. "Because deciding whether or not to have a baby is a very personal decision and it's not anyone else's business," I said.

Riley nodded. "Okay."

They really were awesome kids.

Sadie was thrilled when she got home from work, slipped off her shoes, and was greeted by her daughters holding out cupcakes they'd made just for her.

"Look at those! I can't decide which one I like more. They're almost too pretty to eat," she said. "Let's put them on a plate so I can get a picture of them."

Sadie arranged the cupcakes on a pretty plate and set them up to take some pictures on her phone.

"I don't think I can eat them by myself. I might need some help," she said, winking at me.

"I'll help!" Riley said.

"Me too!" Zoey yelled. I mean, they'd literally eaten half the frosting from the bowl when they thought that I wasn't looking, but I wasn't going to snitch on them.

"Okay my loves. I'll see you on Monday, okay?" I gave both of them hugs and told Sadie to call me if she needed anything.

I walked out as Sadie was unwrapping the first cupcake and started cutting it into thirds.

～

WHEN I GOT BACK HOME, I couldn't contain my excitement. Sadie had the girls all weekend, so I was off and had two days to myself.

Joy, Sydney, and I were going to the beach in Castleton tomorrow, and then Sunday my only plans were sitting by the pool under an umbrella, drinking Arnold Palmers, and reading until my eyes bled. I might take a dip too. Mark had a quick business trip, so I had the entire house to myself. I could walk around naked if I wanted, but I wouldn't because then the security cameras might pick it up and that would be an awkward conversation with my boss.

After I left Sadie's house, I stopped by Arrowbridge House of Pizza to grab garlic knots, a Greek salad, and a meat lover's pizza for one.

Mark had already left by the time I got back, so I checked the house before heading over to the guest house.

Times like this made me wish I had a dog, or that Mark had caved into the twin's demand for a dog. Being here alone at this massive house was disconcerting to say the least. Sure, we had one of the best security systems money could buy, but still. You never knew.

Mark would tell me that I'd watched too much True Crime, but he wasn't the woman alone in the really nice house with lots of things people would want to steal.

To make myself feel better, I turned on all the lights and put the TV on loud as I put my food on the coffee table, grabbed a soda and sat down on the couch. I could have invited Joy and Sydney over, or even to stay with me this weekend, but I wanted to test myself by being alone.

I was really bad at it. When I was in college, I'd lived in the dorm all four years mostly because I liked being around so many people. There was always someone to talk to. Then when I graduated, I'd lived with Liam until I got this job and then I'd moved into the guest house and become part of the Jewel family.

Someone else might think it was sad that I was a thirty-year-old woman who was bad at being alone, but I wasn't going to apologize for my comfort zone. When I'd been growing up with just one brother, I'd always dreamed of having a bunch of siblings. All of us fighting and stepping over each other and crowding into the same rooms. That was probably other people's nightmare, but that had been my dream. Maybe it's why I liked books so much. They'd been my companions when I'd wished for more.

I let out a breath, deciding that was enough navel gazing for one Friday night. I popped a garlic knot into my mouth and tried to find the trashiest thing I could to watch to soothe my loneliness.

Chapter Five

Saturday morning, I made myself a huge, beautiful breakfast: pesto eggs on top of grilled bread with smashed avocado and sundried tomatoes and crispy parmesan potatoes and a bowl of berries. I also brought out the fancy coffee and made sure to froth the milk for a beautiful cloudlike latte.

Did I eat my breakfast by the pool in a robe like I owned this place? Yes I did. Did I also make myself a mimosa? Yes I did.

Life could be too bleak not to take joy in doing little things for yourself.

Once I cleaned up from my fabulous breakfast, I put on my favorite swimsuit, covered myself in sunscreen, threw on a kaftan and headed out to the beach to be with my buddies.

Joy was already lounging when I got there and I found her way on one side of the beach away from a lot of people.

I was huffing and puffing as I dragged my shit over the sand toward her.

"Did you have to be all the way over here?" I asked, dropping my chair and beach bag.

"It's more private this way. Plus, fewer small children playing or tossing a frisbee in our faces."

She did have a point.

I set up my chair and sat down with a sigh.

"I needed this," I said.

"Don't you live right next to a pool?"

"This is different," I said, pulling my hat out of my bag and putting it on to protect my face from the sun. "The beach is just…good for the soul. Reminds us of how big the universe is."

Joy gave me a look. "It's too early for you to be waxing poetic like this." She reached into her cooler and pulled out a cold drink.

"It's never too early for me to wax poetic," I said, putting my arms over my head and stretching.

"Why are you all the way over here?" someone called, and we both looked up to see Sydney dragging her stuff over the sand and looking disgruntled from behind her sunglasses.

"Privacy," Joy said, getting up to help her.

Sydney sat down on my left and sighed with relief as she sat down in her chair.

"You just missed Layne writing poetry about the ocean," Joy said, opening the cooler again.

"I wasn't," I told Syd.

"I need a minute to catch my breath," Syd said, fanning herself. "Do you have any water?"

Joy tossed her a bottle and I grabbed a seltzer water for myself.

"Mmm, this is perfect," Syd said, tipping her face up. "I don't have to think about pottery dildos all day long."

"You know, that could be a whole new avenue for your mom. Pottery after dark," I said. "She could set up a secret room and you'd have to have a password to come in and see the naughty pots."

Sydney snorted. "Don't give her any ideas."

"I got called a 'peddler of filth' the other day," Joy said. "That was fun. Some guy got mad at a book with a shirtless dude on the cover. I told him that he shouldn't buy it if it offended him. He ended up storming out in a huff. Some of these tourists have lost their minds."

We sat for a while and bitched about tourists until we were sweaty, so we went to dip our toes into the ocean. The water was still cold as hell, but there were people swimming.

The three of us managed to get up to our knees and that was as far as we could go.

One of the swimmers started moving toward us and I thought I recognized her.

"Paige?" I asked. She put her hand up and squinted at me.

"Oh, hey! Hi Joy, hi Sydney." She came closer and smiled. Paige was one of Kendra's friends and lived in Castleton.

"Aren't you cold?" Joy asked.

Paige shook her head. "Nope. I'm just built different. Hopefully this one will be too." She put her hand on her expanding belly. I didn't know how far along she was, but she was so petite that she looked like she was ready to pop at any moment.

"Okay, now I'm getting cold," she said, shivering. "Where are you sitting? Esme and I will come say hello."

I pointed and she waved as she headed back up the beach toward her wife, Esme, who had a large towel held out and waiting for her.

"They're so cute," Joy said. "I love it when they have their book club. I mean, their Non Book Club. I don't get it, but that group is great."

The three of us also decided the water was too cold, so we got out and took a little walk up and down the beach to warm up.

I watched families building sandcastles, and little kids riding the waves with boogie boards. Everyone was having a good time and the energy was rubbing off on me.

We ventured over the rocks at the other end of the beach to look for seashells and to gaze into the tidepools. All three of us got hungry and headed to the snack bar for burgers, hot dogs, fries, onion rings, and sodas with just the right amount of ice.

The three of us claimed a picnic table in the shade and ate so fast that none of us really said anything until we were full. Paige and Esme had come by to say hello before heading out since Esme had to work that night.

"Last onion ring," I said, holding up the container. Joy and Syd fought each other for it. Joy won and Syd pouted.

"Would an ice cream make you feel better?" I asked.

"Maybe," Sydney said. "I'd have to eat it to find out."

We took our ice creams back to our chairs and did a sunblock reapplication once we'd finished.

"Nap time," Sydney announced, pulling a blanket out of her bag and putting it down next to her chair. "Wake me if I start to sizzle."

Joy pulled out a paperback, our next book club selection, and I opened my latest read on my ereader.

Something at the edge of my vision distracted me for a second and I looked up. A woman had gone in swimming and was emerging from the water, pushing her hair back from her face.

Fuck, she was hot. She walked out of the water, the waves crashing around her. Her bikini was white and had so many cutouts that it was barely covering anything. Not that she should cover anything, because her body was incredible. My mouth went dry and I couldn't look away. There was something about this woman. The way she walked, like liquid sex. She was hot and she knew it and wanted everyone to know she knew it.

I could feel sweat trickling down my body that had nothing to do with the sun beating down on me.

I knew I was absolutely ogling this woman, but it was hard not to. She came closer and then I realized her face looked familiar.

Fuck. Fuck, fuck, fuuuuuuccccckkkkkkkkkk.

I wanted to dive under my chair, but that wasn't an option, so I just looked down at my phone as quickly as I could and hoped my sunglasses hid most of my face and that she hadn't seen me.

My heart pounded louder than the waves against the sand as I waited for her to walk away.

"You okay over there?" Joy asked, looking over at me as I hyperventilated.

"Is she gone?" I asked as quietly as I could.

"Who?"

"Honor. She was right here," I said, my voice low. Joy sat up and looked around before I could tell her not to be so obvious.

"Do you want the good news or the bad news?" Joy asked.

"What's the good news?" I asked.

"Um, sorry, there isn't any good news because she's coming this way. Sorry."

I slid lower in my chair, wishing for the powers of invisibility.

A shadow fell across me and there was no way I couldn't look up.

"Got a day off?" Honor asked. She'd gotten a towel and was using it on her body to dry herself. My mouth went completely dry as she brushed it across her chest, drawing attention to her boobs. Honor moved slowly with a little smirk on her face.

"Yes, I get most weekends off," I said, somehow finding my voice. "What are you doing here?"

"I like the beach. Doesn't everyone?" she said, her eyes flicking to Joy, who was watching this exchange with a little too much glee on her face. Even Sydney had woken up and seemed to be watching to see what was going to happen.

"I'm sure there are people who don't like the beach," I said. What a weird conversation this was. Not my fault, because I couldn't think when she was just standing there in her swimsuit like that, saltwater still trickling down her body.

"Well," Honor said, tipping her head back and running the towel over her hair. "You have a lovely afternoon."

She nodded at Syd and Joy and walked back toward her spot, which was further to the right of us. She must have gotten here when we were at the snack bar or else she would have walked right past us.

I let out a shaky breath.

"What the hell was that?" Joy asked, turning to me.

"Seriously, she's…something else," Syd said, hopping back into her chair. "I woke up at the right time."

"I'm so glad you're enjoying this," I grumbled.

"What is her deal, though?" Joy said, putting her book aside.

"Like I said, no idea. I've tried to figure her out and she just keeps perplexing me. All I do know is that she's a bitch and I hope she gets sand in her ass," I said.

Both Joy and Syd burst out laughing.

∾

WHEN WE'D HAD ENOUGH of the sun, we packed up our stuff, rinsed off our feet, and headed to our cars.

"Did you want to get dinner in Castleton?" Joy asked. "We can say hi to Esme if she's working later."

Our favorite place to eat in Castleton was the Pine State Bar and Grille, where Paige's wife, Esme, was the bartender most nights. She made incredible drinks, and she also gave us good deals, so it was only natural to head over there from the beach, even though we were kind of sweaty and sandy from the beach. That was to be expected in Castleton.

We walked in and were seated after a short wait. We told our server that we wanted to grab drinks from the bar and went over to find Esme working, her dark hair flashing red highlights under the neon signs above the bar.

"What's the special tonight?" I asked as she smiled and came over to take care of us.

"Shark Bite," Esme said. "It's been a hit this summer."

I checked with Joy and Syd and that's what they wanted.

"You got it," Esme said, slapping the bar. She wore a ripped black tank top and shredded black jeans shorts. I wondered if she ever wore colors off the clock. Probably not. All-black seemed to be her thing. Even her bathing suit and towel had been black.

Esme brought our drinks back and we held them up to the light.

"Not going to lie, I thought about mixing corn syrup with the grenadine to make the blood look more realistic," Esme said.

"I like the way your mind works," Joy said, shoving a few bucks in the tip jar. I agreed to pay for this round and gave Esme my card.

She was called away by other customers so we didn't really get to chat with her, so we took our drinks back to our table so we could order.

I was still irritated about Honor showing up during my beach day. My weekends were Honor free and she'd ruined that.

"Why are you pouting?" Joy asked, nudging my shoulder as I ate my summer berry salad with chicken.

"I'm not pouting," I said, finishing the last of my Shark Bite and switching to water.

"You are," Syd said, pointing her fork at me.

I sighed. "Honor just ruins things. She's a ruiner. A ruiner of things."

"Oh, come on, she didn't ruin anything. She showed up for five minutes and barely said anything," Joy said. "Don't let her get under your skin. That's what she wants."

Yeah, it was what she wanted, and I couldn't seem to help giving it to her. It wasn't my fault she was trying to ruin Mark's life for money. And I had no doubt at all that she'd ignore the twins and wouldn't even attempt to be a decent stepmother to them. Honor wasn't exactly the maternal type. She'd want to ship them off to boarding school in Europe or some shit. Not that Mark and Sadie would let that happen, but still. I'd seen people completely change when they married a partner with strong beliefs.

"Another round?" I asked.

They both cheered.

∼

AFTER I GOT HOME from dinner, I rinsed off quickly and then filled up my tub with the best smelling bath bomb, a lemonade with crushed raspberries and mint, a bowl of popcorn, and a little stand that held up my ereader so I could chill in the tub with my book. I even put on one of my favorite playlists of music that mellowed me out.

I floated in the tub, pretending to be a mermaid for a while like I did when I was a kid.

I wasn't thinking about Honor at all. Not even a little bit. Not for a second.

∼

SUNDAY I MADE another fancy breakfast of mixed berry pancakes with maple whipped cream and crumbled bacon, and a mimosa with my coffee.

The sun had decided to be nice to me and was out in full force. I was worried that the day would be cloudy, but there was barely a dot of white in the sky.

I put on my most drapey caftan and took the rest of my coffee to my favorite spot beside the pool. I did get up and stick my feet in for a little while, but soon retreated to the shade of an umbrella, and the first of my books for the day. I'd made a list of what I wanted to get through and I had a schedule to keep.

It turned out to be a little too quiet outside, so I put on the speakers with my playlist again. I tapped my feet to the beat of the music and sipped the giant jug of ice water I'd brought out with me.

Yeah, I could function as a rich person. Someone who had inherited wealth, though, so I didn't have to actually do anything for it. Mark worked way too hard and had to talk to far too many people. Definitely not for me.

Perhaps I could take a leaf out of Honor's book and marry rich. There seemed to be a shortage of rich women looking for a wife in Arrowbridge, though. I'd have to go hunting.

My perfect day couldn't last forever, though, and as the sun moved across the sky, my time alone ticked by. I cringed when I heard a car pull into the driveway but put on a smile when Mark got out and waved to me before going into the house.

I could stay out by the pool and do my own thing, but I went back to the guest house and ate a bunch of watermelon over the sink instead.

The twins had been sending me messages all weekend in the family group chat with their parents. It was sweet, really. I did miss them and would be happy to pick them up from their mom's house tomorrow morning. The weather was going to be crappy, so I was going to be an asshole and make them clean their room and then reward them with a marathon of their favorite show and a charcuterie board that we were going to make together. I wasn't like a regular nanny, I was a cool nanny.

∼

RILEY AND ZOEY acted like they hadn't seen me in a million years and clutched me for dear life when I picked them up.

"They missed you a little bit," Sadie said as she got ready for work.

"I missed them," I said, kissing each of them on the head. "You got all your stuff?"

They nodded and ran over to hug their mom. I saw the sadness in Sadie's eyes as she told them that she'd see them later this week. Even though having divorced parents was all the girls had ever known, it was hard on them, and hard on Mark and Sadie.

Maybe that was what enraged me so much about Honor's obvious ploy to marry Mark. Sure, he was single and fair game, but she didn't want him. She just wanted his money.

I couldn't think about it too much, or my eye would start twitching.

The twins piled into my car and we headed back to their dad's house in the rain.

"Okay, everything upstairs and it's time to clean."

You would have thought I'd asked them to scrub the toilets with their bare hands. The dramatics over picking up a few socks and organizing some papers was truly unreal.

"The sooner you get it done, the sooner it's done. See how that works?" I asked. They were too old for me to sit and direct them, but I did check on them to make sure they were staying on task.

It took three times longer to get their rooms to a normal level of clean than I anticipated.

"Oh my god, I do not get paid enough for this," I said under my breath.

"Can we be done now?" Riley asked as I did my final inspection.

"Much better," I said. Even if it wasn't perfect, it was close enough and I didn't have any more fight in me.

"Good job," I said, high fiving both of them.

"We're hungry," Zoey said.

"Let's go do something about that," I said as we all went downstairs.

Mark came out to make himself lunch as I was arranging cheese slices on a tray for the girls as they fought over which movie they were going to watch first.

"I miss the days when they were happy with finger paints," I said as he assembled a sandwich on the counter.

Mark sighed. "Me too. I don't know what I'm going to do when they're teenagers. What do teen girls even like?"

I shrugged. "I haven't been a teen girl in a long time, so I'm not a lot of help. Things are so different now. There's a new social media app every single day and each one is weirder and more concerning than the last."

I shuddered.

Mark grunted and sliced his sandwich in half. "Sometimes I definitely consider getting rid of all technology and moving to the woods."

"Don't blame you," I said. He nodded and went back to his office.

I handed the tray off to the girls, who were on the floor with their giant beanbag chairs. I lounged on the couch and stole bites from their plate and let the movie play as I looked at my own social media apps. I was only human after all.

I heard someone in the kitchen and judging from the clack

of heels on the hardwood, it was Honor. I peered over the back of the couch as she got herself a glass of water.

I hated admitting it, but she looked really pretty today. Honor always dressed like a sexy secretary from some 1950s dream. I had no idea if her clothes were really vintage or not, but I wouldn't have been surprised if they were.

Today her dress was black with capped sleeves and it skimmed her body like it was poured on. Her heels were gold with red bottoms, of course. Why she wore heels when she didn't have to was a mystery, but maybe she liked them. I could imagine it would make you feel powerful to wear shoes that made such a definitive sound. Like a kind of armor.

Honor stared out the windows at the rain, which was coming down hard. Lightning forked the sky and she startled.

"Pause it," Zoey said as she got up from her beanbag chair. I turned to watch Riley pause the movie and when I turned back, Honor was gone.

∼

THE RAIN LASTED ALL DAY, but the movies entertained the twins until it was time for me to get cook dinner. I popped into Mark's office to let him know it would be ready soon, but he was on the phone.

"Can you let him know dinner is in ten?" I asked Honor. She didn't take her eyes from her laptop as she nodded.

Then, for some reason that I blamed on the rainy weather or hormones, I said, "you could stay, if you're hungry."

That made her look up.

She blinked once at me, and I realized I'd caught her completely off guard.

"No thank you," she said, but it took her a few seconds. Phew.

Mark got off the phone and groaned. "Stay if you want,

Honor. No pressure, though. I know you didn't sign up for family dinners."

"Thanks, I'm having dinner with my sister," she said, staring so hard at her laptop screen that I thought she was trying to glare a hole through it.

She had a sister? That was news to me.

"Right, of course," Mark said, nodding. "Well, she's welcome here as well."

"Thank you for the offer," she said. "That's very kind of you."

Gone was the seductive lilt of her voice. Now she sounded…actually grateful? Weird.

I scurried back to the kitchen and started making plates for the twins. Honor came out a few minutes later with her bag over her shoulder. The rain had finally tapered to a drizzle, but she didn't appear to have an umbrella or a coat.

"Do you want to borrow an umbrella?" I asked. I knew Honor wouldn't want to disrupt her coif or get her dress wet.

Honor looked at me and narrowed her eyes. "I'm not afraid to get my hair wet," she said, her voice harsh. She never would have talked that way if Mark had been in the room. No, she saved that special tone just for me.

"Jesus, I just offered you an umbrella," I said. "I'm sorry for trying to be nice."

Honor opened her mouth, probably to snap at me, but then she closed it.

"Thank you." The words sounded like they were ripped from her tongue. As if they were the last words she wanted to say, but she said them anyway.

"You're welcome," I said, making up a plate for Mark.

Honor opened the door and walked into the rain without another word.

If I said I didn't watch her walk to her car, I would have been lying.

THANKFULLY, the rain didn't last, and I was able to get the girls outside for the rest of the week. They had sleepaway camp the following week, so I was also taking my own little vacation. Joy and Sydney had also planned a few days off, so we were heading to a beachside cabin for a few days for a girl's trip. We always joked about how boring we were, but the three of us just happened to like to chill out and talk and read together and try new restaurants rather than do other things. We had planned a few activities, including a whale watch, so we were getting some adventure in.

Since they wouldn't be seeing their mom for her week while they were at camp, I took them over to her house on Friday night so she could have them for the weekend.

"How's it going?" I asked as the girls threw themselves at their mom and she gave them big hugs.

"Come to the kitchen with me," she said after she'd had her little reunion with the twins and sent them to their room for a few minutes.

"Another bad date?" I asked.

Sadie sighed as she poured me a glass of iced tea.

"It's impossible. Impossible!" she threw her hands in the air. "There are no decent men, or at least no decent men that are attracted to me. They're all creeps and jerks."

"I'm so sorry. It's awful out there."

Sadie sighed and sipped her iced tea. "It's fine. Maybe I'm just not meant to find love again. I had it and…" she trailed off.

"Do you think you and Mark would ever?" I asked.

Sadie shook her head. "I used to think, maybe? But not now. I tried, you know. After everything blew up. I realized that I missed him, and I was still in love with him. And I didn't want to break up our marriage, deal with joint custody. But once he said he was done, he was done. Mark doesn't change his mind. Stubborn man."

"Well, he hasn't gotten involved with anyone else," I pointed out.

"I know. I guess a tiny part of me will always have hope that we could get past everything and come back together." She shrugged one shoulder and then I heard a noise.

Sadie and I both turned at the same time.

"How long have you been lurking there?" Sadie asked. Her question was met by giggles.

"I'll let you take that one," I said, pushing away from the counter.

Sadie made them come out and gave them a lecture about eavesdropping before I gave them hugs and told them I'd see them the following week.

"We'll text you," they promised, but I knew they were going to be so busy that they wouldn't.

"You have fun and be nice to the other kids."

They both rolled their eyes. "Mom already gave us a speech."

I was sure she did.

"Then I hope you have an absolute blast and you have so much fun and I want to know every single thing when you come back." I gave them huge hugs again and then headed back to the guest house.

THE REST of my weekend was spent cleaning the shit out of my house, packing for my trip, and making sure Mark had everything he could need while I was gone.

"You do know I am a grown man?" he said when I was showing him where I kept some of the cleaning products.

"Yes, and when was the last time you cleaned your own toilets?" I asked.

That shut him up.

Once I had him all up to date on everything, I gave him the lists and the map of the grocery store.

"This is too much," he said. "I know where things are at the grocery store." He still took the map and the list and promised he would not call me unless it was an absolute emergency.

"Good man," I said, giving his shoulder a squeeze.

"And you have a good time with Joy and Sydney. I'm always telling you that you need to take more time off."

"I know, and I don't listen to you," I said.

"You have to force yourself to take time off because one day you'll wake up and you're almost forty and you can't remember the last time you took a day off."

That was a good point. I didn't want to wake up and realize that I'd worked my life away. Since my job was so entwined with my life, it was easy to blur those boundaries.

Sunday afternoon I loaded up my car and went to downtown Arrowbridge to grab Joy and Sydney. As usual, Syd was bringing twice as much crap as Joy and I were.

"What could you possibly have in here?" I asked, hefting one of her bags into the trunk of my car. I was a control freak when it came to driving so I'd insisted that I be in charge of that part of our trip.

"You know I like to be prepared for things," Sydney said.

"I know, I'm the same way, but this is a whole other level," I said, finally getting the bag into my car with another heave that strained my back.

While I was dealing with Syd's bags, Joy went to the café next to the bookstore and grabbed us all iced coffees and pastries for the road.

Joy was a great navigator and had looked up and marked where we could take pit stops, and had made out our schedule for the week. I was more than happy to let her be in charge of that.

"We good to go?" I asked as Sydney shut my trunk.

"Yes," she said, panting.

The three of us piled into the car and fought about what we were going to listen to until I put on a random nostalgia playlist and we headed out.

Chapter Six

OUR FIRST STOP was for dinner at diner that gave the impression it was a hole-in-the-wall, but actually had been featured in shows and in articles and had won a bunch of awards.

We gorged ourselves on plates of fried chicken and fried pickles and french fries smothered in gravy and cheese. It took us a little bit of time to get up from the table and go back to the car after we'd finished.

We didn't make it to the cottage until later that night and we were all pretty tired from the drive.

"I can't wait to see what it looks like in the morning," Joy said as I got the keys out of the lockbox attached to the front porch.

The cottage was just as quaint and cute as it had looked in the pictures online, and I was itching to check out the private beach located down a little path that was too dark to navigate now.

We got our shit inside and found a welcome basket of goodies and sweet note from our host.

"Shall we?" I asked, pulling out some of the groceries we'd gotten for our stay.

"Definitely," Joy said as Sydney dragged yet another bag into the cottage.

I started mixing dark and stormies for us and since the night was still pretty warm, we took them out to the porch to look at the stars.

There were a few mosquitoes and black flies out, so I lit the citronella candles.

"Here's to vacation," I said, raising my glass.

"Amen," Joy said.

"Cheers to that," Sydney said, and we all tapped our glasses together.

∽

THE COTTAGE WAS SMALL, but it did have three bedrooms, so we each got our own room. We'd done Rock, Paper, Scissors and I'd gotten the biggest room that also had the private bathroom. Joy and Syd had to share a bathroom between both of their rooms.

After we'd had drinks, I'd crashed in my room on the first floor, completely passing out until I heard the noises of someone in the kitchen the next morning. I'd remembered to crack the window open last night, and a cool breeze tinged with the salt of the ocean caressed my face.

Perfect.

I hit the bathroom and then went out into the main living area with an open plan living room, little dining area, and kitchen and found Joy and Sydney working on breakfast.

"Good morning my dears," I said, stretching my arms over my head.

"Coffee?" Joy asked.

"Please," I said. She made me a cup as Sydney stood at the stove and flipped a pan of fluffy scrambled eggs.

"Did you sleep in so you wouldn't have to do the cooking?" Joy asked as I sipped my coffee.

"No, but it seems to have worked out for me, though," I said. I enjoyed cooking, and intended on doing plenty of it this week, but right now it was nice to sit back and let someone else be in charge of it.

"Okay, we are ready," Sydney said, and we filled our plates with warm croissants, eggs, bacon, and fried potatoes.

"I found a blender in the cabinet, one of those really fancy ones. We can make juice later if we want," Joy said as I shoved eggs in my mouth.

"We could go into town and grab some stuff," Syd said.

The three of us finished breakfast and put our suits on to go check out the beach.

It was tiny, but the sand was soft and smooth, and we splashed in the waves until it was time for lunch.

We took showers in shifts and then dressed up for an afternoon of exploring the little downtown, which was within walking distance of the cottage. Our host had even provided tote bags to carry our treasures home in.

The three of us strolled up and down the street, taking our time and looking at everything. There was a term for this town, and it was "tourist trap" and we were happy to be tourists and pretend we didn't live just a few hours away and had access to many of the items that filled the various little stores we ducked into.

"Do I need this? I think I need this," I said, holding up a bag made from old sails that had a blue octopus on one side and an outline of the state of Maine on the other.

"You absolutely need that, and I need this one," Joy said, holding up another bag with a red anchor on it. Syd chose the bag with black nautical stripes.

"This is much less permanent than getting tattoos to commemorate this trip," Joy said.

"We could still get tattoos," Syd said.

"Let's see how the rest of the week goes," I said, and we all laughed.

∼

DINNER THAT NIGHT was at a restaurant with a huge deck right on the ocean, and included clams, lobster, sweet corn on the cob, rolls, and buckets of butter.

The three of us wore the silly plastic bibs and took a ton of pictures and sipped chilled wine as the sun set.

"Are we doing dessert?" I asked.

"I always have room for pie," Joy said.

"Ditto," Syd said, so we ordered blueberry pie with vanilla ice cream.

"We should get going before it gets too dark," I said as we split the bill and gathered up our things. In addition to our new bags, we'd also bought a bunch of silly trinkets, and I'd gotten gifts for the twins because I couldn't help myself.

We piled on the couch in the cottage and watched a movie until we were all struggling to stay awake and decided to head to our rooms for the night.

I tried to read, but my eyes would not stay open, so I plugged my ereader in to charge and called it a night.

∼

THE NEXT FEW days were bliss. We traded off making meals and choosing where to eat for dinner. Joy had packed each day with shopping and beach time and other fun things nearby.

We did a short nature hike one afternoon, visited a lighthouse, and got very wet on a whale watch where we only saw one whale.

"At least we got to see seals and puffins?" Joy said when we got back, completely drenched and somewhat disappointed.

"Yeah, it's not really a guarantee that you're going to see a whale. It's not like they can pay the whales to show up," I said. "Although, that seems like it would be a good deal for the boats and the whales. They could be paid in fish."

Joy snorted.

"Did you get video?" Sydney asked.

"Oh yeah, the twins are going to die," I said, showing her the only video I got of the whale surfacing.

"What do you think Honor has been up to this week?" Joy asked.

I made a face. "I've been trying not to think about her. She's probably thrilled that I'm out of the house so she can really sink her claws into Mark. I wouldn't put it past her to cast a spell on him or something."

"She shouldn't fuck with magic," Sydney said, shaking her head. "You don't want to mess with love spells."

"You sound like you might be speaking from personal experience?" Joy said, giving Sydney a look.

"Don't do it," was all she would say.

I gave Joy a look and decided to ask more about that later.

∼

I'D TOLD myself I wasn't going to think about Honor all week, but it was like my brain was refusing to let me do that. I'd just be doing something random and her face would pop into my head. Or I'd wonder what she was doing at that moment. Or I'd wonder how many creative ways she'd find to insult whatever I was doing at the time.

I wondered when her last vacation was. As much as I couldn't stand her, she was a hard worker. She busted her ass for Mark and stayed late and came in on weekends and did her damn job. What did Honor do when she wasn't at work? Probably had a shrine to Mark in her house that she worshipped at or something.

She'd mentioned a sister and I wondered if she was older or younger. Did they get along? It was so weird to imagine Honor's life outside of what I knew about her. Like, what did she do on the weekends? Was she the kind of person who slept late, or was she up with the sun and getting shit done? What did she eat for breakfast? Did she immediately fold her laundry when it came out of the dryer, or did she let it hang out in a basket for a few days?

Something told me she folded her laundry perfectly and put it away when it was still warm. I bet she had a special folding system she learned from an organizing book. I'd done my best to teach the twins folding techniques, but I'd eventually given up and had just let them have chaos if that's how they wanted their clothes to be.

Joy snapped her fingers in front of my face.

"You there?"

"Yeah," I said. "Just pondering."

"Pondering anything in particular?" Syd asked. It was Thursday night and we were chilling on the porch after we'd made individual pizzas in the really fancy oven.

"Just thinking about the twins," I said, which wasn't a lie. I had been thinking about them plenty of times.

"How are they doing at camp?" Joy asked.

"I've gotten exactly three texts, and one of them was just a blurry picture of nothing. They promised and promised they'd text me every hour of every day and I knew things were going to change when they got there. It just means they're too busy having fun, which is what I wanted anyway."

"Or they've escaped camp and are on the run from the law and can't contact you," Syd said.

"Why? Why would you say that?" I asked.

Sydney just shrugged. "That's what I would do if I had an identical twin. Crimes."

"I mean, they have had their share of shenanigans," I said. "But I don't think they'd do anything criminal."

At least I hoped not. I hoped I'd set a good example for them. Plus, they were eleven. How much trouble could they really get into?

∼

MARK AND SADIE did check in with me a few times, just asking how things were going. And then there was Liam, who demanded a video chat with all three of us on Friday night.

"Don't you have anything better to do?" I asked him.

"I'm going out tomorrow night," he said. Liam was kind of a homebody like me, so we would encourage each other to do shit. I mean, I did plenty of things with Joy and Syd, but he said that didn't count because they were my comfort zone, apparently.

"Ohhh, you have a date?" I asked. Liam rolled his eyes, but his cheeks got red. "Ohhh, you *are* going on a date!"

Joy and Syd both laughed and threw questions at him.

"Jesus, calm down," Liam said. "It's not a big deal."

"Tell me everything," I said.

"Yes, and tell us too because we want to know," Joy said.

Her name was Gwen, and she came into the coffee shop every morning and ordered a matcha latte and one day she'd slipped him her number, in an effortlessly cool move that I had to admire. She was a labor and delivery nurse and adored her job.

"So far I approve, but I'm gonna want to meet her," I said.

Liam groaned. "I haven't even gone on a date with her yet. No way am I letting her meet you yet." He shook his head violently.

"Fine, fine. But if I happen to show up to get coffee some morning and she just happens to be there..."

Liam glared at me. "I swear to god, if you do that, you are no longer my sister."

I laughed. "I'm not out to sabotage your life. I think she sounds like a great girl, and I wish you luck on your date. Where are you taking her?"

"So they have these kitten cuddle hours at the animal shelter, and she mentioned how much she loves animals, so we're doing that, and then hitting up the burger place my friend Kenny runs, and then if she wants to hang out we might take a walk on the beach or if she's done, then I'll take her home."

All of my romance book reading definitely rubbed off on him, I was proud to say.

"Good boy," I said, and he made a face at me.

"You know that I'm an adult, right? With a full-time job and everything? I have a retirement plan," he said.

"Sorry, you'll always be my baby brother," I said. "That's how being a big sister works."

"It's true," Joy said. "My sisters will never treat me like an adult."

"I'm an only child, but I like to think I give off the aura of an older sister," Sydney said. "Sometimes I wish I'd had an older sister that my mom could pour all of her hopes and ambitions into. Maybe she would have been good at pottery."

Syd's voice was light, but that was a seriously touchy subject with her and her mom.

"Don't be sad, Syd," Joy said, putting her head on Sydney's shoulder. "This is not a trip for sadness. This is a trip for relaxation and friendship."

"What she said," I agreed.

"You're the best," Sydney said, putting her arms around both of us and squishing us together in a hug.

"Hello? I'm still here," Liam said. "Not to interrupt the

friendfest, but I should probably let you go. Don't do anything I wouldn't do."

"Have fun on your date and I want to hear all the details. Love you."

"Love you, too," he said through a laugh and ended the call.

∼

OUR LAST FULL day was spent doing a book crawl. It was like a bar crawl, but you went to different small bookstores and bought something in each one.

One of Kendra's bookseller friends had come up with it as a way to get people to visit multiple independent bookstores in Maine and it had really taken off.

Unfortunately, the first place didn't have a romance section and was kind of rude when we asked about it. We still wanted to be nice, so I found a craft book I thought the twins would like, Joy got some bookmarks for herself, and Syd bought a vegan cookbook, despite not being vegan.

"It's always good to learn something new," she said.

Our second stop had a robust romance selection, and we went wild, and bought plenty of books to fill the bags we'd bought earlier in the week.

Lunch was at a sushi place that Joy had found with incredible reviews, and once we were served, we found out why. We topped that off with too many bowls of mango ice cream before hitting our last bookstore and then heading back to the cottage to spend the rest of the afternoon and evening reading and eating all the leftovers in the fridge that we'd have to throw out if we didn't consume.

Joy had us doing so many things that it was nice to just chill and read and not talk much. The three of us had always been comfortable with silence together, and I think that was one of the reasons we'd stuck together as friends. We loved one another, yes, but we were also truly comfortable with each other.

∽

"THIS IS the last morning in this kitchen," I said as I made breakfast for the three of us. We were finishing the last of the eggs, and I'd thrown in some spinach and tomatoes and cheese we needed to eat up. Joy was juicing the last of some of our fresh fruit, and Syd was heating up the last of the croissants. There were only two, so she was trying to divide them evenly and having a challenge.

We took our breakfast to the private beach and laid everything out on the towels from the cottage and dragged some chairs from the porch down with us.

We sat with our toes in the water and had our breakfast and I was so sad that this trip was at an end. It seemed like we'd been planning and waiting for it forever and it had gone by in the blink of an eye.

"You know there was one thing we didn't do on this trip," Sydney said, sipping the last of her juice.

"What's that?" I asked. Joy had included everything we'd wanted to do when we'd planned this. What could we be missing?

"None of us got laid," Syd said, and Joy made a face.

"Is that you coming onto one of us, because the answer is no," Joy said.

Sydney rolled her eyes. "Please, neither of you is my type, and if you were, I would have made a move a long, long time ago. No, I'm saying that we should have hit a lesbian bar and hooked up. Isn't that what you're supposed to do on vacation?"

I shared a look with Joy.

"I think that only applies if you travel out of state, or you go to Vegas or the Bahamas," I said.

Syd shrugged one shoulder. "I'm just saying. We could have added hookups into the plan."

Joy made a sputtering noise. "You never said anything when I was making the schedule!"

She was so indignant that it made me laugh.

"This was supposed to be a friend trip, not a hookup trip. If you want to do a hookup trip, I'm going to need to take some more vacation time," I said.

Honestly, the idea didn't really appeal to me. The idea of having sex with someone I'd never see again made me so anxious. But kissing a stranger didn't sound bad. And if my friends wanted to get laid, then I wanted that for them.

"I didn't mean we should take a separate trip. I was just saying that we might have made a little time in this trip for flirting and maybe more," Sydney said.

"Well, there's still time," I said. "We can hit the downtown and go searching for babes."

Both Joy and Sydney stared at me.

"What?" I asked.

"You sounded like a dude from a really old movie right there and it was creepy," Joy said. "Let's not do that if we go out."

"What would you say, then?" I asked.

Joy thought about that for a moment. "I'd say we were looking for connections. Sparks. Someone that catches your eye."

"Aw, that's sweet," I said.

"Eyes and tits. That's what I look for," Sydney said.

"Syd!" Joy and I said at the same time.

"What? Should I lie and say I'm looking for a sparkling personality? The visual is what hits me first. Sorry."

I shook my head at her, and Joy laughed.

"What do you look for then?" Sydney asked me.

"I don't know!" I said. I was feeling very put on the spot. "It's been such a long time since I had a crush I don't even know if I can get them anymore. I'll probably just end up some spinster with some cats and my books and I wouldn't hate that."

"Spinsters are awesome," Joy said. "They get to spend their disposable income and solve murders."

"Sounds good to me," Sydney said.

The conversation moved on and I was glad. What I didn't tell my friends was that living alone, being alone, was my greatest fear. What if no one fell in love with me? What if I lived the rest of my life alone? I wouldn't be able to do it. I just couldn't.

But I lied to my friends and said I'd be happy to live alone because telling them that I was so scared of the prospect was too embarrassing.

We did one last walk through the downtown (no trawling for babes) and had a late brunch of lobster eggs benedict at a lovely little restaurant.

Packing up took forever because Sydney had to fit everything back into her bags. I wasn't going to lie, she had brought some useful things, like her first aid kit. Other things she brought, like her waffle iron, were pretty useless in the end.

I made sure to write a little thank you note for our hosts before we checked out and made sure that we hadn't left anything behind.

"Goodbye cottage," I said as I closed the door and then dropped the keys in the lockbox.

"We'll just have to make this a yearly trip," Joy said, putting her arm around me as we walked to the car.

"I love that idea," I said.

"Me too. I'll bring less stuff next time," Sydney said, closing the trunk with an effort.

"I think my car would appreciate that," I said as we got in.

Chapter Seven

"I'm home," I said as I walked into the guest house. I was greeted with silence. Ugh.

I dumped my laundry in the washer and turned it on and texted Liam that I'd made it back home in one piece.

He had been pretty tight-lipped about his date, but I knew that it had gone well, since they were going out next week on Thursday to see a local band. So far, so good. If things kept up, I definitely was going to pester him to meet her. Since our parents weren't involved in our lives, he needed someone from his family to give their stamp of approval on his choice of dating partner.

The twins weren't coming home until late Sunday night, so I had hours to kill, and I was bored out of my mind after only a few minutes. Not even any of my books could hold my attention. It was like I had an itch I couldn't reach.

At last, I got a text from the twins that they were almost here. Sadie had picked them up from camp so she could have the drive with them before she dropped them off with their dad.

By the time Sadie's car pulled into the driveway, I was vibrating with excitement.

I threw myself out of the guest house and across the yard to where they were getting out of the car.

Mark got to hug them first, as was right, but they threw themselves at me and I breathed a sigh of relief that they were in one piece.

"Did you have a good time?" I asked, looking at both of their faces. "Looks like the camp wasn't really good on sunscreen." They were both tanner than they'd been when they'd left, and they both had peeling skin on their noses.

"I've already read them the riot act," Sadie said as she pulled one of their bags out of the car. Mark rushed over to take it from her and I watched as their eyes locked and they shared what can only be described as a moment.

I cleared my throat and ushered the twins inside, giving Sadie and Mark some time.

There might be hope for them yet.

"I know you're tired, but can you give me the highlights?" I asked the twins as we sat down on the couch.

"We caught two of the counselors hooking up, but we didn't say anything," Riley said.

"Oh," I said. "Um, let's shelve that one for now. Did you have fun?"

Did they ever. From swimming to horseback riding to learning how to row a canoe, they'd done it all and had the bug bites and bruises to prove it.

Mark came in a few minutes later and we all craned our necks to watch him.

He had the girl's bags slung over his shoulder. "Did you pick up rocks and bring them home?"

"No," both girls said at the same time.

"Yeah, that's not suspicious," I said, giving Mark a look. He narrowed his eyes before taking the bags upstairs.

"Okay, now that your dad is gone, did you get into any trouble?" I asked.

They rolled their eyes at the exact same time. "We know that you'd tell Dad. And we didn't do anything bad."

"Yeah? No switching clothes and names and pretending to be each other?" One of the reasons I thought that they kept the same haircut was so they could play pranks. Too bad for them that both I and their parents could tell them apart without even trying. There were the tiniest subtle differences that they couldn't pull off. Cute that they tried though.

"Okay, we did it for an afternoon. It was fun," Riley said, smiling.

"I won't tell. And since you didn't get sent home from camp early, I'm assuming you didn't get kicked out."

"We were good!" Zoey said, and I gave her a hug.

I laughed and hugged them both again.

"How was your vacation?" Riley finally asked. I told them everything appropriate for eleven-year-old ears, and gave them their presents, which they absolutely loved.

"We brought you something from camp too," Riley said, jumping up and heading upstairs.

She came back down with something behind her back.

"If you brought me a frog or a bug, I'm going to murder you and make it look like an accident," I said, getting stressed out.

"It's not a bug," Riley said. "Calm down and hold out your hand."

I held out my hand but was ready to drop whatever it was if she was lying to me.

Riley dropped something small into my hand and I looked down to find a woven bracelet with a few beads on it that spelled something.

"Oh, Riley," I said, realizing the letters spelled my name and there were also little rainbow heart beads.

"We made it gay for you," Zoey said.

"You girls," I said, squeezing them both. "This is so much better than a frog."

"We made one for Mom too. She cried," Zoey said.

"I bet she did," I said a little sniffly myself.

Mark told them it was time to shower and get ready for bed and they whined and protested, but finally agreed. I got more hugs and they helped me tie on my bracelet.

"Thanks for coming over," Mark said. "I know they were missing you."

"I missed them too." I stood up and told him I'd see him tomorrow morning and went back to the guest house feeling a lot better as I played with the new bracelet on my wrist.

～

MONDAY MORNING CAME TOO SOON, but there wasn't much could do about it.

I got myself up and dressed and over to the house to make pancakes for my monsters, who were exhausted from camp.

Since they would not be dragged from bed, I was a nice nanny and brought it up to them on a tray.

"Now don't think this is happening every day. This is a special welcome back from camp breakfast," I said as I carefully set the tray down on Riley's bed. Zoey had climbed in with her, as they often did. More mornings than not I'd find them in the same bed together. Like they slept better when they weren't separated.

Neither of them was very awake, so I left them to their food and went back down to clean up and found Honor arriving.

"Oh," she said as she saw me coming down the stairs. "Good morning." Normally she didn't even give me the courtesy of a nod, so this was new.

"Good morning?" I said and it sounded like a question.

I reached the downstairs and I thought she was going to brush right by after all that stimulating conversation, but she didn't. She paused, clutching onto her bag as if it was a life raft.

Why was she being so weird?

"Did you have a nice vacation?"

I stared at her. Had she gotten a personality transplant? Had she been taken over by a parasite? Was she in some sort of self-improvement program that emphasized small talk?

"Yes?" I said hesitantly.

"Good," she said, and then she rushed past me as if her hair was on fire.

The fuck?

∽

I WAS VERY aware of Honor for the rest of the day. I kept waiting for her to pop up and awkwardly ask me about the weather or something.

The day passed pretty uneventfully, since the twins weren't up for much. They decided movies in the living room was the order of the day, and I had no problem with that. My time was taken up with unpacking their camp bags and starting all their laundry. How they'd managed to get their clothes so grubby, I didn't know. At least they had evidence they'd had a good time.

Honor didn't come out of the office until the afternoon, and I hoped she hadn't been avoiding coming out to avoid me. Fuck, why was she so hard to read? Why was it so hard to figure her out?

When she did emerge, I tried not to look at her.

She went for her usual glass of water, and it was like I could hear her every single movement.

"Layne?" one of the twins said.

"What?" I said, jumping. I'd been pretending to pick some dead leaves off one of the houseplants.

"Can we have some soda?" Zoey popped her head up and pouted at me.

"You know your parent's rule about soda," I said. "You can have water or iced tea or lemonade or seltzer water."

Zoey huffed and asked for seltzer and then Riley wanted some too, so I went to the fridge and got them out. Normally I wasn't their drink fetcher, but I was willing to do it today.

Honor was still in the kitchen when I moved to the fridge to get the cold drinks.

"You wait on them now too?" she said.

"What?" I pretended I hadn't heard her over the noise of the fridge.

"Nothing," Honor said when I closed the fridge.

"No, what did you say?" I set the cold cans down on the counter and leaned on it. "You've never been scared to speak your mind before. Lay it on me."

I gestured for her to tell me the truth.

"What's that?" she asked, pointing to my bracelet.

"The twins made it for me at camp," I said, showing her. Why was I telling her? I didn't need to talk to her. Every time I talked to her, I got annoyed.

"That's...sweet," she said, and I couldn't tell if she was being sarcastic.

"They're good kids," I said. I wanted to say so much more, but I closed my mouth.

Honor didn't respond, but Riley called for me.

"Sorry, I have to get back to being a servant," I said to Honor, emphasizing the last word.

Before she could say anything else, I picked up the cans and took them back into the living room.

"Thank you," Riley said as I handed over the can. Zoey

Kissed By Her

thanked me as well and I sat down next to them on the couch for a few minutes.

What was Honor's deal? Had she missed me or something? One of these days I was going to straight up ask her and see what happened.

I brooded about Honor for the rest of the day. The twins actually took a nap and only woke up when it was time for dinner.

I went to alert Mark and accidentally made eye contact with Honor.

"I'll be done in a few minutes," Honor said.

"Fine, that's good," Mark said, standing up and stretching. I kept telling him that he needed to get a standing desk, but he was stubborn as hell and it was going to catch up with him one of these days.

I left the room without asking Honor to stay, so I was pretty proud of myself for not doing that and adding to the strangeness between us.

I wish the twins had been here last week to see what Honor had been up to with their dad. Not that I would condone spying, but they could have done a little eavesdropping and just doing a general vibe check.

Now I'll never know what moves she was putting on Mark. Seeing as how he wasn't all over her, and nothing seemed to change in his demeanor, I guess whatever she tried didn't work.

That made me feel good.

How long would it take Honor to accept that Mark just didn't want her?

I was handing plates to the girls when Mark and Honor came out of the office.

"Honor is going to stay for dinner if that's okay with everyone?" Mark said.

I refused to make eye contact with Riley and Zoey because

I knew I would lose my composure. Instead, I grabbed another plate and handed it to Honor.

"Of course, she's welcome," I said through clenched teeth. Honor, at least, looked a little embarrassed, which was new.

"I appreciate it," she said, her voice softer than I'd ever heard it.

"Sure," I said, holding back any other comments. The twins didn't respond, but I gave them looks and they went to get napkins and silverware and a glass so Honor could join us at the dining table.

"This looks really good," Honor said as she sat down after arranging the food on her plate like she was a chef at a restaurant. It didn't escape my notice that she made sure none of her food was touching the other food on her plate. The twins had gone through a phase when they were kids like that. I'd gone out and found plates with separators to make them happy. They were still in a cabinet somewhere. Part of me wanted to ask if Honor would like one.

"Thank you," I said to Honor. It wasn't anything special, just my citrus and fresh herb chicken with saffron rice and veggies with goat cheese. Sounded much fancier than it actually was. Honestly, one of the upsides of cooking for a rich family was that I could buy all the fancy ingredients I wanted and experiment. Mark was a smart guy, but he had no idea what the price of an average banana was.

With Honor around, the conversation was stilted, and that was irritating. Mark did his best to include her, but it didn't really work. Maybe this was her clue that she didn't fit into this family and she should stop trying.

At least the twins saved us with plenty of stories about camp.

"And then Maxie got her period and some people started calling her "Maxie pad" so we had to make them stop," Riley said, and Honor choked on her rice.

"I'm not sure that's an appropriate thing to talk about at the dinner table," Mark said, his face a little red. He was in for such a rude awakening when the twins got a little older. It was going to be bras and tampons and hormones as far as the eye could see.

"Are you saying periods, a normal bodily function, aren't appropriate, Dad?" Riley said, giving her father a sassy look.

Mark opened his mouth and then closed it. I'd never seen his face get this red before.

"What your father is saying is that maybe we shouldn't talk about it right now," I said, jumping in to rescue him. Riley huffed and Zoey laughed.

Honor hadn't said a word and I hoped she was scandalized.

"Another girl got food poisoning. That was bad," Zoey said. "She was in the bathroom all night."

Mark dropped his fork on his plate.

"Okay, that's definitely not something we need to talk about while we're eating. How about nice stories?"

"Like the girl who pretended she was sick and spent all her time masturbating in her bunk?" Riley said and I gasped. Honor swore under her breath and I thought Mark was going to die. He clutched his chest like he was having some kind of episode.

"What?" Riley said. "It's true."

Mark made a bunch of noises that I think were supposed to be words, but he couldn't say anything coherent for a little bit.

"Why don't you take your plates up to your room," he finally said, his voice sounding strangled and his face turning from red to shade of purple.

"Okay!" Riley said, hopping up and taking her plate as Zoey followed suit. They were both giggling, and I was starting to get suspicious.

"I'm so sorry, Honor. They're not normally like this," Mark said.

"It's fine," Honor said, wiping her mouth with her napkin. "I was their age once, too."

"I'm sure you were better behaved," Mark grumbled, shaking his head. "I don't know what I'm going to do with them."

"I'll go talk to them," I said, putting my hand on his arm and getting up from the table.

"No, Layne, you don't have to do that. They're my daughters. I'll deal with it when we're done."

I wanted to argue that he had to go talk to them now, but I wasn't going to question his parenting skills. He was their dad, and I was their nanny.

We three adults finished our food in mostly silence and I grabbed our plates and put away the leftovers as Mark went to talk to the twins.

Honor carried a few plates into the kitchen and lingered.

"I guess I shouldn't have stayed," Honor said as I put the rice into a container.

"Maybe not," I said.

Honor sighed. "Can you tell Mark that I went home? I don't really want to stick around if he's going to make them apologize."

Yeah, that would probably be pretty embarrassing, I had to admit.

"Sure," I said, and she nodded once at me before grabbing her bag and rushing out to her car.

Mark came back downstairs with the twins following him, pretending to hang their heads, but I saw them sharing smiles back and forth. Oh, they knew exactly what they'd done.

"Where's Honor?" Mark asked.

"She had to get home," I said, loading the dishwasher.

Mark nodded.

"Well, you're off the hook for apologizing to her in person, but you're both going to write apology notes."

"For what?" Riley asked.

Mark's eyes narrowed and he crossed his arms.

"You know what. You're not as crafty as you think you are, my girls."

Riley and Zoey looked up at Mark with big, innocent eyes.

"We were just making conversation," Zoey said.

I rolled my eyes. They were really laying it on thick.

"You will both, independently, write notes. In separate rooms. Go," Mark said, laying on his Dad Voice that shut down any disagreement.

Once the two had gone off to take care of his assignment, Mark looked at me.

"Do you think that was good?" he asked. "Every time I think I've got this parenting thing nailed, something new comes up and I'm completely unprepared."

"You should talk to Sadie. Ask what she'd do," I said.

Mark nodded. "You're right. I should at least let her know about this new behavior so she can be on the lookout for it."

He pulled out his phone to call Sadie, and I was happy about that.

"I'm going to head out. Good luck with all of that."

Mark nodded as he called Sadie, and I left him to deal with his kids.

Chapter Eight

"So, what were you trying to do?" I asked the twins the next morning when I woke them up for breakfast. "If you were trying to make Honor uncomfortable, congrats. If you were trying to be subtle about it, you failed."

I got identical innocent faces again.

"We weren't trying to do anything," Riley said.

"Yes, you were," I said. "Come on, tell me the plan." Obviously, they had a plan.

Riley and Zoey shared a look.

"You can't tell Dad," Riley said.

"How about you tell me what you're doing and then I'll decide if I need to involve your dad," I said, sitting on the bed. I needed to get breakfast going, but this was more important.

"We're trying to get Mom and Dad back together," Riley finally said.

I gestured for her to continue. "Go on."

"We know that Honor wants to marry Dad. It's really obvious," Riley said.

"Really obvious," I agreed.

"So we need to make her go away, and we need to get Dad

and Mom alone together," Zoey said. So far, this plan made sense.

"And how are you going to do that?" I asked.

"Drive Honor away, and at the same time, Dad will have to talk to Mom more. We don't care if we get in trouble as long as it works," Riley said.

"We don't want Honor as our stepmom," Zoey said, making a face. "She doesn't like us."

I couldn't argue with their reasoning.

"And she just wants Dad's money," Riley added.

This was all true.

"Are you going to tell Dad?" Zoey asked.

I sighed. This was a dilemma.

"Okay, so I'm not going to tell your dad, on a few conditions." They both looked at me eagerly.

"You can't harass Honor. Yes, she's trying to marry your dad for his money, but your dad is a smart man. And I think if he doesn't give her any hint that he's interested, she'll move on." I hoped.

"As far as trying to get your parents back together? That's something they're going to have to figure out, too. I know that would be the ideal situation, but there's very little that the two of you can do to make that happen."

I was trying really hard to give them the right advice, even if I was totally in support of their plan and their motives.

Riley and Zoey shared one of their twin looks and I waited for them to be done.

"Okay?" I asked.

"Okay," they both said in unison. The twinkle in their eyes told me that they were lying, and I chose to ignore it.

HONOR DIDN'T ASK to stay for dinner the rest of the week, which I was grateful for. Next week was book club, and I had no idea if she was going to show up again. Our book this month was a contemporary romance between two former friends that reunite in their small town years later during a real estate deal. It had all the small-town charm that reminded me of Arrowbridge, and I was looking forward to seeing if everyone else loved it as much as I did.

Would Honor be there? A cute romance didn't seem like her kind of thing, but maybe she'd related to the real estate agent who will stop at nothing to do her job well. That was Honor all right.

Liam video called me during his lunch break on Friday to give me an update on his date with Gwen the previous evening.

"You're looking rough," I told him as he waved to me.

"It was a late night," he said, his voice a little hoarse.

"I'm guessing that's because you had a good time?" I asked.

He smiled and gave me a thumbs up as he leaned against the brick wall of the coffee shop.

"Yeah, she's so great, Layne." He might be tired, but that didn't stop him from gushing about Gwen's many positive qualities and I could see he had it bad. Really bad. Liam hadn't fallen hard for someone in a while and I was excited for him. It also took some of the worry off my shoulders that I carried for him. If Liam found someone to be with, someone to take care of and would take care of him? That was all I wanted. Once he was taken care of, then I could work on finding that for myself.

"She's just so great, Layne."

"You think I might get to meet her soon?" I asked.

"I don't know, is that too much? I don't want to freak her out." He was too cute.

"I don't think it's too much. I mean, we don't have to make

it a big dinner thing, it could just be me stopping into the coffee shop if she's there to say hi. I won't interrogate her."

Liam narrowed his eyes. "You could always just stalk her social media like a normal person."

"What makes you think I haven't?" Who was I, some kind of amateur? The minute I'd figured out who she was when she'd started liking his pages, I'd been looking through her feed. Just to make sure I didn't see any red flags.

"You're such a freak," he said, shaking his head. "Listen, I gotta go. I'll let you know about meeting Gwen."

"Tell her that I'm nice!" I said and he ended the call. "Mean."

"Who's mean?" Riley said, popping out of the pool and reaching for a towel. Zoey joined her a few seconds later.

"My brother. He's got a new girlfriend and I want to meet her."

"We should get to meet her," Riley said, sitting down on one of the chairs. Zoey flopped next to her on the same chair.

"If you act like you did with Honor the other night, then you're never going to meet her," I said, glaring at them.

They both just giggled. Completely unrepentant.

I didn't know how the apology notes had gone over with Honor. She'd been really scarce, and I knew she was absolutely avoiding the twins. I guess their little stunt had worked.

An alarm went off on my phone and I realized it was time for me to start dinner.

"Okay my babies, shower time." They didn't want to go inside, but I shoved them through the door and pointed upstairs.

The second their door slammed, I heard the office door close and Honor appeared.

"They're in the shower so you're safe," I said.

She rolled her eyes and went to get some water.

"I'm not scared of them," she said.

"You should be. They have devious minds and there's two of them," I said.

"I'm not going to be bullied by children," she said, filling her glass.

"Underestimate them at your own peril." I pulled out the steak that had been thawing in the fridge. That was going on the stove and would be sliced up for sandwiches with arugula and garlic aioli and steak fries on the side.

Honor just sort of watched me, and after a few minutes I turned.

"What? Do you think I'm your personal Master Chef?"

"No," she said, putting her glass in the sink.

"Then what are you doing?" I asked.

"Nothing," she said.

"That's what the twins say when they're up to something," I told her.

Honor huffed and left the kitchen without another word.

∼

SATURDAY NIGHT I went over to Joy and Sydney's for dinner and to hang out.

"I bet you Honor is going to come to book club again. I should have asked her about it on Friday, but she was being all weird," I said as Joy handed me a plate filled with salad. She'd made panzanella with a gorgeous tomato vinaigrette and chicken on top.

"Weirder than normal?" Sydney asked as we all sat on the couch. Their place was small and they'd rather have more room for books than a dining room set. The couch was more comfortable anyway, and Clementine would come and fall asleep in your lap, which was always nice.

"Yeah, it was much less odd when she didn't talk to me.

Now she's just kind of awkwardly attempting small talk but she's really bad at it?"

I shook my head and stabbed a lettuce leaf with my fork.

"Not everyone is a good conversationalist, but at least she's trying?" Joy said.

"I wish she would go back to treating me like dirt," I said.

"Maybe she likes you," Sydney said.

I burst out laughing. "No way. She can't *stand* me."

"It's just an idea," Syd said in a sing-song voice. "Think about it."

I absolutely would not.

∽

MY NOT THINKING about it lasted all of a few hours. Once I was back in the guest house, Syd's words wouldn't leave me alone.

It was completely absurd, obviously. Completely.

Even if she did like me, which she didn't, I didn't want her to like me. She liked Mark! She wanted to marry Mark!

Ridiculous.

∽

LIAM FINALLY AGREED to hang out with me on Sunday, since Gwen had picked up an extra shift at the hospital. He asked if he could come over and do a few laps in the pool and I asked him if he could pick up dinner. He agreed and showed up with two different kinds of tacos, elote, and drinks, so he really went all out.

"You're my favorite brother," I said as we sat by the pool. The girls were at a friend's house and Mark was off somewhere, which was unusual. I didn't keep tabs on him all the time, but it was unusual for him to be out on a Sunday evening.

"I'm literally your only brother," he said, squeezing some more sour cream on his taco.

"And yet, you're still my favorite," I said, grinning at him.

He snorted and carefully sat next to the pool with his feet in the water.

"Don't you dare drop that in the water or else I'm going to have to fish it out," I said.

"I won't, I won't," he said.

"How's Gwen?" I asked.

"Beautiful," he said, and I had to stop myself from squealing in delight.

"Is she ready to meet me yet?" I asked.

"Uh, actually she brought it up because she wants to meet you, I guess? I don't know why," he said, and I wanted to throw a taco at him, but that would be a waste of a good taco.

"Hey, I'm a fucking delight. She should want to meet me. I'll bring her books too. Just tell me what she likes," I said.

"She likes messed up shit. Lots and lots of horror." That was slightly out of my wheelhouse, but I could make do.

"Cool, can do. I'll grab a few things, and you can check and make sure she doesn't have them already."

"You don't have to do that," he said.

"No, but I want to. It's my way of welcoming her into the family."

He snorted. "She's not joining the family. We've literally been dating for a few weeks."

"Sometimes when you know, you know," I said.

"And sometimes you should date someone longer and find out if you actually like them before you marry them and spend the rest of your lives making each other miserable," he said, giving me a significant look.

He was talking about our parents. They got married just a few months into dating and stayed married, in spite of completely hating each other. The next few decades were spent resenting each other and not doing anything to change or improve the situation. As far as Liam and I were concerned, they deserved each other.

"Hey, just because we had shitty role models, doesn't mean that it can't work out for some people. There's lots of happy couples that got together quickly that are still happy."

"Yeah, okay, whatever. I'm not going to rush, and I don't think Gwen wants to either. So there." He got up and grabbed another taco.

"Elote please," I said, holding out my plate. He got it for me and then sat back down next to me in the lounge chair.

He couldn't stop talking about Gwen and it was the best thing. We finished all the tacos and Liam dusted off his hands before hopping in the pool. I didn't know how he could swim after filling up on tacos, but more power to him.

I watched him cut through the pool with practiced strokes and finished my food. The air had developed a chill, so as soon as Liam was done, he headed for my shower in the guest house and I put on my pajamas and made tea for both of us.

Liam came out in a different outfit and took the cup of tea I offered him.

"You can stay if you want," I said.

He shook his head. "Nah, it's not that far to my place. I'd rather sleep in my bed than on your couch. No offense."

"Hey, it's not even my couch. It's Mark's couch."

"Not going to lie, it's still weird that you live in his house, technically. I know it's separate, but still a little weird, Layne."

I shrugged. "It's not forever. And it's so much nicer than anything I could afford. Not that I am against getting furniture from thrift stores and the side of the road, but I've gotten used to this." I gestured around me. "It's almost like living in a hotel."

"But it's not yours."

"I guess I don't care about that as much," I said. We'd had

this conversation a few times before. Liam and I just had different values when it came to living spaces. Hell, I didn't even know what I would want if I had a million dollars to decorate a place. One minute I liked lots of birds and flowers, and the next I liked something more geometric, and then I liked something sleeker, and then I liked antiques. I could never seem to make up my mind, so it was a good thing I wasn't in charge of decorating. I'd end with a big old mess.

Liam hung around until he finished his tea and I sent him off again and made him promise me that we'd set up a time to meet Gwen in a non-threatening and lowkey way.

"Love you, baby brother," I said, hugging him.

"I'm not a baby anymore," he said as he leaned down to hug me.

"You'll always be my little bro," I said, reaching up to pat him on the head.

~

THE TWINS SPENT the next several days with their heads together, whispering.

"What are you doing?" I asked, when they were quiet for a particularly long time.

"Nothing," they chorused, which sent up all the red flags. Whenever kids were quiet, and they said they were up to nothing, that meant they were probably setting their pillows on fire or trading bitcoins online.

By Thursday, I knew something was definitely afoot, and I didn't think I was going to like it.

They had barely made eye contact with me all day, so I ambushed them during lunch.

"So, what are you plotting," I said as I held out their plates. They shared a look.

"Nothing," they said.

"No way, not buying it. Try that on someone younger who doesn't know you. Hit me with it."

"We're not doing anything," Riley said. "We're just um…"

"We want to buy a horse!" Zoey blurted out. "We loved riding one at camp, so we've been thinking about how we can ask our parents and how we could earn money to take care of it."

I narrowed my eyes and stared at both of them, waiting for either one to blink. The twins gave me identical wide-eyed looks.

"And what are you going to name this horse?" I asked.

"Lightning!" they said at the same time.

"Impressive performance," I said, handing over the plates. "But I'm not buying it. If you're going to go after Honor again, I'm going to have to object."

"We're not," Riley said, and that I did believe. At least for now.

They shared another look and finally, Zoey's shoulders slumped.

"We want to take Mom and Dad on a date," she said.

"You mean like a family date?" I asked. They both nodded.

"That's actually really sweet. Like all of you go out to dinner?"

They shook their heads. "We want to pretend that we're all going out together, but then we'll leave and they'll have to eat alone together," Riley said, a devious smile forming on her face.

"And how are you going to do that?" I asked. "When you leave, they could just bail."

"That's why we're going to put them on a boat," Riley said. "We'll all get on and then the two of us will jump off at the last second! It will totally work."

I didn't know about that.

"You want to take your father's boat?" I asked. He had a beautiful schooner (because of course he did).

"No, we want them to be totally focused on one another. So we're going to book a sunset cruise for four, and then it will just be for two!"

I could see all kinds of potential problems with this plan. I had to do something.

"I'm not saying this is a bad idea. I'm just saying that I think you need some adult supervision. And if you tell either of your parents that I helped you, I will fill your underwear drawer with spiders," I said.

That wasn't much of a threat because they knew I'd never follow through. Still, I hoped the visual would get my point across.

"Can you help us get the boat?" Riley asked.

"Sure. You paying for it?" I didn't even know why I was asking. These kids had plenty of money. Not that their parents held out their wallets, but they got plenty for allowance and holidays and so forth. Plus, they had tons in savings because what did they need to buy? They didn't have bills.

"We'll send you money," Riley said, getting out her phone.

"Sounds good. So you pick a date and a boat and I'll get the tickets. There's no guarantee this is going to work, and I don't want you to be disappointed. Keep your expectations reasonable." I put one hand on each twin's shoulder.

They were bubbling with excitement for this new plan.

"Oh, and if you're getting off the boat, I should probably be there to pick you up so you're not just sitting on a dock alone for two hours without supervision," I said. "So you'll have to get me a ticket too, to make it plausible."

They groaned. This wasn't going to be cheap, but that was their problem.

"I'll take you out for ice cream," I said.

They both squealed and hugged me in unison.

"You are too much," I said, hugging them back.

∼

"DO you really think it's a good idea to get involved?" Joy said as I helped her set up the chairs for book club on Thursday night.

"I'm not really involved. I mean, they're going to do something whether I help them or not, so it's better if I supervise their plan so they don't do something completely drastic." I shuddered to think what those two could get up to if they didn't have me to reign them in.

Joy nodded and went to set the cups out. "I guess that makes sense." Sydney arrived and brought a tray of s'mores brownies with her.

"You angel," I said, reaching for one.

"They're not that special. I used a box mix," she said, setting the rest of the brownies down on the table.

More people started arriving and I kept twitching anytime the door opened.

"Do you know if she's coming?" Syd asked as I stress-ate my second brownie.

"I didn't get a chance to ask. She was completely avoiding me all week." I'd tried to ask her those few times I'd seen her, but the words had stuck in my throat and I hadn't been able to.

The door opened again as I reached for my third brownie and there she was, but tonight she looked…different.

I'd never seen Honor in anything other than a dress or a skirt. She wore jeans and a blouse with delicate pearl buttons and fluttery sleeves.

Jeans. On Honor.

I'd thought she looked incredible in her office wear, but Honor in jeans was something else entirely.

Of course, she still had heels on, but these were delicate

little strappy things with crystals on them. You wouldn't think they'd work with her outfit, but they did.

"Breathe, Layne," Joy said, hitting me on the arm. I gasped in a breath.

That bitch had actually made me forget to breathe. What the hell?

Honor adjusted her bag and walked in, nodding at people as she took her seat.

"Are you going to go talk to her?" Joy asked.

"What? No. Why would I do that?"

"To be nice?" Joy said and I looked at her as if she'd grown a second head. "You could be the bigger person. And hasn't she been trying to reach out?"

"I don't want to be the bigger person. I like being small," I muttered.

Joy gave me a silent look. Okay, fine. I grabbed a napkin and grabbed another brownie. She probably hated brownies as much as she hated happiness.

I walked over to Honor and she looked up as if she'd been expecting me.

"I brought you a brownie," I said, like a dumbass as I held it out to her.

Honor's eyes flicked down to the brownie and then back up to my face. Her eyes narrowed.

"You didn't let the twins poison it, did you?" she said. "You know I found fake plastic vomit on my car and a rubber snake in my purse this week. I wouldn't put anything past those two."

"Pft. As if I'd participate in such an obvious ploy as poison. It's okay if you don't like brownies. The brownie was more of a metaphor." I didn't say anything about the other pranks.

Honor sat there for a beat and then took the brownie from my hand.

"I've never eaten a metaphor before," she said, and I almost laughed.

"I'm sorry about the twins," I said, not sure what the fuck I was doing apologizing. I hadn't done anything.

"It's fine. I understand. I was young once too. And I have a sister. We used to play pranks too."

Right, the sister.

"I have a younger brother," I said and since it was weird to keep standing while she was sitting, so I took the seat next to her, which happened to be on the other side of Sydney.

"My sister is younger too," she said. Interesting. I didn't get older sister vibes from her, but I did get first-born child vibes.

"Does she live around here?" I asked.

Honor shook her head. "She lives with me when she's not in college during the summer, but she's going to be a junior this year at school in Boston."

I couldn't believe that Honor was talking to me like a regular person. Then she took a bite of the brownie and kept going.

"She hasn't declared a major yet and I'm apparently being a nag for asking her to think about it. I told her I'll support whatever she picks as long as she picks something and follows through on it."

Honor took a breath and I could tell that was something she'd been holding onto.

"She sounds like a pain in the ass," I said, and Honor let out a shocked laugh that was so lovely it almost made my toes curl. I'd never heard her laugh before, and maybe if I had, she might have pissed me off less.

Honor's laugh was the kind of thing you wished you could hold onto.

"She is a pain in the ass, but I love her." Honor shrugged one shoulder and took another bite.

I was about to tell her about my brother when book club started, and I couldn't.

Honor pulled her paperback copy out of her bag and I

noticed that there were little tabs sticking to the pages. Oh, she'd made notes. She had prepared for this.

Would I expect anything less from her? No. Not after what'd I'd seen when she worked with Mark.

I was torn between my desire to gush about how much I loved the book, and my desire to watch Honor and see what she was going to say.

This time she did talk, and her observations were insightful. As I'd suspected, she had identified with the realtor character, but she did criticize her for some of the decisions she made. It was strange to hear her saying that the character should have put love over her job. Who was this Honor? She wasn't the same person I saw every day at the house.

This Honor wore jeans and thought love was important and laughed and had a sister who annoyed her.

I didn't know what to do with this Honor. The one who glared at me and didn't speak to me because I was beneath her notice was much easier to deal with.

I got myself a little cup of wine when everything wrapped up and I felt someone behind me.

"Thanks for not poisoning the brownie," a voice said in my ear and I almost dropped the cup of wine, but I was able to keep my hold on it at the last second.

Turning, I met Honor's eyes. They were such a beautiful icy blue that they almost looked like they were colored contacts. I didn't think they were.

"You're welcome," I said. "I guess you liked this book, huh?"

Why was I suddenly so terrible at talking?

"I did. When do we vote on what the next book will be?" At every meeting, we took suggestions for the next book, and then the votes were counted in the next few days via email so anyone who hadn't attended could have a say.

"You'll get an email tomorrow," I said. "Which one are you

picking?"

Honor reached for the last brownie. "I'm not telling you. I don't want you to influence my vote."

I pretended to gasp. "I would never do that. Hey, have you ever read anything by Skylar Alyssa?"

She shook her head.

"Well, if you liked this month's read, then you'll love her. Come on."

I walked toward the Skylar Alyssa shelf and hoped that Honor would follow me.

It hadn't escaped my notice that Joy and Sydney had been cleaning up and had left me and Honor alone.

She did follow me to the shelves, which had a sign that said LOCAL AUTHOR on it.

"She comes in and signs a lot too," I said, picking up the first book in the most recent series. "Try this one."

Honor took the book from me, our fingers brushing.

She read the back and nodded. "I'll give it a try."

This time I followed Honor to the register. Joy skipped over and rung up the book.

"She's doing a signing in a few weeks if you want to come and meet her," Joy said.

"I'll think about it," Honor said, and Joy beamed at me before going back to finish cleaning up.

"I didn't think sapphic romances would be, um, your kind of thing," I blurted out. It was something I'd been thinking about since she showed up at the first one. I mean, it wasn't like we advertised as a queers-only book club, so she might not have known when she first came. But she was back now and seemed to want to keep coming.

"What kind of books did you think were my kind of thing?" she asked with an arched eyebrow.

"Ones on how to marry your boss?" I asked and the playfulness was gone in a second.

Honor leaned close to me and I could see the rage ignite in her eyes.

"You—" she said, but she didn't continue.

"Me?" I said as I moved closer to her, as if drawn to her inner flame.

"You," Honor said and then I was almost knocked off my feet as she kissed me. No, she didn't just kiss me. Her mouth attacked mine. Almost as if she was angry at me and was punishing me with her lips.

The kiss shocked me, but then my brain registered that Honor was kissing me and I...I liked it. A lot. Her mouth was plush and firm and hot and delicious. I hadn't been kissed in a long time, and for a second I forgot what to do, but then her tongue licked the seam of my lips and with a moan, I opened up and Honor Conroy's tongue was in my mouth.

Honor Conroy's tongue was in my fucking mouth and the world had gone completely bonkers. Before I knew what was happening, the kiss was over, and I was blinking my eyes open in a daze.

Honor stormed out of the bookstore without another word as I pressed my hand against my mouth.

~

"WHAT JUST HAPPENED?" Joy asked as I stared out the door and wondered if I should go after Honor.

"I don't even know," I said. "Did that just happen?"

"Honor sucking your face off? Yeah, that happened," Sydney said.

"I need to go home," I said as Joy and Sydney stared at me.

"Call me to let me know you got there safely," Joy said as I grabbed my bag and walked out to my car, still completely perplexed and more turned on than I'd been in my entire life.

What the actual hell?

Chapter Nine

THE NEXT MORNING, I made sure to linger in the kitchen so I'd see Honor when she walked in. I'd pulled up a blank message to text her and ask why she'd kissed me at least a hundred times the previous night but figured that this was the kind of thing you talked about in person. My brain was incapable of thinking about anything other than that kiss and the questions it created. Was it a mistake? What did it mean for her plans with Mark? Was Honor even queer? Too many questions and only Honor had the answers. I also wanted to apologize for the shitty comment that had led to the kiss. The outcome might have been good, but it was still a nasty thing to say and I didn't feel good about it.

Honor was back to her beautiful self with a sleek dark blue sheath dress and her heels when she arrived. My eyes went instantly to her mouth and that deep red lip stain.

I needed to go over to Sadie's and watch the twins, but I wanted to deal with Honor first.

"Hey," I said as she made to walk right past me to the office. My voice stopped her.

"Can we talk about last night?" I asked.

Honor shook her head. "Not now," she said before rushing down the hall. Maybe I should have given her another brownie to get her to open up. I did a quick search of the cabinets and we didn't really have anything brownie-like on hand.

Hm. Nothing I could do about it now, but I did think about it as I drove to Sadie's.

∽

THE TWINS HAD FOUND a boat they wanted to rent and asked me to email the company to find out about available dates after their mom had left for work. I typed out an email and showed them that I sent it.

"What are we doing today?" Riley asked. That was the eternal question. If I didn't plan things out, it probably would have made me homicidal hearing it every single day.

"How does going to the library, then lunch, then bringing your mom lunch at the shop and then going to the movies sound?" I asked, and their faces both lit up.

I made sure their rooms were clean before we headed out. The Arrowbridge Library had gotten a grant a few years ago to add on a really nice teen space. Not only did they have plenty of books for the kids, but they also had computers they could use, and tablets to rent, and even a TV with a few games on it.

Whenever the twins were bored, I shoved them in the teen room and told them to have fun. There were always other kids in there from school, and many a rainy day had been spent here.

They also did movies in the middle of the day in the small theater and they made sure they weren't just for little kids.

I returned a few books and said hi to the volunteer as the twins headed for the teen room when they spotted a few of their friends.

I hit the New Releases table looking for anything that might catch my fancy. As many books as I bought, I also borrowed heavily from the library. It was the perfect way to check out a new author without the commitment of buying a book.

I didn't see anything I liked, so I just sort of wandered around and then chatted with one of the librarians, who was my age and always took my advice on what they might want to order. I was doing my best to distract my mind from thoughts about kissing Honor, but I wasn't doing a great job at it.

Looking for something different that might capture my attention, I hit the non-fiction section for a random book and found one on the radium girls that looked intriguing, if a little depressing.

There was some new art on the walls that I looked at before going back to the circulation desk to check out my book and chat with the librarian before grabbing the twins and heading to Nick's Pizza for lunch.

I checked my emails and I had a message back from the boat company for the twins.

"Okay, here are the dates," I said, reading them off. "I'll just forward you the email." I sent it to them, and they started plotting again as I finished my pizza.

"So how are you going to play this?" I asked as we threw out the trash and left the pizza place.

"We're going to tell them that we have a surprise for them and that it's really important," Riley said. "They can't say no to both of us."

I snorted. They really were confident.

"Sounds like a plan," I said as they skipped ahead of me to walk into the boutique.

Sadie was arranging some jewelry on the counter and her face lit up as the girls went over to hug her.

"What are you two up to? You look like you've been plotting." Never underestimate the instincts of a mother.

They shared a look.

"We want to do something with you and Dad. A special surprise," Riley said as her mom brushed her hair back from her face.

"Oh do you now?" she said, looking at Zoey. "What kind of surprise?"

"Mom," Riley said, rolling her eyes. "It's not a surprise if we tell you what it is."

"Do you know anything about this?" Sadie said, turning her attention to me. I'd been looking at some of the racks of clothes. I bought way too much stuff from this store because I couldn't help myself.

"It's good, I promise. Nothing nefarious," I said. The twins grinned at me.

Sadie looked back down at her daughters. "Okay, when is this surprise happening?" The twins jumped up and down and chattered away, telling her how happy they were and how much she was going to love it.

I thought about telling her what they were really planning, but I kept my mouth shut.

Hopefully I wouldn't get fired.

∽

AFTER I TOOK Riley and Zoey to see the latest animated movie all the kids were excited about and then deposited them back with their mom, I hit the Yellow Roof Grocery store for a box of brownie mix, cookie dough, Oreos, and hurried back to Mark's.

He and Honor were still working, so I did my best to make the brownies as fast as possible, but they were still in the oven when Honor came out with her bag over her shoulder.

"Wait," I said, looking at the timer on my phone. Ten minutes still to go.

"Excuse me?" Honor said, freezing. I guess I'd been a little aggressive, but I'd been so sure that I could get these brownies baked before she came out.

"Sorry. I, um, do you have anywhere to be?" I asked.

Honor stared at me and then set her bag down on a chair. "Why?"

"Um, I need you to wait like fifteen minutes," I said, hoping she couldn't smell the scent of chocolate wafting from the oven.

Honor narrowed her eyes. "Again, I ask, why?"

"Fuck it, I'm making you apology brownies. This time I made them from scratch. And we need to talk about the other thing." I didn't want Mark to come out and hear me talking about kissing, so I kept things vague on purpose.

Honor looked right at the box I'd left on the counter.

"Okay, so I made them from a box, but they're slutty brownies!"

Honor crossed her arms. "Do I even want to ask?"

"You've never had slutty brownies? They're the best. Kind of a bitch to make, but your eyes are going to roll back in your head, trust me."

Honor did not look like she believed me, but she did take several steps toward me.

"So yeah. I made you slutty apology brownies," I said, and Honor let out a snort.

"I'm not sure whether to be flattered or insulted," she said, and then she was in the kitchen, and there didn't seem to be enough room to breathe.

"Why not both?" I asked.

The timer still had a few minutes to go, but she wasn't leaving.

"Well now I have no choice but to find out what makes

these brownies so slutty," Honor said. I couldn't lie, the way she said the word "slutty" was sexy.

"If you want, we could go over to the guest house to try them. Or you could just take the pan home and bring it back when you're done. We still need to talk more about what else happened."

I hadn't intended on inviting her over to my place but the words just kind of came out of my mouth. We did need privacy for our discussion, so it made sense.

Honor was silent for a beat and then she nodded. "Okay."

Well shit, now I had to hope that my house was clean. I thought it was, but with my luck there was a pair of underwear in the middle of the couch or one of my vibrators in the drying rack by the sink.

At last, the timer went off and I brought out the brownies.

"They smell really good at least," Honor said.

"No poison either," I said cheerfully.

Mark came out of his office and looked from me to Honor and back.

"Brownies?" Mark asked.

"Oh, uh, yeah. I made them in here because your oven is better," I said. For some reason I didn't think Honor would like Mark knowing she was going to hang out with me, so I covered.

"Is something wrong with your oven? I can get someone here to look at it," he said. I waved him off.

"No, it's fine. This one is just more efficient. Makes for gooier brownies," I said. He nodded and then got a phone call that he took back down the hall.

"Shall we make our escape?" I said to Honor. She looked back toward where Mark had disappeared.

"I'm not sure if I should leave yet. He might need something."

I rolled my eyes. "He's a grown man and he has your

phone number. Come on."

I picked up the still-hot pan with oven mitts and headed out the door, not waiting for her.

Then I got stuck because I couldn't get through the door because my hands were full.

"Need a hand?" Honor asked.

"Please," I said, and she reached around me to open the door and then got ahead of me as we headed for the guest house.

"Sorry for the mess," I said the second she stepped inside. It wouldn't have mattered if my house was cleaner than it had ever been. I would still apologize for mess.

Honor turned slowly as I set the pan of brownies down on the counter.

"It's nice," she said.

"Is that a compliment?" I asked.

"Maybe," she said, smiling.

"The brownies have to cool for a few more minutes before we can slice them," I said. "Did you want some tea or water or anything?"

When I woke up this morning, I did not think that I would be serving Honor drinks and brownies in my house, but if you asked me before last night if she would have kissed me, I would have said that was out of the question, too.

"Tea is fine," she said, and she sat right down on my couch.

"Don't those hurt your feet?" I asked, nodding toward her feet as I filled the kettle and pulled out two mugs and my tea selection.

"No," she said, looking down. "You just get used to them."

"Huh," I said. I wore heels on occasion, but those occasions were rare.

My phone vibrated with a message from my brother, making me jump.

Do you want to meet Gwen this weekend? She

wants to go to the beach on Sunday and you could stop by.

I smiled as I answered him, telling him that yes, absolutely I wanted to meet her.

Honor got up from the couch and joined me in the kitchen. The kettle went off and I added the water to both cups.

"Pick your poison," I said, showing her the options.

"Funny," she said, picking my favorite black tea and adding it to her cup. I didn't need that much caffeine this late in the day, so I went for an herbal mix.

"Is it strange living so close to where you work?" Honor asked.

"I think I'm just so used to it at this point that it's just my life," I said, dipping my teabag in and out of the water.

"How long have you worked for them?" Honor asked. I guess she wasn't so bad at small talk after all. We were going to have to warm up a little until we got to talking about the kiss.

"They hired me right after the twins were born. When they were still together. Then they got divorced and I was hoping they weren't going to get rid of me because I was so in love with the girls at that point. Fortunately, they decided to keep me, and I think it really helped having someone stable who was going to both places."

I got out a knife and started cutting up the brownies.

"You are absolutely mangling them," Honor said, holding her hand out.

"This is my kitchen. I wield the knives," I said, but now I was stressed out about my brownie-cutting abilities.

"Center or corner?" I asked.

"Center. Obviously," she said, as if that was the only answer.

"Okay then," I said. "Honor has strong opinions on brownies. Noted."

I levered out the center brownie for her and got a plate.

"I have strong opinions on a lot of things," Honor said, taking the plate from me.

"I'm not shocked," I said, getting my own brownie that had corners on both sides. I liked the crunch. Honor and I carried our treats and tea over to the couch and sat down together.

"I'm waiting," I said as Honor stared at the brownie on her plate.

"If I eat this, will it make me slutty?" she asked, picking up the brownie and bringing it to her lips.

"Let's hope so," I blurted out before I could think better of what those words would mean.

Honor raised one eyebrow before taking a bite of the brownie.

"Slutty?" I asked as she chewed and swallowed.

"Very," she said. "I think I've been ruined for regular brownies now. Slutty only from here on out."

I laughed and then ate my own brownie. It was really good.

"Do you still want an answer?" she asked as we both looked down at our empty plates. I was ready for seconds. Sure, it was time for dinner and I should be doing that, but also, brownies were amazing. As a grown woman, I could eat brownies for dinner if I wanted to.

"To what?" I asked, licking a brownie crumb off my thumb. Was she ready to talk about the kiss now? I'd been holding back on blurting it out, and it had been killing me.

"About what kind of books I like," she said, and I knew we weren't talking about books.

"What kind of books do you like, Honor?" I asked.

"I like books about all kinds of people. I might prefer books about woman, but I've been known to read books with all genders."

Oh.

"So you don't discriminate," I said.

"But I prefer sapphic romance," she said.

"Got it."

That took me a second to digest. "I like sapphic romance only," I said. I mean, I absolutely did read all kinds of romance, but right now books were a metaphor and I was going with it.

Honor nodded. "Glad we got that out of the way."

"Yeah, that's good information to know," I said, and suddenly it was too hot in here. I got up to open a window and turn the fan on.

"So are we going to talk about the other thing?" I asked.

"What other thing would that be?" Honor asked.

"The fact that you kissed me?"

Honor refused to meet my eyes. "No," she said.

"Why not?"

She didn't answer and I wasn't going to beg and plead and force her. I almost thought about going over and kissing her again, but my emotions about the whole thing were still so confusing.

To give myself some space from her, I went to the kitchen.

"Do you want another brownie?" I asked, and my voice sounded like it belonged to someone else.

"Sure," Honor said, finally breaking her silence.

"Did you want dinner? I could make something," I said as I selected brownies for both of us. There wasn't another middle piece, so I just cut a corner piece and cut off the edge for her. Like she was one of the twins and I was cutting off the crust.

"No, you don't need to do that. I'll have something when I get home."

"Where do you live?" I asked, and she just got up and came to lean on the kitchen counter. I was too restless to sit down right now.

"Not that far. You know Seagull Lane?"

I did. "Are you anywhere near Lorna Rose?"

That made Honor smile. "She's my neighbor. I adore her."

Lorna Rose was a local legend. She was a million years old (no one knew quite how old) and she was known for making and selling jam out of her garage, and for raising fancy chickens that she sold and had shown around the country when she was younger.

"I feed her chickens sometimes," Honor said, and I almost fell over.

"I literally can't picture that," I said. "Do you have a farmer outfit?"

Honor shook her head. "No. I do have regular clothes you know. You've seen me in them."

"Once," I said. "I only ever see you in work clothes."

"I promise you, I do have clothes that I don't wear to work. I've got a whole wardrobe that you've never seen."

"Well, some of us don't have that many clothes, or fashion sense," I said, and she laughed. "Sadie does her best with me, but I'm going to choose comfort every time. When the twins were babies, I don't think I wore anything but yoga pants and shorts. And I had to bring multiple outfits because one of them was always spitting up or making a mess all over me."

"You really love them," Honor said.

"Yeah, I do. I know they're not mine, but I know I'm part of their family and always will be. No matter what happens in the future." Ugh, I didn't like talking about that part.

"What's that face?" Honor asked.

"Oh, I just don't like thinking about what's going to happen when the girls are old enough to not need me anymore. Scares the shit out of me."

I didn't know why I was telling her this. "They've been my life for over ten years, and I can't imagine waking up every day and not making them breakfast and getting them off to school and making sure their rooms are clean."

I shuddered.

"Fuck," I said, feeling tears prick at the corners of my eyes.

"Mark would never get rid of you," she said.

"Oh, I know he might keep me on as a housekeeper, but I don't know if that would be enough, you know? I just… I took this job at a time when I needed it and I never expected to fall in love with the family and work for them so long. I'm supposed to have plans and ambitions and I have nothing!"

I threw my hands up in the air.

"Sorry. I didn't mean to just dump that on you," I said, feeling my face getting red.

Honor nodded. "It's okay. I don't mind."

"You don't?" I asked, skeptical.

"It's nice to have someone to talk to," she said.

"Right now, I'm the only one who's doing the talking. What have you been holding onto that you want to get off your chest?" Maybe me opening up would have the same effect on her?

My eyes automatically looked down at said chest. It was a very nice one, I had to admit.

"Is this just a ploy to talk about my chest?" Honor asked, and I hurriedly moved my eyes back up to her face.

"Not intentionally," I said. "But stop changing the subject. You talk to people like you're dodging bullets."

Honor's lips thinned.

"It's not my fault that I've had to dodge a lot of conversational bullets in my life."

I waved my hand for her to elaborate. "Such as?"

Honor sat back and regarded me. "You should know that I don't trust people."

Shocking.

"Yeah, I can kind of tell. You're not exactly the warmest person, Honor."

"I know what people call me. I know you think I'm an ice-cold bitch. I know you think I'm mean. I know you think I'm a gold-digger. None of those things is news to me."

"I figured."

"I'm not going to apologize for who I am and who I've become. A lot of my choices about who I am now were taken away from me."

Well, that was interesting. Honor was so tight-lipped about everything, but especially her family. Hell, I didn't even know where she grew up. I didn't know if her parents were still alive or anything.

"Liam and I are estranged from our parents. Let's just say they didn't take his transition well and it was better for the two of us to strike out on our own. I know he's grown, but I still feel like I have to take care of him."

Talking about Liam's transition wasn't something I talked about with a lot of people. You never knew when someone could turn on a dime and reveal themselves as a secret transphobe, but Honor already knew Liam was trans.

"I'm sorry about that," she said. "Families can be toxic."

"Yes, they can."

Silence fell between us.

"My mother has been married six times," she said. Now we were getting somewhere.

"She taught me that the best way to get what I wanted was to ingratiate myself with someone who had money or power or both. I learned about prenups while I was playing with dolls."

That was a little messed up.

"I learned that in order to have what you wanted, you had to find a man and make him happy."

Everything started to fall into place.

"That's what I did, for a while. Then I decided to go to college and get a good degree and do it on my own. That lasted as long as a few weeks after graduation, when I couldn't find a job. My loans came due soon, and I could barely pay them, let alone my rent. So I found myself a boyfriend that had money that didn't mind me moving in with him after only a few weeks of dating. He was a good man, I don't want you to get me wrong. I made sure I picked someone I wasn't in love with. Never fall in love, that's what my mother whispered to me. I could love my children, but never fall in love with a man. Ever. That was paramount. No love. Just security."

Honor took a breath. I took one as well. I'd been completely still, stunned that she was telling me all this. It was as if our kiss had unlocked something in her. She might say she didn't trust me, but right now she was acting like she did.

"The one flaw in my plan was that he didn't want to marry me. So I had to search for a new place. I decided I needed to get away. Be somewhere new. I don't know how I found Mark's ad for a job, but I did and when I walked into his house, I saw my future before me."

It took everything in me to not make some kind of comment. I clenched my teeth so hard they hurt.

"Mark is just the kind of man I always pictured myself marrying. And nothing was going to stand in the way of that and then you…" she trailed off and I could see her starting to breathe faster. Her face got red and the waves of anger radiated off her.

"You fucked up everything, Layne. Completely fucked my plan."

Somehow I found my words. "How did I do that?"

Instead of answering, Honor stood up.

"I need to go. I need to get out of here. Thank you for the brownies." She snatched her bag and headed for the door.

"Wait, what's happening?" I asked, but she ignored me, pulling her keys out of her bag.

"Honor!" I yelled as she rushed toward her car and got in. I wasn't going to throw myself in the path of a moving vehicle, so I just let her go. She backed out and then she was gone, leaving me with half a tray of slutty brownies and a whole lot of questions.

Chapter Ten

Joy had to work at the bookshop on Saturday, but I grabbed Sydney so I could talk to at least one of my friends to process what went down with Honor.

"Joy is going to be so mad she missed this," Sydney said as she poured me a glass of iced tea.

"You can fill her in later."

I told Sydney most of what I'd talked about with Honor, leaving a few things out. Honor would definitely be pissed if I shared all her business with my friends, so I kept things vague.

"So then she just fucking bolted and I don't know what to do," I said. Why did I keep getting into situations with Honor that completely confused me? Dealing with her made me feel like I didn't know what the hell I was doing.

"Did you chase after her?"

"No, she was in her car. I wasn't chasing her car like a dog."

Sydney thought for a few moments. "Sounds like she's mad at you for distracting her from her nefarious plans and there's not a whole lot you can do about that anger. Not your fault she finds you attractive and kissed you."

"Wait, she finds me attractive?" I asked and Sydney stared at me.

"Obviously, Layne. When was the last time you passionately kissed someone you didn't find attractive?"

I mean, never, but still.

"But she acts like I'm garbage. Like I'm beneath her."

"Maybe she did that to try and put some distance between you and her feelings."

Well, shit.

I hadn't considered that.

"This whole thing is confusing as fuck and I don't like it," I said, putting my head in my hands. "Why couldn't I just fall for a nice Arrowbridge girl and buy a Subaru and get a couple of dogs?"

"Oh Layne, you wouldn't be happy with a local girl and a few dogs. Remember your first crush?"

I thought back to the first girl I'd ever fallen for. She'd been the prettiest girl in school, but also the meanest. "Oh."

Sydney gave me a significant look. "Exactly."

"So, my type is hot and mean?" I asked. "What does that say about me?"

"The heart wants what the heart wants," Sydney said.

"Whoa, hold on here. Who's talking about my heart? We were talking about Honor being weird."

My heart started to race a little and I didn't know why.

"We can't talk about her feelings without talking about yours, Layne."

I guess she had a point. I didn't want to talk about my feelings. They were too tangled right now.

"Obviously she's gorgeous, and I guess we've established that she's my type, but other than that..." I trailed off, thinking.

"I mean, I guess she's a hard worker. I can appreciate that. And she has goals, even if they're completely weird and twisted goals. Her taste in books is excellent. She told me she feeds Lorna Rose's chickens," I said.

"Anything else?" Sydney asked.

"I don't know. She's just..." I couldn't put Honor into neat, safe words. Partly because I hadn't figured her out yet, and partly because words seemed inadequate for describing her.

"There it is," Sydney said, pointing at me. "You like her. Admit it."

I made grumbling sounds and finally rolled my eyes. "Okay, I will admit, I am intrigued by her. I'm not saying that I like her."

Sydney sighed. "So, what are you going to do now?"

"I don't know, that's why I came to talk to you," I said, and then finished my glass of iced tea.

"I can't tell you what to do, you know that. You wouldn't listen to me anyway."

Syd was right; I didn't have a good track record of taking advice.

"Fine, what would you do? Should I make more brownies?" I'd stress-eaten the rest of the pan last night and this morning for breakfast. At this point, my body was about sixty percent slutty brownie. I was starting to get lightheaded.

"Well, I'd give her some space and then approach her in a few days in a neutral setting and ask if she wants to talk. If not, let it go. She's got her own shit to deal with that doesn't involve you, and she might need to work it out on her own."

I didn't like sitting back and not fixing things. I never had. When Liam had transitioned, I'd read every freaking thing I could about it, and had gone with him to his appointments and made sure that his doctors were treating him right all through getting on T and during his top surgery. When the twins had an issue at school, I let their parents deal with it first, but I also made sure they were okay, and knew that I supported them. If something was broken in the guest house, I tried to fix it first using online instruction videos before asking Mark to take a look. More than once at the bookstore when Joy was busy, I'd helped a customer and just pretended I worked there. Kendra had to tell me to stop because she couldn't afford to hire me.

I liked fixing things. I liked helping. Letting Honor work out her own shit went against my natural instincts.

"I don't like it," I said.

Sydney patted me on the arm. "I know, I know. Would some food make you feel better?"

"Yeah," I said. "And maybe a nap. Sometimes I wonder if I'm just an overgrown toddler."

"We all are," Syd said, going to the fridge.

~

SYDNEY MADE a quick chopped salad with what she had on hand and we ate it out of big bowls with lots of croutons while Clementine begged at our feet until Syd put food in her bowl.

"And how about you? Seen anyone who strikes your fancy?" I asked. Enough about me. I was curious what was going on with her.

She shrugged and picked up a crouton with her fingers, crunching down on it.

"I don't know. I guess I like to keep things casual."

"And have you been casual with anyone recently?" I asked.

She shook her head. "No. Maybe I'm getting too old for hookups."

"You're twenty-six," I said. "You're hardly decrepit."

"I just want to go to a bar and have a quick and hot fuck in the bathroom, is that too much to ask?" Sydney said, setting down her empty bowl.

"You can go out and do that, you know," I said.

She sighed. "I guess."

"Go get it," I said, bumping her shoulder. "You're young

and you're hot and you should have what you want. I fully support your sexcapades."

Sydney snorted. "I'll think about it."

"Would you like Joy and I to go with you?" I asked. "I mean, we'd stay at the bar and let you do your thing, but we could be your wing women. Since we didn't do any of that on our vacation."

"You'd get me laid? Aw, you're such a good friend," Sydney said, giving me a hug.

"I've got your back, doll," I said.

∼

I STILL DIDN'T HAVE a clear course of action, but I stopped by to see Joy near the end of her shift.

"There have been developments with Honor," I said as she organized the children's area. Kids were always pulling the stuffed animals and toys out to play with, so keeping the area clean was a constant struggle. "I talked to Syd, so she can fill you in."

"Do you need advice?" Joy asked.

"No, I think I'm going to just wing it," I said. "Syd told me to do nothing, but that's not really my style."

"Your style doesn't always work," Joy pointed out.

"Hey, that's rude," I said, but she waited patiently. "Okay, fine. You may be right. But I don't have to like it."

"That's fair," Joy said with a laugh.

A customer wandered over needing help, so I let her get back to work and headed back home. Seagull Lane wasn't on my way, but I did a little detour and turned down the road without really thinking about it.

Lorna Rose's house was easy to spot, mostly due to the signs about jam and the chickens. She had a beautiful coop for them that took up a lot of the yard next to the house.

I pretended I was stopping for jam and looked at the houses all around Lorna's. One was basically abandoned and overgrown and looked like no one had been in there for ages. The one across the street had a FOR SALE sign on it and a bunch of workers replacing the roof. I didn't think that was Honor's house.

On the other side was a teensy cottage that had some peeling paint in parts but had Honor's car parked in the driveway.

Shocked, I sat in my car in front of Lorna's and tried to process this cottage with the image I'd constructed of Honor as a person with means to live in a much nicer house.

Not that this was bad, by any means. The lawn had been mowed and there were blooming flowers in the window boxes. Still, there were cracks around the edges and the place looked shabby, for lack of a better term.

In my mind, I'd pictured Honor in a huge house, maybe with lake views. Someplace white and modern and intimidating.

The cottage had been a bright yellow at one point, but the paint had faded and desperately needed to be updated.

Before either Lorna or Honor could come out to see why I was parked on the side of the road, I pulled into the driveway across the street and turned around, heading back to the guest house with way too many thoughts.

~

ON SUNDAY, I made a nice big breakfast and then got ready to meet Liam and Gwen at the beach. I'd told him I was just stopping by, but I intended to spend at least a few hours with them if I could.

"Are you moving to the beach?" Liam asked as I dragged my ass and my stuff across the sand.

"Shut up and help me," I said, and he rushed over to take some shit from me.

A beautiful girl with the biggest smile and short reddish curls got up from her chair.

"Hi, I'm Gwen. You must be Layne. I'm so happy to meet you."

I dropped my crap next to Liam's chair.

"It's so nice to meet you too. I've heard nothing but wonderful things from Liam," I said, and he glared at me.

"Oh, have you been talking about me?" Gwen said, smiling and turning to Liam.

"Bragging is more like it," I said, and Liam smacked me on the arm.

"You knew this was going to happen when you invited me," I said.

"And now I'm having regrets," Liam said, slumping down in his chair as I got myself set up in the sand.

"So you're saying nice things about me?" Gwen said, reaching out to squeeze Liam's arm.

He made a grumbling sound and I shared a look with Gwen.

"Someone is being a grump today," I said, pulling some snacks out of my bag. "Have some chips." I handed him the bag. They were barbecue, his favorite.

"Don't be a grump," Gwen said, pushing his hair back from his face in a sweet gesture. They might have only been dating for a short time, but after being with them for a few minutes, their chemistry was easy and clear as day.

Liam warmed up after a few minutes and I chatted with Gwen about her work as a nurse and how she and Liam met.

"I can't drink that much caffeine, so I kept just handing them out to the other nurses."

"You didn't have to keep buying coffee and matcha as an excuse to talk to me," Liam said.

"I know, but I was trying to be subtle," she said with a laugh.

"You came in four times in one day," Liam said, chuckling.

"You were just too cute. Couldn't resist," she said, messing up his hair.

"He is really cute," I said, agreeing with her.

Liam smiled at Gwen and scowled at me.

The three of us sat for a little while longer and then headed to the water. Liam wanted to swim out a little bit, but Gwen and I stayed where the water was a little shallow and I asked her more about her life.

"Sorry, I'm not trying to interrogate you or anything, so just tell me if I should stop," I said. "I'm also just really excited to meet you."

"Can I tell you a secret?" Gwen said, floating closer to me. I wish I'd brought our inflatable rafts from the house so we could just lay out, but I hadn't remembered them this morning.

"Of course," I said.

"I was really excited to meet you too. Liam talks about you all the time," Gwen said.

"I'm a little obsessed with him. Maybe that's weird for an older sister, but I don't care. He's an awesome guy."

"He is," she said, looking out where we could still see Liam's head bobbing above the waves and his arms as they cut through the water.

Gwen sighed. "I really like him."

"Don't worry," I whispered. "I won't tell."

"Thanks," Gwen said, her cheeks pink.

∼

THE THREE OF us had lunch at the snack bar and Liam revealed that he'd already met Gwen's parents and her siblings. She was one of four, and they were all very close.

"My mom is ready to adopt him," Gwen said as Liam carried the tray of food to an empty picnic table under an umbrella.

"I may be willing to share custody," I said as Liam went red.

"I did not anticipate the two of you ganging up on me," he said, grabbing a few fries.

"You should have," I said, and Gwen nodded.

Oh, I definitely approved.

∼

GWEN GOT a hug from me as we packed up our cars and prepared to leave.

"It was so nice to meet you," Gwen said. "We should do something together soon."

"Absolutely. You both can come over and I can make dinner," I said.

"Sounds good," Liam said, and I gave him a big hug.

"She's a keeper," I whispered in his ear.

He released me from the hug and smiled. "I know."

Chapter Eleven

THE TWINS HAD SOMEHOW GOTTEN both of their parents on board for this surprise boat ride, so I went ahead and booked five tickets for the sunset schooner cruise. The twins said that it was more plausible if I was going with them, so five tickets it was. They included a fresh lobster dinner and wine for the legal adults, which I was sad about missing.

The girls were true to their word and sent me the money to pay, so everything was all set for this plan to get their parents together again.

Since everything was organized, I thought their sneaking and plotting would be over, but it wasn't.

"What are you up to?" I kept asking them, but they kept telling me nothing.

Then I heard a scream on Wednesday coming from Mark's office. The twins had gotten picked up a few minutes before for a playdate with one of their friends, so the only other person screaming could have been Honor.

I rushed to the office and found Honor shaking her head and Mark looking at the floor where her purse had been dropped, spilling everywhere.

"What is it?" I asked. Mark bent down and picked up something small, holding it out to me.

"Looks like someone dumped a bunch of fake spiders in Honor's bag," he said, his mouth a thin line.

"Oh," I said, and joined him on the floor to pick one of the plastic spiders up. They did look terrifyingly realistic.

"I'm so sorry, Honor. I'll have to have another chat with them," Mark said.

It was obvious what the girls had done.

"Did you know anything about this?" Mark asked.

"Absolutely not," I said.

Those little brats. I didn't know how they'd gotten their hands on the fake spiders, but I wanted to know. The snakes and fake vomit were one thing, but this was a prank too far.

"I'm okay, I'm fine," Honor said, quickly pulling herself together.

"I'll take care of it," I said, starting to pluck the spiders off the floor.

I got all of Honor's shit back into her bag and handed it to her.

She looked pissed, but that wasn't an unfamiliar expression on her face in my experience.

Sorry, I mouthed before leaving the room as quietly as I could.

The spiders were dumped in the trash, and I wanted to send the twins a text that they were both in big trouble, but they needed to hear from their parents first. Mark had probably already called Sadie to discuss this latest issue.

The pranks were bad, but they were making Mark and Sadie have to talk to each other a lot, so maybe the twins were more devious than I thought.

Honor came out a little later for water.

"You good?" I asked. The fake spiders had made me forget all about what happened when she came over on Friday, and then seeing her house on Sunday. She didn't know about that part, though.

"I'm fine. It would take more than a few little spiders to freak me out. You should tell them that." A little shudder went down her spine, though.

Honor downed an entire glass of water and braced her hands on the counter.

"I'm sorry for running out on you on Friday," she said.

"Wait, you apologizing to me? This feels weird. I'm not used to it," I said.

She gave me a tiny smile. "Well, I didn't bring any slutty apology brownies."

"Then I do not forgive you. I can only accept apologies that include brownies." I shrugged and Honor laughed.

"Then I guess I'm out of luck."

The tension was broken, and we hadn't really talked about everything, but the mood was lighter, so I guess that was something.

I briefly considered asking if she wanted to hang out later, but I wasn't going to be done until the twins were in bed, so it would be pretty late.

"Now you owe me brownies. I expect them this week sometime," I said.

Honor gave me a smile that made my stomach drop to my feet and my hands go numb.

"How about Friday night? That seemed to work for us last time."

"Deal," she said. "I should get back to work."

"Hopefully with 100 percent less spiders."

She threw a smile over her shoulder. "Here's hoping."

THE TWINS GOT in big trouble that night, got their allowance taken away, and were sent to their room to consider what they'd done. Mark was also going to check their room to search out any other prank materials.

I went upstairs to deliver their dinner and handed the tray over.

"You've got to leave Honor alone. Getting your parents together is one thing, but these pranks have to stop. Do you have anything else?"

They both shook their heads.

"We got rid of everything," Riley said, pointing to the trash can. I glanced in there and found several fake snakes, fart items, fake bugs, and a bunch of other things.

"Did you buy out a prank store?" I asked.

"We got a kit when we were at camp," Riley said.

I groaned and picked up the trash can so I could empty it into the main trash so they couldn't fish anything out.

"Can we keep the fake blood?" Zoey asked.

"Absolutely not," I said and shut the door behind me.

∽

THE REST of the week dragged, and I definitely got up early on Friday to make sure my house was clean and that I had everything I needed. This time I was going to make brownies and kick things up a notch by topping them with ice cream.

"Good morning," Honor said when she came through the door. The twins were sitting at the counter eating their breakfast. They both looked up and mumbled "good morning."

"Good morning," I said, making up my own plate. "Bacon?"

"No, thank you," she said and gave me a little nod before she headed to the office.

I turned back to find the twins staring at me.

"What? Do I have something on my face?"

They looked at each other and then gave me identical smirks.

"Nothing," they chimed in unison.

~

THE GIRLS HAD another sleepover this weekend, but it wasn't starting until Saturday afternoon, and it was a smaller group this time, thank goodness. Just three girls were going to be coming over, so it was a lot easier to manage.

The whole day on Friday I kept watching the clock. Riley and Zoey had spent much of the day in the pool, which gave me time to clean and get other shit done.

They had cold sandwiches for lunch and then hit the showers before sitting down to watch some show they'd recently gotten obsessed with. It had cartoon vampires or something and was actually pretty good. They'd also gotten into graphic novels, so they'd begged me to take them to the library to get more since they blew through them so fast.

At least they were reading and not planning on setting Honor's hair on fire.

Finally, it was time for me to make dinner and I was almost done for the day. Honor had popped out of the office much more than usual today, probably because Mark had gone off to play golf. I guess that was all part of his job, and he honestly hated it, but he put on a smile and did it anyway, then came back and ranted about how much he hated golf courses. It was our little ritual.

"You excited to hear how much fun Mark didn't have today?" I asked her when she finally emerged from the office to come and watch me cook. On tap for tonight was baked macaroni and cheese, one of the twin's favorite, biscuits, and a big old salad with whatever veggies I had in the fridge. I was kind of winging it, which I didn't normally do. I'd been distracted all day and forgot to take the chicken out for what I'd planned to make.

"I keep telling him that he needs to suggest other activities, but he always gives in and goes to the club," Honor said, shaking her head. "For such a successful man, he can be really bad at saying no sometimes."

"Right? He's so random about it. Like the twins will convince him to say yes to something, but he'll be like 'absolutely not' for something else. It was way worse when they were younger, let me tell you. He had a steep learning curve in becoming a dad."

Our conversation was cut short by Mark's arrival. Riley and Zoey wandered into the kitchen a few minutes later to see how dinner was coming.

Honor said goodbye to everyone, and I didn't have a chance to tell her that she could go over to my place and wait for me and hang out. Her car pulled out of the driveway and I pulled up a new text message. Honor and I had exchanged texts a few times when I couldn't get in touch with Mark. The last one was from months ago.

My door is open if you want to go next door and chill until I'm done here, I sent.

She didn't respond for at least ten minutes.

Went home to change. Be back later.

That made sense.

"Who are you texting?" Riley asked, trying to peer at my phone.

"None of your business," I said. "It's rude to look at other people's phones."

Mark finished up in his office and I finally got dinner on the table and ate as fast as I could.

"I have plans tonight, do you mind if I dip out a little early?" I asked Mark.

"Of course. I think loading the dishwasher would be a nice thing for Riley and Zoey to do," he said, giving them both looks.

They protested, but then he reminded them about the spider incident and that quieted them down.

I did help them a little and took my plates and put them in the sink before saying goodnight and walking over to the guest house.

"Hello?" I said as I opened the door. No one answered. Honor must still be at her house.

I went to my kitchen to pull out some bowls and spoons and so forth to make the brownie sundaes.

A few minutes later, there was a soft knock at the door.

"Hey," I said, and Honor kept glancing back at the main house. She'd changed into jeans and a nice shirt and a pair of espadrilles.

"Hey," she said, pushing inside. "I had to park my car up the road in a ditch and walk."

"Why?" I asked.

"So Mark wouldn't look out the window and wonder what I was doing still parked in his driveway," she said.

Right.

"So you don't want Mark to know you're here," I said, confirming my suspicions.

"I just think it would lead to a lot of questions, don't you think?"

It absolutely would, and I didn't have any answers and I still didn't know what the fuck was even happening between us.

"Hopefully you won't get attacked by a moose on your walk back," I said.

Honor glared at me. I gave her a big smile. "Want a brownie sundae?"

"Is it slutty?" she asked, following me into the kitchen.

"It can be slutty if we want it to be," I said. "I've got a ton of toppings. Don't tell Mark that I might have stolen some of them from his house."

Honor pretended to zip her lips.

"You're spoiling me with all these desserts," she said.

"Life is short, eat more desserts," I said.

"You should put that on a bumper sticker," Honor said as I set a middle brownie in her bowl for her.

"Maybe I should."

I pulled the ice cream out of the freezer and let her pick her flavor. She chose French vanilla, which didn't really surprise me. I went for the cookie dough and then loaded my bowl with sprinkles, crushed Oreos, whipped cream, nuts, and multiple cherries.

Honor stuck with the brownie, ice cream, whipped cream, and one cherry placed carefully on top.

Her bowl looked like art. Mine looked like a mess.

Honor and I took our bowls to the couch again.

"Did you want to watch something?" I asked.

"Sure. I'm not picky."

I stared at her. "Yeah, you are."

Honor rolled her eyes. "I'm trying to be polite."

"Stop it, it's freaking me out," I said and that made her laugh.

"Okay, but you can't make fun of me," she said.

"I can't promise that I won't mock your viewing choices until I know what you want to watch," I said. I would pretty much watch anything, but I was dying to know what she would be embarrassed about.

"So it's a show from the '90s that I never really watched about this woman who becomes a nanny for a rich guy and his three kids."

She didn't even need to say anything else. I pulled it up on my TV and had to scroll back to the first episode.

"Anyplace you want to start? I've seen it way too many

times. I could probably just quote the episodes for you. Do a dramatic reenactment with voices."

Honor snorted. "It makes sense that you'd like that show."

"I mean, I'm not trying to marry my boss and I wish I had her closet, but yeah," I said.

Honor gestured for the remote to select an episode and I gave it to her. I hurried to eat my sundae before it completely melted as Honor found the episode she wanted.

"I didn't think you were a sitcom kind of person," I said.

"I don't like a lot of them, but I really like this one. I don't know. I marathoned it back when I went through my big breakup and couldn't get off the couch."

I tried picturing that and couldn't.

"My brother and I would watch it when we were sick home from school. I didn't start rewatching until a few years ago," I said.

Honor settled into the couch and I watched as she slipped her shoes off and then tucked her feet up under her.

Her eyes focused on the screen as she laughed at something on the show. She still ate her ice cream carefully, but her posture was completely different than it had been when she'd first walked in.

I went back to my own sundae and tried to watch the show, but I couldn't stop glancing at Honor every time she laughed. Fuck, I loved that sound. Completely infectious.

"I wish I could pull off an outfit like that," Honor said, nodding at the character on the screen wearing a sweater set in bold blocks of color.

"You could pull it off," I said.

"I don't think so," she said, shaking her head.

"Oh, come on, you're gorgeous. You'd work it," I said, rolling my eyes.

Honor set her empty bowl down on the coffee table.

"Was that a compliment?"

"Can the truth be a compliment?" I asked, tilting my head to the side.

Honor sighed.

"What? You're gorgeous. This is an objective fact," I said.

"I think many people would disagree with you."

"Those people are entitled to their opinions. They're wrong, but they can think that," I said. Why were we fighting about this? How ridiculous.

"You sure know how to flatter a woman," Honor said, shaking her head.

"Like I said, it's not flattery if it's true."

"I give up," Honor said, chuckling softly.

"Do you want another brownie? Or a drink?"

"A drink would be great," she said, and I made some more tea as Honor watched the show and then brought it back to her.

"Thank you," she said. "You've fed me twice now, so I'm going to have to repay you."

"Invite me over," I said, feeling a little bold.

"How about I take you out?" Honor said.

"Is there something wrong with your house? Is it haunted?" I whispered the last part.

"It's not haunted. Ghosts aren't real."

I gasped. "Okay, we need to have a conversation about that later, but back to your house."

"I don't invite people over," Honor said. "I like my privacy."

Fine. If she wanted to set that boundary, then I wasn't going to be an asshole about it.

"That's fair. Do I get to choose the restaurant?" I asked.

"I get veto power," she said. "I'm not eating at any restaurant that has a singing fish on the wall."

I burst out laughing. "Okay, no singing fish. That's fair."

She told me about some of her favorite places to eat and we agreed on a few of them.

"Wait," I said holding my hand up. "I need to get one thing clear."

I met Honor's eyes and I could tell she knew exactly what I was going to ask.

I opened my mouth and asked the question. "Is this a date?"

Honor didn't look away from my eyes. "Do you want it to be?"

I opened my mouth and then closed it. "I don't know! You're a really confusing person, Honor, I hope you know that."

She nodded and looked down at her hands in her lap. "I do. Believe me, I do."

"Because one minute you're trying to seduce Mark and be his second wife and the next you're kissing me and telling me you like women and now we're here eating ice cream and it's just…very fucking confusing."

I took a deep breath and waited for her to answer. Honor looked up from her hands.

"I'm very fucking confused, Layne," she said. Honor cursing was kind of hot.

"You confuse me," she whispered. "What I said about you fucking up my plans, I was being honest. Yes, I thought about marrying Mark. You can think I'm a horrible person, that's fine. But then you were there, and you were annoying and distracting and you were always around, and it wasn't easy to think about Mark anymore."

I had to remind myself to breathe.

"Me?" I looked down at myself.

Honor nodded. "Yes, you. Give yourself some credit. You have a confidence about you that you aren't even aware of. And you are so good with those kids and they love you so much. You care for your friends and you take care of this family and you're always trying to make everyone's life better. It's so different from what I'm used to."

Right. Her mother.

"I learned that you should never be kind to someone unless you were going to get something out of them. You never expect anything from people. You give without thought of reciprocation."

"I do?" I asked. The way Honor was describing me, it sounded like I was some kind of saint, which was definitely not true.

"You're a good person, Layne. A genuinely good person. They are rare in this world, and I guess I find your qualities irresistible."

"I'm irresistible?" I squeaked. How was this even happening?

Honor sighed. "You are, and believe me, I tried. The more you teased me and the more time I spent around you, the harder it became to think about anything else but you."

My mouth dropped open. This was a lot of information to absorb at once.

"I don't even know what to say," I told her. "I think I'm in shock right now."

Honor's face got red. "I'm not very happy about it myself. You weren't in my plans."

"I'm sorry?" I said. "Should I make you some more slutty brownies?"

"I had something different in mind," she said before pushing herself up on the couch and leaning over to me. Honor brushed her fingers across my cheeks before barely brushing her lips across mine.

This kiss was a polar opposite to our first one. That kiss had been vicious and angry. More of a combustion than a kiss.

This kiss was tender and sweet and completely threw me

off guard. I didn't know what to do with this kind of kiss from Honor.

My lungs stuttered like a car engine on a cold day. Honor left little delicate kisses on my lips and then pulled back.

"Should I stop?" she asked, her hand still on my cheek.

"No, but you're kissing like you're scared of me," I said. "It's weird."

Honor smiled. "I am scared of you, Layne." Her voice was barely above a whisper.

"That's bullshit," I said, and decided to take matters into my own hands.

I didn't kiss her with quite as much force as the first time, but still, she took my breath away. I had to dig my fingers into her waist because I needed something to hold onto.

She hesitated for a fraction of a second and then surrendered and kissed me fully.

There she is, I thought.

Those timid kisses had irritated me because Honor wasn't timid about anything, ever. Honor was fierce and she went after what she wanted. It was an insult to kiss me with such little effort. I deserved more.

Despite me being the one to start this kiss, Honor quickly took control and then her tongue was invading my mouth and caressing mine and she was reaching and searching and demanding more from me.

She could have it. She could have it all.

It was the easiest thing in the world for me to completely surrender to her.

Honor suckled on my bottom lip and then slowly dragged it through her teeth and I let out a whimper in response that made her smile against my mouth before biting my lip again and then pulling back.

"There you go, completely fucking up my plan," she said, huffing out a laugh.

I let her go and she eased back, sitting with her feet directly under her.

Honor had a satisfied smile on her face.

"Well, you don't have to look so smug," I said.

"There's a difference between smug and satisfied," she said.

"What's the difference?" I asked.

"Does it matter?"

I shrugged. I couldn't really even follow this conversation. I was still dizzy from the kiss.

"I'm still confused," I admitted. "Are you not going after Mark anymore? Because I think the twins would be really happy to hear that."

Honor moved further away from me on the couch and I had to stop myself from grabbing her to pull her back.

I shouldn't have said anything, but I needed to know before any of this went further.

"Fuck, Layne. Do we have to do this now?" Honor rubbed her forehead as if she was rubbing away a potential headache.

"I'm not going to make out with you if you're still trying to marry my boss. I have standards."

Honor glared at me, but I held my ground.

"Fine, I'm not going to try to marry Mark. Happy?"

I held out my hand, my pinky stuck out straight. Honor looked at my pinky like she'd never seen one before.

"You gotta promise," I said. "I make the twins do this all the time. And Liam."

"You're making me promise like a child," she said.

"No, I'm making you promise like I make people in my life promise things. You want to be in my life, get used to it."

Honor sat there for a second, but then she lifted her hand and linked her pinky with mine. I locked mine around hers and wouldn't let her go right away.

"There's a second step. Now you kiss your thumb," I said, showing her how to do it.

"This is ridiculous," she said, but then she kissed her thumb.

"And now we seal it," I said, reaching my thumb out and pressing it against hers.

"You spend too much time around children," Honor said.

"Yes, I do. It's literally my job," I said. "Occupational hazard." I shook the wrist with the bracelet that the twins had made me.

She tried not to smile and failed.

"Glad we got that out of the way. Oh, and I'm pretty sure that Mark is still in love with Sadie and I'm still rooting for their second-chance romance," I said.

Honor frowned. "Yeah, I know. He's a really good man, though. I could have loved him."

"I get it. He's easy to love. But he's not for you to love. His heart's already taken."

She sighed and rubbed her forehead again.

"That makes sense. You couldn't have told me that a few months ago?"

Was she serious?

"I tried! You wouldn't listen to me!"

Honor laughed and then let out a groaning sound. "I guess I picked the wrong Mark, literally."

"You should probably stop looking at men like they're going to save you. Save yourself, Honor. Be independent."

"I'd love to. But I'm putting my sister through college. She depends on me," she said. "Our mother won't help her because she doesn't believe in college."

"I don't think your sister would want you to marry a man you don't love just to make sure she doesn't have student loan debt. I know I'd kill Liam if he tried to do something like that." I reached out and rubbed her arm.

"I want her life to be better," Honor said.

"Christ, do I get that. I really do." Honor and I had more in common than I'd ever thought.

"Being an older sister isn't for wimps," I said.

Honor shook her head. "No, it's not."

I smiled at her. "Want to make out again?"

She let out a startled laugh. "How could I resist when you put it that way?"

"Get over here," I said, crooking my finger at her.

～

HONOR and I did a lot of kissing that night. My lips got quite a workout, and I could tell they were a little swollen when I kissed her goodnight.

"You sure you don't want me to walk you to your car?" I asked her for the third time.

"No, I'm a big girl and I can do it. I keep a knife in my purse," she said, pulling it out and showing me.

"Jesus. I won't mess with you," I said. Honor holding a knife was hot too. Or maybe it was everything she did.

"Good," she said, and kissed me again. "Thanks for the brownies, even if they weren't slutty."

"You're welcome."

I watched her pick her way across the yard, even though the lights in the main house were off. If Mark so much as glanced at the security cameras, he would see her, so honestly, trying to sneak was useless.

I figured letting Honor feel like she was being subtle was worth it. Mostly so she'd feel like she could sneak back to my place anytime she wanted to. I really liked the idea of that.

Made it to my car in one piece. Heading home xx

Seeing those two x's made me smile.

Get home safe. Keep an eye out for moose xxx

I figured I should one-up her with one more x.

Chapter Twelve

I slept in on Saturday because I'd stayed up way too late thinking about kissing Honor. The woman was good at everything, but she definitely excelled at kissing. Like I would expect anything less.

Now that she'd promised me she wasn't going after Mark, a flood of all kinds of thoughts had rushed through me like a tidal wave.

I didn't think it was a stretch to say that Honor liked me, and I liked her. Neither of us wanted to like each other, but I guess life had other ideas. Her plan to seduce and marry Mark had been a bad one, so at least she'd abandoned it. Now the twins could work their mission to get their parents together again. I had more hope than ever that it was going to happen.

I lay in bed and smiled, wondering what Honor was doing. She probably woke up early and got lots done. Maybe an early yoga session. Honor definitely seemed like someone who did yoga.

Imagining her in all kinds of poses had me hot and bothered and throwing off my covers. My hand strayed under the waistband of my sleep shorts to find that I was already wet and just one stroke of my hand had my legs trembling.

Gently I circled my clit and then slid two fingers inside before going back to my clit. When it came to masturbation, I had a routine honed over years of practice. Having good visualization material was key, and Honor gave me plenty.

With just a few hard thrusts of my fingers and a little love for my clit, I came hard, my entire body overtaken by pleasure and release.

I opened my eyes as I came down and stared at the ceiling. My masturbation habit was very healthy, but I couldn't remember coming that intensely in a while. Since it felt so good, I decided to go for round two before I had to get up and change out of my shorts and put on a fresh outfit. Not a bad way to start the day at all, and I floated into the kitchen in post-orgasm haze.

I made some pancakes with a quick fresh berry compote and some bacon with my morning coffee. Soon I'd be supervising Riley and Zoey's sleepover, but I had the morning to myself, so I decided to hit the farmers' market while I had time.

Joy was spending the day shopping at the mall an hour away with her mom and sisters, and Sydney had to cover at the pottery studio, so I was flying solo. I didn't really feel like going alone, but Liam already had plans with Gwen, and I assumed the twins would get bored.

Want to come to the farmers' market with me?

I sent the text to Honor before I could second-guess myself.

Meet you there in half an hour? she replied.

One of the things about Honor that was so attractive was her decisiveness. Maybe that was why I'd been so irritated when she'd kissed me so hesitantly last night.

Deal I sent.

NORMALLY I WOULDN'T WORRY about what I looked like when I went to the farmers' market, but today I was meeting Honor and I wanted to spruce up a little bit. It shouldn't matter, seeing as how she'd witnessed me in all my everyday casualness for months, but I felt like looking cute for her.

I did a quick but pretty braid with my hair and slid on my sunflower dress that made my boobs look really good and swirled when I moved. My aviators were scratched to hell and didn't really go with my outfit, but they were my favorite, so I put them on and grabbed my tote bags anyway.

～

"GOOD TIMING," I said as I got out of my car and saw Honor parked a few spots away from me in the grocery store lot.

Main Street was blocked off for the various sellers and artisans, so finding parking right now was rough. I'd had to go around several times and wait for someone to leave.

"Nice to see you," she said, pulling out her own reusable bags.

"You ready?" I asked, going over to her. She wore a dress as well, but it was more loose-fitting than her work clothes and made of something soft and floaty.

"Ready," she said, holding up her bags. I didn't know if I was allowed to kiss her in public, so I waited for her to make a move.

"Really?" she said after a few seconds of awkwardness.

"What?" I asked.

"You were all about kissing me last night and now you've lost your nerve?" she said.

"I didn't know if it was allowed!" I said, startling some people nearby who were getting out of their car.

Honor stepped closer to me. "You don't have to kiss me if you don't want to."

Kissed By Her

"I do want to," I said, and then I leaned forward and kissed her. Honor inhaled through her nose in shock, but she didn't pull away. I slanted my mouth over hers, deepening the kiss before pulling back.

"There," I said. "Is that allowed?"

"It's encouraged," she said, her voice a little breathless. Good. I liked seeing her that way.

"Glad we figured that out," I said, transferring my tote bags to one hand and holding out my other to her.

"Are we doing this?" she asked.

"Yes," I said, wiggling my fingers. Maybe she wasn't a hand-holder. Maybe she thought that kind of PDA was too much.

The entire town was pretty much milling around today, so if she took my hand, that was a public declaration that we had some kind of relationship.

Honor looked up and down the street and the longer she stood there, the more I could see her panicking.

"It's okay. I'm sorry, that was probably too much," I said.

"I want to," Honor said. "But I need more time."

"You got it," I said, trying not to feel hurt. Things between us were so new, so fresh. I needed to hit the brakes so I didn't scare her off.

"Come help me pick out some good tomatoes," I said, and she gave me a smile.

"Sure."

~

WE SAW JUST ABOUT EVERYONE, and it took way longer than I anticipated to make it to all the tables and booths. I picked up the most gorgeous heirloom tomatoes that I was going to make a big caprese salad with, some basil to go with it, a block of local sheep's milk cheese, a bag of croissants, and a candle from a local maker.

Sydney and her mom had a booth out in front of the pottery store that Sydney was manning to sell a few smaller pottery pieces like ornaments and coffee cups.

"You should go and say hello," Honor told me, bumping my shoulder with hers. She'd barely bought anything, and I wanted to ask about it.

"Will you come with me?" I asked. If she and I were going to be a thing, I wanted my friends to know about it. I mean, they already knew about the kiss, so seeing me and Honor together wasn't going to be that big of a shock.

"As long as you don't put me on the spot," Honor said.

I nodded and we walked up to Sydney's table. She stood up to stretch her arms and beamed when I waved at her.

"Thank god, can you do me a huge favor and stand here so I can go pee?"

"Yeah, no problem," I said.

"Hi, Honor," Sydney said with a wink before she vanished into the pottery shop to use the bathroom.

Honor gave me a look.

"What? I didn't say anything to her. I mean, she and Joy know about us kissing because they were literally there, but they don't know that you came over last night or that we're doing whatever we're doing."

Not much of what I said made sense.

"Are you upset?" I asked, pulling her behind the table where Syd had been standing. The crowd was a slow-moving tide that moved past the table, with a few people stopping and lingering for a moment before moving on.

"No, I'm not upset," Honor said, doing that forehead-rubbing move again.

"Should we go? I feel like I've fucked up somehow, but I'm not really sure what to do about it," I said.

Honor sighed. "You didn't fuck anything up, stop doing that. Stop trying to fix something that isn't broken. I'm just reeling from how things have changed between us, and you seem to be full-steam ahead and I'm trying to catch up."

She had a point. "Maybe it would help to talk about our expectations."

Sydney came back and gave me a hug. "Thank you so much. Can you do me another huge favor?"

"Of course," I said, turning away from Honor for a second.

"Can you get me an iced coffee? I would love you forever."

"You already love me forever," I said.

"I'll love you for forever, forever," she said.

I laughed. "Okay. We'll be right back."

Sydney waved and sat back down in her chair with a sigh as a woman picked up a mug and asked her how much it was.

The line for the coffee shop was horrendous, so we ended up waiting outside.

"I'm not ready to be public," Honor finally said. "I'm still not sure what I want."

"Okay," I said. "Thank you for telling me."

Honor cringed. "And now I feel like a bitch."

"I hate to break this to you, but you kind of are a bitch. It's cool, it's one of the things I like about you." I leaned into her and stroked her arm.

"Being a bitch is in my genetic code," she said. "Letting myself have feelings is not. This is new and, honestly, you scare the shit out of me."

She said the words in a low voice so no one could overhear her.

"That makes two of us that are terrified, so you're in good company." The line moved and we made it inside the shop.

"Be patient with me," Honor said. "Please. Because I really like you, Layne. I can't even believe I'm saying that, but I do."

"I like you too," I said. "I think."

She glared at me and the line moved again.

"Oh look, they have brownies on the menu. What kind would you like? My treat."

"More apology brownies?"

"No. Just regular brownies."

She brushed her fingers across my shoulder in a sweet gesture. "Seems like a letdown after eating slutty apology brownies."

"The brownies can be slutty if you want them to be. You just have to believe," I said, and Honor laughed.

At last, we made it to the front of the line, and I ordered coffee for Syd, but also got some for myself and Honor and two brownies.

After I paid and picked up our order, I delivered the coffee to Sydney and she sung her song of gratitude.

"Listen, I have to get going to supervise the twin's sleepover, but we'll talk tomorrow?"

"Oh, we will definitely be talking tomorrow," Syd said, smirking at Honor.

"Stop making things weird, Syd," I said, hitting her on the arm.

"I'm not being weird," she said.

"Yeah, you are. Goodbye," I said, walking back down the sidewalk with Honor as we sipped our coffee.

"Do you really have to go?" Honor asked. "I don't want to keep you from your job."

I checked the time on my phone. "No, I have some time. I just decided I wanted to spend it with you instead of dealing with a million questions from Sydney."

Part of the street was taken up with chairs and tables so people could sit and eat, and I took one and sat down.

Honor joined me, pulling her brownie out of the bag from

the coffee shop. It had extra chocolate chips in it and was still warm.

"You and your friends are really close," Honor said.

"I mean, yeah. That's how best friends work," I said.

Honor studied her brownie. "I don't really have friends. Other than my sister. My mom always told me that other kids would try to stab me in the back and hurt me and take things away from me."

"Your mom is a real asshole," I said, sipping my coffee. I was going to need the buzz to get through the sleepover later.

"I know that now," Honor said, breaking off a little bit of the brownie. "At the time I thought everything she said was right and true and by the time I figured out how much she'd messed me up, it felt like it was too late to try and fix it."

"Oh, we can fix this," I said. "You've already started trying to make friends by joining book club."

"I joined book club so I could see you," she said in a low voice.

"I'm sorry, what was that?" I cupped my ear and leaned over the table.

"I joined book club so I could see you, okay? Are you happy?"

"You totally like me," I said, smiling. "That's adorable."

Her face went red, but she was smiling too.

"Did you really join book club because of me?"

"I told myself it was to make friends, but it was mostly for you."

"But you didn't like me," I said.

"Oh, I did. I just lied to myself about it for a while," she said, licking a little bit of chocolate off her lips.

I really, really wanted to kiss her right now.

"I think I did the same thing. Maybe that's why I was so pissy about you going after Mark. Because I wanted you for myself."

Honor rested one arm on the table, and I reached out and ran my fingers up and down the inside of her arm.

"Mmmm, you wanted me?"

"Yes, maybe all your seduction tactics bounced off Mark and hit me instead. Good job."

Honor snorted and shook her head. "I should have aimed better."

I stroked her open palm. "Oh, I think you aimed just fine."

∼

HONOR DID KISS me when we went back to our cars.

"Have fun with those monsters," she said.

"They absolutely can be monsters," I said. "What would you have done if you really married Mark?"

She leaned against her car. "I hadn't thought that far ahead."

"That seems kind of important," I said. "Look, I'm not trying to be a jerk, but those girls are really important to me."

Honor met my eyes with her bright blue ones. "I know. The longer I think about my plans with Mark, the more I see how shallow and silly they were. My mother would be ashamed of me for not being more conniving."

"Your goal should be to disappoint your mom from here on out. She's the worst." If I ever met this woman, I didn't know what I would do. Probably end up in jail for fighting her.

"I'm beginning to see that," she said, reaching out and tucking some of my hair behind my ear. "I don't know how to do relationships. Or friends. Or being a regular person."

"That's okay. I can teach you about all of it. You're a smart woman, you'll figure it out. First lesson is stop trying to marry rich guys."

She laughed and then nodded. "Okay, I think I can do that. What's the second lesson?"

"Kiss me," I said.

"That's the second lesson?" Honor said, squinting at me.

"Yes, come here." I put my fingers under her chin and drew her face down to mine.

Honor kissed me until I was buzzing with the feel of her mouth on mine and the taste of chocolate on her tongue.

"I like the second lesson," she said when she leaned back.

"Me too," I said. "Fuck, I wish I could stay here kissing you all day, but I have to go."

"I understand." Honor kissed me one more time.

"You're probably going to get a shit ton of messages from me tonight, so I'm sorry in advance. Supervising sleepovers tests my patience sometimes."

Honor shuddered at the thought.

We finally parted and got in our separate vehicles and I drove back to the house, the memory of Honor's kiss still on my lips.

∼

FORTUNATELY FOR ME, the girls just wanted to play in the pool and watch movies and eat a ton of junk food, which I was happy to supply.

My supervision extended to mostly making sure they didn't drown or disappear as a group in the bathroom to conjure a ghost or something.

"You seem happy today," Mark said as he sat down beside me with a plate of food. Instead of ordering pizza, he'd thrown a bunch of burgers and hotdogs and corn on the grill to make everyone happy. One of the twin's friends was vegan, so he'd also grilled a vegan patty and hot dog for her. Tomorrow morning, I was cooking up a vegan veggie egg scramble and vegan bacon for everyone.

"Do I?" I asked.

"You do," he said, and I wanted to hide my face.

"Just having a good weekend," I said.

"Mmm," he said, but he kept glancing at me.

Part of me wanted to throw myself in the pool, but then it would be really obvious that I was hiding something, so I just sat there and pretended to be chill. Inside I was not chill.

Could people tell I'd been making out with Honor? Had I changed that much since last night? Did I have kissing cooties or something? Was I, a grown woman, considering that I'd been infected by cooties?

One of the kids did a cannonball into the pool, making me jump.

Get a grip, Layne.

∼

AS I'D PROMISED, I did end up texting Honor a bunch of times as the night wore on.

I couldn't help it. There were so many random things that I needed to tell her about.

I asked her which book she voted on for book club and that opened up a whole door about our favorite books, and what we'd felt when we'd read our first queer romance and which book characters had definitely made us gay.

My cheeks were sore from smiling.

Riley flopped down in the chair next to me and Zoey took the other.

"Are you in love?" Riley asked me when I looked up from my phone.

"What?" I said, almost sliding off my chair. "What are you talking about?"

"You just have a grin on your face, and you seem really happy, so we wanted to know if you were in love," Zoey said matter-of-factly.

"No, I'm not in love," I choked out. I definitely wasn't. Love didn't happen like it did in their favorite animated movies.

Riley and Zoey looked at each other and shrugged. "Okay."

The good thing about them being so young was that they tended to move on from things pretty quickly.

They hopped back in the pool and I was left to my chaotic thoughts.

～

THERE WERE no incidents during the night, and everyone commented on how good the vegan breakfast was before I sent the other kids back to their parents and told Mark I was "clocking out" to enjoy what I had left of the weekend.

I met Joy and Sydney at their apartment so we could just chill and have dinner. I brought the caprese salad I'd made with the heirloom tomatoes and the basil.

Joy had made baked eggplant, and the minute I walked in she was already ranting about her family.

"I just…I've had it! They're all up my ass because I'm not in a relationship and I don't know how much more I can take."

I waved and set the tray down with the salad in it. Sydney gave me a look that said Joy was just getting started. She always got going when she cooked for some reason. Under normal circumstances, Joy was a sweet little ball of sunshine, but her family knew how to push every single one of her buttons.

"What did they do now?" I asked and Sydney glared at me for getting Joy going. I told her that Joy needed to talk this shit out so she didn't bottle it up, but Sydney thought that talking about it just made things worse.

"The usual," Joy said, making a lot of clattering noises that seemed excessive for the cooking process. She took on a mocking tone, pretending to be her mom or one of her sisters. "Joy, we just love and care about you and we don't want you to be alone. Someday you're going to wake up and realize that you don't have anyone to share your life with."

She let out a growl and finally stopped moving. I saw that Sydney had already taken the knives away. Good thinking.

"And they act like I don't have anyone, just because I'm not dating anyone. Oh, and don't even get them started on bugging me about my wedding date."

"We've already said that one of us will go with you," Sydney said carefully.

"That's not going to cut it," Joy said, crossing her arms and leaning against the counter. "They're going to want to see someone new. You know single ladies who would pretend to be my date for my sister's wedding?"

She laughed, but I thought she was serious.

"We'll ask around," Sydney said. "So, Layne, how are things going with Honor?"

Seems like someone was desperate to change the subject.

"What *is* going on with Honor?" Joy asked, her attention from her own troubles diverted by potentially juicy information.

"Honestly, things are kind of new? And weird. But good!" They both looked at each other and then at me.

"Honor doesn't know if she wants to do the whole relationship thing, so we're kind of...doing whatever. She likes me, I like her, and that's about as far as we've gotten. It's only been a few days."

Joy squealed and gave me a hug. "I'm happy for you. I'm going to reserve judgment until we all hang out together and I can get to know her better. If you like her, we like her. Right, Syd?"

"I'm on the fence, but I fully support you getting some," Sydney said, coming over to hug me.

"Aw, thanks. You're both the best. And she's not as terrible as I made her out to be."

"Yeah, I think that's your hormones talking, but that's okay," Syd said, giving me a squeeze and then letting go.

∽

HONOR KEPT TEXTING me during dinner, and I couldn't help but answer.

"Wow, you are in it deep," Sydney said as I looked up from a meme picture she'd sent me. Over the past day or so, I'd realized that Honor had a cutting sense of humor that I appreciated. Sure, it could be a little dark, but all the best people were.

"I am not," I said.

"Don't listen to her," Joy said. "She's just jealous."

"Absolutely not," Sydney said. "I don't need all of that stuff." She pointed at me with her fork.

"What stuff?" I asked.

"The flirting and the getting to know everything about each other and the long conversations about nothing. I don't need it. That stuff's too complicated. Give me a quick hot bang and I'm good."

Joy and I shared a look and decided not to comment.

"To each their own," I said. The thing was, if what Syd really wanted was a hookup, I would absolutely be for that. But I knew she was lonely. I knew she wished she had someone to hang out with that wasn't me or Joy. Someone to be her emergency contact and to trust all her secrets with. Sydney kept protesting that she didn't need a relationship so often and so loudly that I wasn't sure who she was trying to convince.

∽

I DIDN'T STAY that late at Joy and Sydney's and I told myself it was because I was tired, but it was also because I wanted to lay in bed and send messages back and forth with Honor.

I was so curious what she did when she wasn't at work, and she hadn't really answered my curiosity yet.

What else did you do today? I asked, trying to get a window into her life.

Took my sister to go shopping for some school things she needed for next year. She's getting an apartment, so now she needs all kinds of things, she responded.

When Liam had gotten his first place, I'd helped him out, so I didn't really have a leg to stand on when it came to being an older sister helping a younger sibling with finances.

If I hadn't helped Liam, he would still be sleeping on a mattress on the floor and have a futon in the living room, I sent.

His confusion when I said that he couldn't keep his grungy, saggy futon and expect to ever have a serious girlfriend as an adult still made me laugh.

Honor and I shared our older sister woes, and I was starting to get a better picture of her. Thought I had yet to meet her sister, I could tell that she didn't quite have the same level of ambition that Honor did. Even though Honor told me her whole thing had been to marry rich, she'd still gone to school and had built a career. She told me it was to put her in the company of rich guys, but there were a lot of other ways to do that that didn't involve getting a college degree and going into debt.

What Honor said and what she did were often at odds with each other and I didn't know if she was aware of it.

Interesting.

I should probably go to sleep at some point. I have some monsters to take care of tomorrow, I sent.

And I have to manage their father, Honor replied, and I laughed.

It took a team of two of us to handle the Jewel family.

Chapter Thirteen

Honor came in for work as I was finishing up the twin's breakfast and making sure they had anything they might need for their week at Sadie's. Mostly they had two of everything, but things like their phones and tablets had to travel to each house.

"Go check your room," I said, pushing them upstairs. I waited until the door slammed before looking at Honor.

"Hi," I said, stepping close to her. Making out at work was probably forbidden, but it didn't stop me from wanting to. In fact, it made the urge worse. The idea of pulling her into a random room and making out with her was tantalizing.

"Good morning," she said in a prim voice. Oh. She was putting up a barrier. We probably should have talked about this at some point. I guess I just got so lost in flirting with her, I forgot about logistics.

I saluted her. "Good morning."

That made her smile and roll her eyes. "You don't have to be quite that formal, Layne."

I leaned forward and whispered. "Okay, but how formal should I be? A handshake? A curtsy?" I put one leg behind the other and tried to execute a curtsy like I'd seen in the movies.

"I can't even deal with you right now. It's too early," Honor said, and turned to go into the office.

"You want to come over later?" I asked in a low voice.

"Maybe. Let me see how my day goes," she said, and just before she turned to walk down the hall, she brushed her fingers across my lips. It wasn't a kiss, but it still made me tremble.

"Have a good day, Layne," she said, winking before she disappeared.

I stood there for a second, completely stunned. I didn't even notice when the twins came barreling downstairs with their bags.

"You alive?" Riley asked, snapping her fingers in front of my face.

"Yup," I said, blinking to clear my head. "Did you get everything?"

They nodded in unison.

"Okay, let's go." I grabbed my bag and they followed me out to the car, but I couldn't help glancing through the window in Mark's office. Honor was standing next to his desk, nodding and completely focused on her work.

Hot. Very hot.

∽

RILEY AND ZOEY called me on being distracted all day. Sadie had left a list of chores for them to do, one of which included helping at the boutique, so I brought them over after lunch.

"Sorry, just have a lot on my mind," I said as I parked the car and the girls hopped out to walk to the boutique.

"Snap out of it," Riley demanded. "You're supposed to be in charge of us. Our parents will get mad if something happens."

She had a good point.

"Then just don't run out into traffic, and we'll be good," I snapped back at her, holding the door of the boutique open.

"No promises," Zoey said in a sing-song voice. I stopped myself from responding

The boutique was packed with a group of women who were on vacation and obviously bored. One was trying on dresses and coming out as the others voted on which ones she looked good in. They were having a good time and as long as they spent money, I didn't think Sadie cared if they made a lot of noise.

She was supervising and handing out glasses of champagne. It was something she did when a group came in that looked like they had cash to spend. Brilliant.

I quickly rushed the girls past Sadie, who waved and mouthed that she'd be with us as soon as she could.

Riley and Zoey followed me into the back, where the offices and the bathroom and the stockroom were.

In addition to the retail store, Sadie also sold her items online, and packing them up to ship was one of her most-hated jobs. She did delegate some of it, but she was currently behind and having the twins help out was free labor and taught them good responsibility. They didn't see it that way, but I knew they really did love helping their mom. Her job was fun, unlike their dad's.

"Okay, let's see what we've got," I said, pulling the stack of printed order forms that would go in the bags off the printer.

"Riley, I need an Audrey dress in purple, size XL," I called out and Riley dashed to find the item. I gave Zoey an order too, and they'd race each other to see who could get the order done first.

The three of us had a good time and we made a dent on the stack before Sadie came back and leaned against the wall.

"They bought a decent amount, so I'm not complaining," she said.

"These are all ready to go," I said, patting the stack of orders that were ready to ship.

"You are an angel and worth your weight in gold," Sadie said, coming over to kiss the top of my head.

"You are welcome," I said.

"I don't know what we would have done without you."

I smiled up at her. "Ditto."

"We're hungry," Riley said, slumping against a shelf of shirts.

"Oh, you are, are you?" Sadie said.

"Yes."

Sadie made eye contact with me.

"They had lunch about an hour ago," I said.

"We're hitting a growth spurt!" Zoey said.

"Yeah!" Riley agreed.

Sadie laughed. "Okay, okay, go see what's back there," she said, pointing at the second office, which was also an employee break room and had a fridge with drinks and a basket with snacks.

They ran off and Sadie shook her head.

"You're still not going to tell me about this big surprise, are you?" Sadie asked.

"My lips are sealed. I wouldn't ruin it."

Sadie sighed. "If this even involves me getting up on a stage, or performing or singing, I'm going to kill you."

I burst out laughing. If there was one thing Sadie hated, it was being put on the spot in public.

"Don't worry. There isn't anything like that. It's much more lowkey."

"Can I get a hint?" she asked just as the twins burst back in with bags of chips and granola bars.

"Whoa, whoa, you do not need all that," Sadie said, going to do her mom duties as the twins protested.

IT WAS A FUN AFTERNOON, and I was in a good mood when I got back to Mark's.

"I'm feeling like a lobster roll from Mulligan's for dinner," Mark said from the kitchen. He had his phone in his hands, probably putting in the order. He'd have to go and pick it up, but it was absolutely worth it.

"If you don't mind, that sounds great," I said. "With onion rings."

Mark smiled. "Of course."

"I'm going to head out," Honor said, emerging from the bathroom. She had her bag over her shoulder. I'd judged her for having it before I'd known that her ex had bought it for her as a surprise and it was actually used. So many of my assumptions about her had been completely wrong.

"Thanks for your work on that contract today. I know it wasn't easy," Mark said, shaking his head. "Why people don't keep multiple copies in multiple places is beyond me. No wonder their company is in shambles."

"Thanks, it was no problem," Honor said and then glanced at me as Mark was occupied with his phone again.

Meet me outside, I mouthed at Honor. She couldn't go home until I'd kissed her at least once.

What? she mouthed back.

Meet. Me. Outside, I said, trying to enunciate.

"Did you say something?" Mark asked, looking up.

"Nope," I said, and decided to use my phone to send a message.

Meet me outside, I sent and heard the sound of Honor's phone.

"Oh," she said, realizing what I'd said. "Well, I'm going to get going."

"I've got to go grab the lobster rolls," Mark said. "Be back in a while."

He left without another word and as soon as I heard the sound of his car pulling out of the driveway, I let out a breath.

"Finally," I said, going over to Honor as she crossed the room to get to me.

"Thinking about you made me almost mess up so many things today," she said as I touched her face.

"Same. The twins called me on it."

"Come here," she said, and then her mouth was on mine and my blood was zinging in my veins.

I sighed into her mouth with relief and she laughed in her throat.

"Miss me?" she said between kisses.

"Maybe a little bit," I said, my fingers pulling on her dress to pull her closer to me.

"You can come share some onion rings with me if you want. I'm not sharing my lobster roll, though," I said.

Honor smiled. "Oh, so you don't like me enough to share your lobster roll?"

"Sorry," I said.

She narrowed her eyes. "What about if I do this?" she asked and leaned in to kiss me again, almost knocking me off-balance. Her tongue was aggressive, slicking its way into my mouth and making me completely melt at her touch.

I might have been the older one, but when it came to kissing, Honor took control and I was fine with letting her have it.

My body sunk into hers and I didn't even know what we'd even been talking about until I opened my eyes and she asked me if she could have some of my lobster roll as she stroked my neck with one hand.

I sighed. "Still no."

Honor huffed out an offended noise.

"It's a really good lobster roll," I said, brushing my thumb back and forth on her chin.

"That doesn't say much for my kissing skills, does it?" she said, staring into my eyes. Honor had so much intensity and it should probably scare me, but it only made my heart race.

"Your kissing skills are excellent. I'd give them five stars out of five."

Honor chuckled and stepped away. "If I can't have some of your lobster roll, I guess I'll just go home and have dinner at my place. It's Lark's turn to cook."

"Lark?" I asked.

"My sister." I hadn't heard her name until now. "I'm sure you'll meet her at some point. I haven't exactly told her about you, but she knows that something is going on. She's being very smug about it. She always said that one day I was going to meet someone that would ruin all my plans."

"Is she smug or satisfied?" I asked her.

Honor shook her head. "It doesn't matter. Either way, she's annoying."

We laughed and she kissed me a few more times before heading back to her place so Mark didn't see her car when he got back.

I puttered around the house and enjoyed the silence until Mark came in with our food.

"So, they actually gave me an extra by accident," he said.

"If you don't want it, I'll take it," I said. I could give it to Honor after all.

"Sure, it's yours," Mark said, handing me the bag.

"Thanks, boss," I said, and he cringed.

"Don't call me that," he said.

I SENT Honor a text as soon as I got back to the guest house that I did have a lobster roll for her and sent a picture of it sitting on a plate.

It must be my lucky night. Be there in a few, she sent.

Figuring I had already said I'd share, I put some onion rings on her plate as well and grabbed some sauce if she wanted it.

I did a quick tidy and then Honor was knocking on my door.

I opened it and found her smiling and wearing the jeans from book club, and a soft t-shirt with a faded design and…

"Hold on, are those sneakers?" I asked. Designer sneakers, but still.

"Like them?" Honor said, holding out her foot and looking down at it.

"They're cute," I said. She looked so casual it was throwing me off. So many sides to Honor Conroy.

"Your lobster roll," I said, holding the plate out to her. "And there's sauce or whatever for the onion rings."

She selected ranch dressing and added some to her plate. I stuck with ketchup.

We both grabbed drinks from the fridge and took out spots on the couch.

"My sister wants to meet you and I had to actually stop her from coming over with me," Honor said, laying a napkin on her lap. Lobster rolls could be a mess to eat.

"Yeah, I'm fine with meeting her," I said. "From what you told me she sounds interesting."

"That's not the word I'd use for her, but sure," she said, chuckling.

"Still hasn't decided on a major?"

Honor put up one hand. "Don't get me started. I want to enjoy this lobster roll."

I snorted. "Okay, then. How was your day?"

Honor told me about the issues they'd had with getting records from one of their new companies to do due diligence.

"They asked if they could fax them to us, can you believe that?"

"What is it, 1972?" I said laughing.

"I know. Everything is digital now. Anyway, we finally got things squared away, but it was a tense couple of hours. How were the twins today?"

I told her about what we'd done today. It wasn't as exciting as writing contracts for lots of money, but it was a job that needed to be done.

"Their mom seems like a good woman," Honor said.

"She is. She really is. I know you haven't seen her much, but I think you'd like her. She was so driven after the divorce that she opened her own boutique when she had two infants. I still don't know where she found the time or energy, but she did the damn thing and it's still successful."

Honor nodded. "I really admire that."

"So, I promised the twins I wouldn't tell, but now that you're not trying to seduce their dad, I can tell you."

Honor raised both eyebrows. "Tell me what?"

"Part of the reason Riley and Zoey were pulling all those pranks on you was to get you away from their dad so he would notice their mom again. They booked a private sunset cruise on a schooner and the plan is to say they're seasick at the last minute and I'm going to take them home and then they'll be stuck on the boat together for at least three hours. They think it'll spark the romance again."

Honor took a dainty bite of her lobster roll and then set it down.

"They're young," was all she said.

"Don't you think it's cute, though?" I asked.

"I think they're going to be disappointed," she said, wiping her mouth. "I don't know why you're going along with it."

"Because if I try and stop them, they'll just come up with something else and they need adult supervision. Like, you weren't here when they both pretended they broke their legs because they didn't want to do a presentation at school." What a complete disaster that had been.

"Still," Honor said. "They're going to get their hearts broken."

I was starting to get annoyed. "Maybe they won't. You haven't seen Mark and Sadie lately. The chemistry is there. It's not out of left field to think that it could reignite."

"We clearly aren't going to agree about this," she said, looking at her plate.

"I'm sorry, I guess I'm just more optimistic than you are. You read lots of romance, don't you believe in love?"

Honor looked up at the ceiling and sighed. "I guess I just don't believe that it's always forever or that as many people experience it as say they do."

I sat back in shock. "What the hell, Honor? If you don't believe in love, then what the fuck are you doing with me?"

She whipped toward me. "Who said anything about love?"

"I mean, in the hypothetical sense," I said quickly.

"Wait, I thought we were talking about Mark and Sadie? Are we talking about us?" she asked.

"Yeah, we should talk about us. I think we should at least be on the same page about whether love exists or not," I said. Obviously, I should have asked some more relevant questions before we kissed the first time.

Too late now.

"Layne," Honor said in a tired voice. "I'm not saying that I don't believe in love at all. I'm just more realistic about it. We have different life experiences that led us to our conclusions."

I hated when she talked all logical and businesslike about something like this.

"So, you do believe in love?" I asked. That was the question I just really needed an answer to. If she didn't, then all of this was over. I couldn't be with someone who didn't think there was a possibility that we could someday be in a committed relationship together.

"I believe in the potential for love, yes, I do. I don't know if I'll get a chance to experience it. I'm not going to hang my hopes on something that might not happen. It's a matter of practicality."

I took a deep breath. While that wasn't the best answer, I could work with it. My new personal goal: make Honor believe in love.

"Okay," I said. "Then that's that." I picked up my lobster roll and took a big bite.

"Is it?" she asked.

I lifted my shoulder, pretending to be casual. "Yeah. I mean, did you want to discuss it further?"

She shook her head. "No."

"So let's move on. Eat your lobster roll, Honor."

"Don't tell me what to do."

"Don't waste good lobster," I fired back, and she smiled at me and we were back to normal. Mostly.

~

HONOR STAYED for a while and chilled with me on the couch, her arm around my shoulder and our legs entwined as we propped them on the ottoman. She wanted to watch more of the sitcom, so I put it on and listened to her laugh.

I couldn't focus on the show because I was seething at all the damage that Honor's mother had done to her. She hadn't been born not believing in love, not believing in having friends.

No, an adult had pounded those ideas into her head and warped her view of the world, and if I ever met that woman, I didn't know what I would do.

I was really curious to meet her sister, to see how she had grown up in the same environment. Did she share Honor's beliefs?

Honor deserved to be loved. To be cherished. To have someone spoil her, and not just with money. Spoil her with attention and care and consideration. She needed someone who valued her, and not just for what she looked like.

I was more than up to that task.

My fingers crept up to her hair and I stroked her scalp with my fingers as she made a little contented noise.

"That feels nice," she said.

I continued to touch her hair as she snuggled closer into me.

"When did you know you liked girls?" I asked her after I'd turned the volume down on the show.

"I'm not sure. I think I always did, but there was a lot of denial. Since I liked boys too, it was easy to convince myself I was straight to fit in."

I nodded.

"What about you?" she asked.

"I remember telling my parents I wanted to marry a princess from a movie, and they were not okay with that idea when I was young, and I think I internalized it. So when I had crushes on girls, I got really good at hiding it. They were so happy when I pretended to date guys, but that got old and then I finally came out freshman year of high school and it didn't go well. My brother came out that same year as trans, so it really was the two of us against the world. Like, on the surface they were supportive, as long as I didn't hold hands with a girlfriend, or as long as my brother didn't ask them to call him Liam instead of his deadname. Their support was conditional on us being quiet queers and as soon as I was old enough to move out, I did. Liam moved in with me as soon as he could. We haven't gone fully no-contact with our parents, but we pretty much only hear from them at Christmas when they send a card and some random presents. They sent me a bunch of oven mitts and random books last year."

My parent's terrible presents were kind of legendary. Every year I'd do an unboxing with Joy and Syd and we'd try and figure out what they'd been thinking when they sent me whatever it was.

Honor leaned into my hand and I scratched lightly at her scalp.

"My sister is queer too," Honor said. "She came out much earlier than I did, so my mom pinned all her hopes on me marrying a rich man and kind of gave up on Lark."

"Why couldn't she just find a rich woman to marry? There are tons of rich queer women."

"My mom hates women. Says they're all a bunch of backstabbers and that marrying a woman was the worst idea," she said, shrugging one shoulder.

"Wow, I can smell the internalized misogyny from here," I said.

Honor laughed without humor. "It all sounds awful when I say it out loud now, but at the time, I thought she was right."

"We all think our parents are right about everything when we're young," I said. "It's not your fault she raised you that way."

"I know," Honor said.

"I don't want you to take this the wrong way, but have you ever thought of going to therapy?" I asked.

"Of course, but I could never really commit to making an appointment. There are so many other people who have terrible problems. What am I going to do, sit there and whine about how my mommy taught me how to marry a rich guy and take his money?"

She made a scoffing noise and I really wanted to argue with her.

"Everyone needs some help sometimes, Honor, and just because other people have worse problems, doesn't mean you don't deserve help."

She lifted one shoulder again and leaned further into me with a yawn.

"I know. Maybe it's time to revisit that. Is that the next step in your Honor Improvement Plan?"

I snorted. "Is that what you're calling it?"

"Isn't that what you're doing?" she asked.

"No. You don't need any improving. I'm just helping you with some of your social and relationship skills."

Honor gave me a look. "So, improvement."

I glared at her. "I'm going to whack you with a pillow."

"Is that part of the program?"

I groaned and then did hit her with a pillow, but it was gentle.

"I don't think I like this part of the program," she said, putting her hands up to protect herself.

"I'm trying to help you be a better person!" I yelled but I was laughing.

"Aha! You *are* trying to improve me," Honor said, and reached for a pillow, holding it up as if she was ready to attack.

I leaped off the couch and brandished the pillow at her.

"Bring it on, bitch," I said.

Honor sat on the couch for a second and I thought she was going to tell me to stop being silly, but then she reached over and grabbed a pillow in her other hand.

"You have underestimated me, Layne Gray," she said in a low voice.

"Oh, have I?" I said, starting to edge backwards. She might

have two pillows, but this was my house and I knew the terrain better than she did.

Honor smiled slowly, a maniacal gleam in her eyes that I'd never seen before.

"You have," she said, just before she dove at me and started pummeling me with both pillows, wind milling her arms and making me run for cover. She chased me into the bedroom as we both laughed and after a short fight that left me short of breath, I went ahead and let her win. Honor raised both pillows in victory.

"I think I win," she said.

"You win," I said, trying to catch my breath. I'd ended up on my back on the bed with Honor over me.

"What do I win?" Honor asked, setting the pillows down on the floor.

"You don't know the rules?" I asked, pushing myself up on my elbows.

"What rules?" Honor asked.

"The winner gets a kiss from the loser," I said. "Everyone knows that."

Honor smiled down at me. "Is that so?"

The next moment she was climbing on the bed, straddling my legs.

"Well, we should follow the rules, shouldn't we?" she asked before she leaned down and kissed me. Her tongue dipped into my mouth.

She might have won the pillow fight, but I was winning right now in the kiss department.

I drove my hips upward, seeking friction.

Honor chuckled in her throat and pulled some hair away from her face so it didn't get in either of our mouths.

Her mouth drifted away from my lips and over my cheeks and down my chin.

I turned my head, giving her access to my neck and she

took my direction. Honor had no shame about kissing and licking her way down my neck, figuring out which spots were most sensitive by the noises I made.

Honor was good at taking direction.

She found one spot that had me gasping and writhing under her and sucked on that spot and I knew that it was going to leave a mark, but I couldn't find it in me to care even a little bit. Let her mark me. I'd wear it proudly.

Honor left one last fluttery kiss on the spot and pulled back, looking down at me.

"How was that for a prize?" she asked, and her breath was a little shaky.

"Yeah, it was good," I said, clumsily patting her cheek.

"Just good?" she asked, her thumb stroking the spot she'd just been kissing on my neck.

"Fantastic? Magnificent? Incredible? How do those words work?"

Honor pretended to think about that.

"They're acceptable."

"Are you angling for another pillow fight?" I asked.

"Only if it gets me a kiss," she said.

"You can have a kiss anytime you want. My lips are ready and waiting." I puckered them at her to illustrate my point.

Honor just smiled and shook her head at me.

"You're ridiculous."

"You like it."

She kissed my puckered lips so I took that as a yes.

∽

"WE SHOULD SLOW DOWN," Honor gasped what might have been minutes or hours or years later. I always lost track of time when I was kissing her.

We'd both ended up horizontal on the bed, our bodies

entwined as our hands went exploring and our mouths came together again and again.

Things were getting hot and heavy and horny, and it took me a second to realize that she'd said something. I was only focused on the fact that she'd stopped kissing me.

"Right, slow," I said, rolling my hips against hers slowly.

She bit her lip and let out a sexy noise. "That wasn't what I meant."

"Mmm, but you liked it anyway," I said.

"Too much," she whispered.

"Should I do it again?" I asked. If she said the word, I would rip her clothes off with my teeth if I had to. I needed to find out if my lurid fantasies of her body matched with reality. I'd seen her in a bathing suit once, but that didn't really count.

Honor closed her eyes and bit her lip again. "I should go. I really should."

"Okay," I said, but she didn't move.

She lay there next to me with her eyes closed, breathing through her nose.

"You gonna move, babe?" I asked, and that made her open her eyes.

"Babe?" she asked.

"Is that okay?"

She pressed her thumb against my bottom lip. "I like it."

I licked her thumb with the tip of my tongue, making her close her eyes again.

"I'm definitely going now." This time, she did get up. "Thank you for the lobster roll. And for everything else. It's nice to have someone to talk to."

"It is," I said.

"You have Joy and Sydney," she pointed out.

"I don't want to make out with either of them," I said.

"No?" she said, standing by the edge of the bed. "Joy is pretty, but I think Sydney is more my type."

"Oh really?" I asked, sitting up fully. "She'll be happy to hear that."

"Don't tell her," Honor said, pointing at me.

"Fine, I won't. Only because her head would get too big. Oh, if you know anyone who's looking for like a quick dirty hookup, Syd's in the market," I said.

"I don't, but I'll keep my eyes out," she said, stroking my face. "I'll see you tomorrow?"

"Yeah. Say hi to Lark for me," I said as I stood up to walk her out.

"I will." She kissed me once more.

"Bye, babe," I said, and she smiled at the term of endearment.

"Bye."

Chapter Fourteen

I WAS ABSOLUTELY FLOATING the next day and I didn't care who knew it. The twins were off to a theme park with some of their friends, so I spent most of the day wandering around Sadie's house doing a few chores before going getting groceries and going back to Mark's.

Honor and I had been texting all day, but I missed seeing her perfect face. Her ass wasn't bad either.

I was still putting the groceries away when she came out for a glass of water.

"Good afternoon," she said.

"Good afternoon," I said, nodding my head in her direction as I closed the fridge. "May I get you something?"

"Layne don't make this awkward," she said, getting her glass of water. "Oh, and Mark was wondering if you could make him a coffee. He ran out of the pods."

I searched the bags and pulled out a new box of Mark's favorite coffee pods. "Voilà."

"Oh, is this like a magic trick? Can you find me that pair of shoes I've had my eye on?"

I pretended to search the bags and then gave her a sad look.

"My powers only work for groceries, sorry."

Honor sighed. "You tried, that's the important part."

"I did try," I said, nodding.

Honor finished her water and lingered in the kitchen, watching me put away the groceries. I finished and folded up the bags and put them back in the drawer where they lived.

"So what are you doing this weekend?" she asked, and my heart leapt.

"I don't know, why?" I asked, copying her pose on the other side of the sink.

"Because my sister has demanded that she wants to meet you."

"Oh really? Well tell her that I would love to meet her."

"Dinner okay?"

"Yeah, she can pick the place if she wants."

"I'll tell her that. She'll be thrilled," Honor said, and I inched closer to her.

"Cool. Can't wait."

I moved until our arms were touching.

"I really want to kiss you right now," I whispered.

"I know," she whispered back.

"Meet me in the downstairs guest bedroom in fifteen minutes?" I asked.

Honor glanced toward Mark's office and then back at me, her face breaking into a smile. "Deal."

She rushed back to the office and I started the countdown. Blood pounded in my veins as I waited for Honor to join me. As a pretense, I fluffed the pillows and messed with the bed and made like I was cleaning as I waited.

What felt like a thousand years later, there was a knock at the door, and I opened it to find Honor. I yanked her inside and shut the door.

"We should have come up with a secret knock," I said.

"Dork," she said as she pushed me up against the door and kissed me, making me forget all about secret knocks and getting caught and everything else but the intensity of her mouth on mine.

Honor's hips drove into mine, increasing the pressure between my legs.

Never thought I'd be this fucking horny at work but here we were.

My hand slid down the front of Honor's dress, and I pulled the hem up just a little as she let out a little moan. Honor was the first one to end the kiss as she stumbled backward from me.

"Sorry," she gasped. "Sorry, I don't think we should fuck at work."

"Right," I said, nodding and trying to catch my own breath. "That's unprofessional."

"Right," she said, her pupils dilated with lust. Her hair was a little disheveled, so I pointed her in the direction of the bathroom that was attached. She went to finger-comb her hair.

"Your lipstick isn't even smudged," I said as I watched her.

"That's why I like this brand," she said, giving herself another once over and pulling her dress back down.

"Do I look like I've been making out?"

"No, I don't think so," I said.

She took a deep breath and let it out. "Good. I'm going back to work."

"Wait," I said as she passed me. She stopped and turned.

"Come to the beach with me tonight. You don't have to wear a bathing suit or anything. We can just take a walk."

"The beach in Castleton?" she asked.

"Yeah."

Honor's smile made my heart stop for a second. It was giddy and sweet.

"Sure," she said before she pulled the door open and went back to Mark's office.

I stayed in the guest room a little bit longer to get myself together.

∼

AFTER I PICKED the twins up and brought them back to Sadie's, I made dinner for them and then sent Honor a message that I'd meet her at the beach in an hour. Sadie was doing inventory at the shop, so she'd stayed late and didn't get home until after Riley and Zoey had eaten.

I handed them off to her and drove to Castleton.

There were still plenty of people at the beach, even though it was late.

I found Honor's car parked further away from everyone else and parked my car right next to hers.

"Hey," I said, getting out. She emerged from the driver's seat wearing another faded t-shirt and jeans with her sneakers.

"You look really cute," I said, going over to kiss her.

"Thanks. Every time I wear something like this, I know my mother is screaming with rage somewhere."

"Your mom controlled what you wore?" I asked, and then I realized it was a silly question. Of course, she had.

"Oh yes. I was wearing designer clothes the minute I was born and if I hadn't gone to private school with uniforms and other wealthy kids, I would have gotten mocked."

"Oh, so you went to private school," I said as we walked toward the sand. We sat down on a bench to take our shoes off so we could squish our toes in the sand.

"My mom also considered boarding school, but she thought she couldn't indoctrinate me properly from a distance, so I stayed closer to home."

Yeah, Honor definitely needed to give therapy a shot, because that was fucked.

"I know I've said this a million times," I said, standing up from the bench and holding out my hand, "but your mom is an absolute monster."

This time, Honor took my hand after a short hesitation.

"I always thought she was just doing what was best for me, in her way. Her methods might have been harsh, but she wanted me to succeed and be taken care of."

Honor gazed out at the rolling waves.

"Sorry. Didn't need to drag the mood down."

I squeezed her hand.

"You're not. I can tell stories about my depressing family, too, if you want. To make things even."

"No, that's fine," she said, pulling me toward the water. She rolled up her jeans and I did the same to my overalls. If Honor hadn't already seen me in overalls a dozen times, I might not have worn them, but she had so there was no reason I couldn't be comfortable. Maybe she liked the lesbian farmer look.

"Chilly," I said, shivering as the waves washed over our feet.

"It's not that bad," Honor said.

"Do you come here to swim a lot?" I asked. "You know Mark would let you use the pool if you wanted. It's heated and everything."

"I know. I just prefer the ocean to any other body of water. Can't explain it. Lakes seem like they have too many germs."

"I'm pretty sure there are just as many germs in the ocean," I said. "And isn't there a giant ball of trash the size of Texas?"

Honor kicked water in my direction.

"Stop trying to ruin the ocean for me," she said. "Or I'll dunk you in it."

"You wouldn't dare," I said, pointing at her and backing away.

"I might," she said. "I'm considering it."

"I will never speak to you again," I said, exiting the water and backing up across the sand. Honor was taller than me, but I definitely had a few pounds on her, so I thought I could hold my own in a fight if it came to that.

"You're no fun," she said, sloshing along in the water next to me.

"I'm so much fun, what are you talking about?" I took her hand again but kept my eye on her. Honor was absolutely the kind of person who would lull you into a false sense of security before she struck.

Honor squeezed my hand. "You are fun. I think I forgot about fun. My sister is always annoying me to have fun. Or at least she was before I started hanging out with you."

"So what you're saying is that I've been I good influence on you," I said, smiling.

"Okay now you're smug *and* satisfied," she said, and I grinned at her. "And it's adorable."

She stopped me and leaned down to kiss me as I pushed up on my toes in the sand.

A rogue wave came up out of nowhere and soaked our ankles, making us both scream.

"The ocean doesn't want us to kiss," I said.

"The ocean can go fuck itself," Honor said, capturing my lips again.

"How would that even work?" I asked when we started walking again. I was a little unsteady on my feet as a result of the kiss. Honor's mouth scrambled my brain.

Honor made a face. "Let's not talk about the ocean anymore."

The two of us lingered on the beach even as it was getting dark.

"I really should head home," Honor kept saying.

"You don't have to, you know," I said. I wasn't suggesting that she had to come over to spend the night and fuck me but wasn't *not* not suggesting it either.

"You're saying I could sleep on the beach? Just make a nice little bed of seaweed like a mermaid?" Honor said.

"You'd make such a hot mermaid," I said as I imagined it. "That's a definite possibility for a Halloween costume," I said.

"I don't do Halloween," she said.

"You do now. As long as you're with me, a couple's costume is required."

Honor sat down on the bench to brush off her feet and put her shoes back on.

"This is sounding like a lot of work," she said.

I pretended to toss my hair. "But I'm worth it."

She snorted as I sat down next to her. "But you're changing the subject."

She looked over at me as I sat down next to her to deal with my shoes.

"Is that too much too soon? Asking you to stay over? We don't have to have sex," I said, and two people walking by gave me dirty looks.

Honor put her socks on and then laced up her sneakers.

"The couch pulls out into a bed," I added.

Honor looked out at the water as if she was gathering her thoughts.

"Wait, have you ever been with a girl before?" I asked, probably a little too loudly, but there was no one around to hear this time.

Honor's face instantly went red and I knew I was right.

"Hey, no pressure."

"Layne!" Honor said, turning fully to face me. "Can you just chill out for a second and stop trying to fill the silence?"

I opened my mouth and then shut it with a snap.

"Sorry," I said.

"Yes," she said in a low voice. "I've never been with a woman before, but I'm not scared about having sex. I guess I just don't know…if I'm ready." She mumbled the last part so low I could barely hear her.

"Hey, no big deal, that's fine. I don't want to rush you at all. I was just offering, in case. But I'll follow your lead when it comes to staying over."

Honor made a disgusted noise. "Now you're just patronizing me, and it feels gross."

Fuck.

"I don't know what to say!" I said. "I want you to feel comfortable with how things are going between us."

"I know, Layne. I know. I just feel like it's so easy for you." She brushed imaginary sand particles off her jeans.

"Oh, I wouldn't say it's been easy. Firstly, it took me how long to realize that I actually liked you? Joy and Syd could have stood in front of me with an electric sign that said LAYNE LIKES HONOR and I would have ignored it."

I was honestly surprised that they hadn't.

"That is true. You were in denial."

I bumped her shoulder with mine. "Not anymore."

"Not anymore," she echoed. "I want you to know that I don't believe sex will be some mystical, magical, life-altering thing. I'm not, like, saving myself or anything."

"Wow, it's good to know that you already know our sex will be mediocre," I said with a laugh. "That really gives me a boost of confidence."

Honor put her head on her legs and let out a muffled scream.

"You okay?" I asked, reaching out to touch her back.

She sat back up. "You know, I'm not normally this bad at making my thoughts clear. I think you do something to my brain."

"Good, that makes two of us. I swear I can't think clearly whenever I'm around you."

Honor leaned in. "Sorry about that."

"You owe me brownies now. For that and for getting me wet earlier."

Honor raised one eyebrow. "Getting you wet is a bad thing now?"

I felt my cheeks flame as she laughed and kissed me hard.

"You have a dirty mind, Honor Conroy," I whispered.

"That's something I will never deny," she said, standing up and this time, she offered me her hand as we walked back to our cars.

Chapter Fifteen

"If you come into this kitchen one more time, I am locking you outside," Liam said as I hovered somewhere around his elbow as he chopped some veggies.

"I'm going, I'm going," I said, putting my hands up and leaving the little galley kitchen to sit down at the dining table for two he had tucked in a corner. Gwen was already sitting there, kicking back with a glass of wine after a long shift. She'd delivered twins and I didn't know how she was still awake.

Since Liam wasn't much of a cook, we'd agreed that pizza with a pre-made crust and topped with veggies and pepperoni was the way to go.

"I'm just glad to not be swimming in placenta," Gwen said, and I gagged. "Sorry. I forget not everyone wants to hear about the graphic details of my job."

"Yeah, I'm definitely set on placenta talk for the rest of my life," I said, shuddering.

"It's not all placenta. When the babies get placed on their parent's chests it's pretty great," she said.

"Okay, I am banning the word 'placenta' until dinner is over," Liam called from the kitchen.

"You got it," Gwen said, raising her wine glass. "I'm just glad they didn't give them cutesy twin names."

"What's an example of cutesy twin names?" I asked, sipping my own wine. Liam's apartment was tiny, but it was tidy and cozy. He knew how to use a vacuum, and with my help on furniture, it looked like a functioning adult lived here. I couldn't take full credit for how he'd turned out as a human, but I could take a little bit.

"Oh, like Molly and Holly. Not bad on their own, but together they're kind of cringe. You don't know how many times I hear what people are going to name their kid and I have to bite my tongue until it bleeds so I don't say anything. We definitely have a secret contest with the other nurses as to the worst name we've ever encountered."

"I know this would never happen, but I almost wish some people would run names by a committee or something. Figure out if the name is going to work for a baby, as well as the adult they might become. Sure, you can change your name when you get older, but it's a pain the ass. I just remember the hoops we had to jump through for Liam," I said.

"Oh, yeah, you're right. I've had a few parents that actually didn't pick a name right away and spent some time with their baby to figure out which fit best. I like that," Gwen said.

"Pizza is in the oven," Liam called, and I heard the slam of the oven door. He washed his hands and set the timer on his phone before grabbing some wine and sitting on the couch since he didn't have any more chairs.

"Thanks for making dinner," I said.

"Thanks for letting me chop vegetables without too much supervision," he said, glaring at me.

I just held up my middle finger at him and Gwen laughed. Even though this was only the second time the three of us were spending time together, she was used to how me and Liam interacted with each other. She had siblings.

"Gwen thinks I should get a cat," Liam said.

"Oh my god, please get a cat. I want to be a cat auntie," I said clasping my hands together in a pleading motion.

"See? I told you it was a good idea," Gwen said.

"What am I going to do with a cat while I'm at work?" Liam asked.

"That's easy," I said. "You get a second cat to play with the first cat and they can keep each other company."

"What she said," Gwen said, pointing at me.

"So now I'm getting two cats?" Liam asked.

"Yes, you're getting two cats," I said.

"It would be cruel to just get one," Gwen said, nodding. "You don't want to be a bad cat dad, do you?"

"No," he said with a sigh. "But if these cats destroy my apartment, I'm blaming both of you."

"They're not going to destroy your apartment," I said.

"I'm going to hold you to that," Liam said.

~

THE REST of the evening was punctuated with pizza and laughs. So much laughing that my stomach actually hurt when I got home. I sent Honor a message that I was home and that Liam and Gwen said hello.

They knew I was seeing someone, because I wasn't really good at hiding it, but I had managed to keep her identity a secret so far.

I didn't want to say "Honor is my girlfriend" until she was ready for me to say it.

That hadn't stopped Liam and Gwen from grilling me about her, though.

It's kind of fun having a secret lover, I sent.

I don't know if I like being referred to as a secret lover, she responded.

Well, come up with a better term for yourself, babe, I sent back.

I like it when you call me babe, she replied.

My secret babe then, I sent.

I can live with that, she responded.

~

MY WEEKEND WAS JAM PACKED, with the schooner cruise with the twins and their parents on Saturday night and then dinner with Honor and Lark on Sunday. I was a little nervous about both events, but I was really stressing about meeting Honor's sister. I really didn't know what to expect. I tried looking her up on social media but couldn't really find anything. At least, not anything under her name. How dare she deprive me of the ability to stalk her online?

I guess I was going to have to wait until Sunday to really find out what Honor's sister was like.

~

"ARE you sure you want to go through with this?" I asked the twins on Saturday as they were getting ready for the dinner. They'd informed Mark and Sadie that they should wear something nice, but since it was going to be chilly on the boat, everyone was bringing coats. Plus, they'd have to wear life jackets, which didn't really go with semi-formal wear.

To keep up the ruse, I was also dressed nice, in a pair of black slacks and a crisp white shirt with thin blue stripes. I had the coat I'd bought at a massive discount from Sadie's boutique a few years ago.

"Yes, it's going to be amazing," Riley said, bouncing on her heels as she applied lip gloss in the mirror. Their parents didn't really have a lot of rules about makeup, but the twins had just started wearing it. I think they were under some pressure from their friends to keep up with the trends. As long as they weren't walking around with eyelashes crusted in too much shitty mascara the way I had when I was their age, I didn't care. Couldn't really help them in the makeup department since I didn't wear much of it myself. Honor would have been a better tutor in that area. Hers looked flawless every single day. If there was one person on this planet that could do a razor-sharp cat eye look, it was Honor.

"You both look great," I said as Riley tugged on her dress. I'd made her put leggings on underneath so her legs didn't get cold. Zoey wore a pair of paperbag waist pants and a cashmere sweater. Both had put their hair up; Riley's in a ponytail and Zoey's in a bun.

There had been some drama about who would wear what earrings, because they absolutely could not wear the same pair and they both wanted to wear the same pair.

"Girls! We've got to go," Mark yelled up the stairs.

"Come on, get your coats," I said as the twins grabbed their winter coats and we walked down the stairs.

"Oh, don't you look lovely," Mark said as the twins came down behind me.

"They do, don't they?" I said. "So grown up."

Both of them beamed at the praise.

"Let's go meet your mother," Mark said, and we headed out to his SUV.

We met Sadie at the boat dock, and she looked gorgeous in a pair of tan pants tucked into boots and a long dark blue raincoat.

"Look at you!" Sadie said, holding her arms out. "Let me look at you. Turn, turn." Each twin did a little spin so Sadie could gush about their outfit.

"Mark, you look nice as well," Sadie said when Mark didn't speak.

"As do you," he finally said, and I caught just the tiniest touch of a blush on his cheeks. I shared a smile with the twins. This was a positive development.

The five of us walked over toward the boat as a group and greeted the captain and met the crew who would be serving us a lobster feast at sea.

Mark helped Sadie onto the boat, and then turned to help the twins.

"Oh, no," Riley said, putting her hand to her stomach. Zoey elbowed her and hissed "not yet!" in her ear.

"What's wrong?" Sadie said, instantly on alert.

"Oh, um," Riley said. "I feel seasick?"

"Sweetie, you're not even in the boat," Sadie said. "And you've never been seasick before. Are you nervous about going on the boat?"

"Yes!" Riley said, seizing on this new excuse. "I'm nervous about going on the boat."

"Me too!" Zoey practically yelled.

"We don't have to go anywhere right now," the captain said. "In fact, we can keep the boat right here in the harbor and still have a lovely evening."

"No!" both girls said at the same time. "We want you to go and enjoy the ride. We'll just stay here with Layne." My arms were seized by small, but strong, hands.

"I can look after them," I said. The twins had given me a script.

Mark and Sadie looked at each other and then burst out laughing.

"Was this all a ploy to get us alone together?" Sadie asked.

"Depends. Are you mad?" Riley asked, trying to hide behind me.

Sadie and Mark shared another look and it was so beautiful

that I wanted to cry. There was a warmth to the way they glanced at one another that had been grown over years of knowing each other and the shared love of their daughters.

"No, we're not mad," Mark said. "You could have just told us that's what you were doing without this whole production."

The crew of the schooner had stepped back, sensing a private family moment.

"I helped," I blurted out, going off-script. "They made the plan themselves, but I helped book the tickets. It was such a sweet idea I couldn't resist."

Please don't fire me, I begged with my eyes.

Mark looked at Sadie and tilted his head. "You want to go on a sunset cruise with me?"

He held out his hand.

"I would," Sadie said, putting her hand in his.

If this were a movie, the orchestra would be playing swelling romantic music right now.

"So you're going?" Riley asked.

"Yes," Mark said, almost unable to take his eyes from Sadie. Oh yeah, this had been a good idea.

"I'll take care of them," I said. "We'll go out and meet you back here."

"Sounds good," Sadie said, finally looking over at us. "Give me hugs before you go."

Riley and Zoey hopped on the boat just to hug their parents and then we stood back as they headed out, waving our arms as if they were going on a long journey.

I put my arms around both of them, pulling them toward me.

"Good job, girls. I think they're going to have a lot to talk about on that boat ride."

"Do you think they'll kiss?" Riley asked. "We should have told them they should kiss."

I laughed. "I don't think it works that way, Rileybug."

"Should we text them?" Zoey said, pulling out her phone.

"No, I think they can figure it out."

∼

SINCE RILEY and Zoey and I were dressed nicely, I took them to a nice restaurant. I'd let them look at the menu ahead of time so they knew there was something they wanted.

"How do you think they're doing?" Riley asked as we were seated at our table. There were no other kids in the restaurant, and I was sure there were some adults that thought children didn't belong in a place like this, but I didn't care. Riley and Zoey had learned restaurant manners when they were young.

"I think that no news is good news," I told her as they picked up the giant menus.

"Zo-go, that's the wine menu, you don't need that," I said, taking the tasseled wine list from Zoey.

"Wine, gross," Zoey said, making a face.

"You're not old enough to drink it anyway," I said, setting the wine list off to the side.

"Do I have to drink it when I get older?" Zoey asked.

"Absolutely not. You don't have to eat or drink anything you don't like. Not even if people tell you that you should like it, okay?" I said.

"Okay," she said, and leaned over Riley's shoulder to ask her what she was going to get.

The small Italian place had both spaghetti and fettuccine alfredo on the menu, so the twins got an order of each so they could share, and I got the lasagna, even though I cringed at the price.

"Can we order a fancy drink?" Riley asked, her eyes lighting up.

"I'll order one too," I said and when the server came over,

we all ordered Shirley Temples with extra lime and an antipasto plate as an appetizer.

Our drinks came, and we all toasted each other. Riley took a picture of me sipping my drink and making a silly face.

One of the unwritten rules of my job was that I was required to be part of their social media whether I wanted to be or not. Sometimes that meant doing silly dances with them, and sometimes that meant participating in some ridiculous challenge. I tried to be a good sport about it.

Riley sent me the picture and I went ahead and forwarded it to Honor because the lighting was working for me and I looked cute.

Mission accomplished. Parents on boat. Out to dinner with the kids.

She responded a few minutes later with a selfie of her own.

Drinking on my porch with my sister. Not as glamorous, she sent, holding up a glass as the setting sun lit up her face.

She was so pretty it was painful to look at her. How could one person be so gorgeous?

Tell Lark I said hello, I responded.

She says hello and that she's looking forward to meeting you tomorrow. I've told her she's not supposed to grill you, but she's not making any promises, she sent.

"Who are you talking to?" Riley asked as our appetizer arrived on a wooden plank that sat in the center of the table.

"Beeswax," I said, reaching for a slice of bread to dip it in some olive oil. Riley and Zoey and I had our own little language that we'd built over so many years together. When someone said "beeswax" it meant "none of your business, drop it."

"You're hiding stuff from us," Riley said, pouting. Zoey looked at her and then started pouting too.

"I'm allowed to have a life that doesn't involve you. That's what's cool about being an adult. I can do what I want."

Their eyes narrowed, obviously not liking that answer.

"Someday you can have your own secrets," I said.

"We have secrets," Riley protested.

"When you get older, the secrets get better. Trust me," I said. "Are you going to eat?"

"Do they have mozzarella sticks?" Zoey asked.

"No, they don't, but this is some nice cheese right there, and some olives and some meat. I can't remember what kind of meat, but it's kind of like pepperoni, I think."

The twins perked up at the idea of cheese and pepperoni and olives and soon they were devouring even the peppers and asking if I could make this for them at home.

"I don't think I can make it as nice as this, but we can do some research and then try it," I said. "I'm sure there's a video we can watch."

One of the great things about the internet was that if you wanted to learn how to do something, there were plenty of people who had made a video on how to do it.

"I'll introduce you to Martha Stewart," I said.

"Who?" Riley asked, shoving a piece of cheese into her mouth.

"You'll see," I said.

∼

DINNER WAS ABSOLUTELY DELICIOUS, if expensive, but I paid the bill and I could ask Mark and Sadie to reimburse me.

As we were leaving the restaurant, Sadie sent a message to me and the kids via the family group chat.

Coming back soon, had a lovely time. Saw a dolphin family!

The message was accompanied by a video that Sadie must have taken of a small pod of dolphins surfacing near the boat and Mark telling Sadie not to get too close to the edge.

Cute. I heard him laugh at something she said, and they did sound like they were having a good time.

I couldn't wait to get every single detail when they got back.

The twins begged for ice cream, so we walked down the street where there was a tiny little ice cream stand next to the dock and I let them get whatever they wanted while I just got a dish of cookie dough. Part of me considered getting a brownie sundae and sending a picture of it to Honor to gloat.

But then I thought about all the brownies I'd eaten with her and how now they felt like a thing we should do together.

~

THE TWINS and I waved madly as Mark and Sadie returned from their voyage. Sadie's hair was windblown, and their cheeks were red, but they were both beaming.

Riley and Zoey ran to hug their parents and I hung back as they talked together as a family.

It never bothered me, standing back sometimes to let them have their time. It was important.

They all walked over to me, and they looked so sweet together, the two girls between their mom and dad.

"How was it?" I asked as Sadie shivered. "Let me get the car started, you both look freezing."

"I haven't been on a boat in forever," Sadie said, getting into the passenger seat of Mark's SUV while the girls hopped in the back. I gave Mark the keys and got in the back too.

Riley and Zoey bombarded their parents with questions, and I watched as Mark and Sadie talked about their "date."

"If you wanted us to be alone together, you could have just told us," Sadie said, giving both girls a significant look.

"You wouldn't have done it if we asked," Riley said, and Sadie and Mark didn't really have a good answer to that.

"You know your mother and I are not together," Mark said.

"We know," they chorused.

"It's nice that you want us to spend time together, but we don't want you to get your hopes up, okay?" Sadie said, echoing Mark's sentiments. For two people who weren't together, they were definitely in synch.

There was a lecture, but I didn't think the twins were paying attention to it.

I didn't miss the looks that passed between Mark and Sadie, and I didn't think it was reading too much into things to say that their looks were heated.

Eventually Sadie said she had to go home, and she'd see the kids on Monday morning. They hugged her and begged her not to go, that she should come back with us, but she put her foot down.

Sadie came to give me a hug as well. "Thanks for looking out for them."

"I knew I needed to get involved so they didn't try to book you plane tickets to Vegas or get ordained online or something really bonkers," I said.

Sadie laughed. "You know them well."

"Oh, I do," I said, hugging her back. "And if you want to give me any details, I'm going to be up for a little while." I gave her a wink and didn't miss that she blushed.

"I have a lot to think about," was all she said.

∽

MARK TOLD the twins that question time was over, and they needed to talk about something else, anything else, on the way back.

That didn't make them happy, but they ended up talking his ear off about the restaurant, so that was something.

I hopped out of the car when we got back and said goodnight to everyone.

"I'm glad it worked out," I said to Mark.

"It did," was his only reply.

"Goodnight," I said, and he waved before taking the girls into the house.

The guest house was too quiet, so I turned on the TV and sent another message to Honor.

Back from my little excursion with the family. Still drinking on the porch? I sent.

Her response was immediate. **We moved our drinking to the living room. Lark won't pick out a movie to watch.**

What are the choices? I asked.

She listed them and I told her which movie she should watch.

Have you seen it? she asked.

About five million times, I responded. The movie was one of my favorites.

Okay, Lark said we could watch that one, she sent.

Happy to be of service, I replied.

We shot messages back and forth like that for the next two hours, and I didn't even think she was watching the movie. That was fine. I'd just make her watch it with me sometime so I could see her reactions.

It was growing increasingly more difficult to not think about Honor. I thought of her when I woke up and made breakfast. I thought of her after she went into the office with Mark. I thought of her when I was alone in the guest house the most. Many of those thoughts involved nudity, but I wasn't ashamed of that. If you couldn't masturbate to the thought of your sort of undefined girlfriend, then what even was the point?

Honor obviously wanted to take things slow, and I was doing my best, but my thoughts about Honor were slow, fast, and everything in between, and it was getting to be a real problem.

Chapter Sixteen

THE NEXT DAY I stood in my bedroom and looked at three different outfits spread out on my bed. It was unusual for me to take a while deciding what to wear, but I was all in my head about it today for some reason.

I wanted to impress both Honor and Lark, but for different reasons. My outfit for Honor should make her think of pulling me away to do dirty things, and my outfit for Lark should convey that I was the kind of woman she wanted dating her older sister.

A dilemma, since there were very few outfits that could speak to both of those needs.

In the end, I decided on a light blue dress that had buttons down the front and hit me about mid-calf and made my boobs look really good. Breezy and casual, but still sexy.

The thick straps hid my bra straps, because there was no way that I could walk around without worrying about one of my boobs trying to make an escape.

The girls were tucked in securely, and I did a double check for underwear lines before sliding my feet into my sandals, adding my favorite sunglasses, and grabbing my bag.

Just as I was going out the door, I nabbed my jean jacket just in case it got chilly.

Honor said that she'd pick me up, which I assumed she was doing so she didn't have to show me her house. I still hadn't told her about that little afternoon excursion, and I wondered how long it would take before she'd actually show it to me.

I hoped she didn't think I would judge her. I couldn't throw stones about anyone's living situation when I was living in a guest house that I didn't pay for. Sure, Mark was rich and had a huge house, but Liam and I had grown up very frugal and had shared a room until I'd moved out for college.

Honor showed up five minutes early, as predicted, and I barely waved before someone jumped out of the passenger seat and came over to me.

"Lark!" Honor yelled, getting out.

I was greeted by a smiling face that was so similar to Honor's that I did a double take. Her cheeks were a little rounder and her hair a few shades darker blonde and pulled into a messy bun.

"I'm sorry, I couldn't wait anymore. Hi, I'm Lark," she said, waving. I'd thought she was going to pull me into a hug, but she stopped just short of doing so.

"Hi, Lark, I'm Layne," I said.

"Lark and Layne sounds like a badass duo," Lark said. "I like it."

"Me too," I said, laughing.

"Sorry," Honor said, cringing as she made her way over.

"For what?" I asked. Honor looked at me and then Lark and back.

"I told her not to make this a big deal," Honor said.

"I'm not making it a big deal, calm down," Lark said. "She's always telling me that I'm too much."

"Oh, really," I said, turning to Honor. "We have that in common."

"When have I ever told you that you're too much?" Honor said to me.

"It's implied," I said. "Doesn't matter, because if I'm too much for someone, they should go find less somewhere else."

"I completely agree," Lark said, beaming. "Should we go? I'm starving."

I liked her instantly.

Honor seemed wary as Lark hopped in the backseat, giving me the front to sit with Honor as she chatted away.

"I've been dying to join book club, but this one said that I wasn't allowed," she said, pointing to Honor as she backed out and pulled onto the road to head to the restaurant.

"I never said that," Honor said.

Lark rolled her eyes. "Okay, fine. But you told me it was your thing and that you needed something that was just yours. And then I found out about you and it all made sense."

I looked over my shoulder and saw a smirk on Lark's face.

"Lark," Honor said in an exasperated voice that made me think of how I interacted with Liam.

"Hey, I'm not going to judge you, I just wish you'd been honest with me, HONOR," Lark said, emphasizing her sister's name.

Honor muttered something under her breath.

"What was that?" Lark said, leaning over between the seats.

I turned and smiled at Honor, who was doing her best to keep her attention on the road with a glare on her face.

"This is going to be fun," I said.

∼

HONOR AND LARK could not have been more opposite. Where Honor was prim and reserved, Lark was gregarious and seemed to say whatever she thought.

By the time we got to the restaurant, I had learned quite about Honor Conroy.

"Why are you like this?" Honor said after Lark had told a funny story about Honor having a goth phase in high school that was short-lived.

"You'd look hot as a goth," I said as we got out of the car at the restaurant.

"She probably still has the black choker and fishnets somewhere," Lark said, wiggling her eyebrows.

"You are walking home," Honor said to Lark as I held the door open for everyone.

~

"I KNOW I'm supposed to ask you a million questions and be all tough and ask about your intentions with my sister, but I'm just grateful someone actually wants to spend time with her that I'm going to beg you not to run away," Lark said as we looked at our menus.

"Are you going to get a drink? I think I'm going to get a drink," Honor said to me, ignoring her sister.

"Sure, I'll get a drink," I said to Honor.

"Surprisingly, I like your sister," I said to Lark. "Takes her a little to warm up, and things definitely improved once I knew she wasn't trying to marry my boss."

"And now you're walking home with Lark," Honor said, not taking her eyes off her menu.

I reached under the table and touched her leg gently.

"I'll be nice," I said, and she softened.

"Okay, this is cute," Lark said, putting her chin in her hands as she watched us from across the table.

Honor hid behind her menu.

The server finally came and we ordered drinks, and Lark seemed to have gotten most of her jokes out of her system and toned herself down a little bit. She asked me about my job and what it was like to take care of twins for so many years.

"It's weird because it very much is a job, but also they feel like my family, so it's a hard balance to keep," I said. "When they were babies, I definitely wasn't good about setting boundaries and I had to do that as they got older. My friends help."

"I feel like I don't know anyone in Arrowbridge, and I've been here the whole summer," Lark said, pouting. "I don't have a car, so it's kind of hard to get around. I mostly hang out with Lorna and the chickens."

She laughed, but I could sense that Lark was lonely under her bravado.

"I'm happy to take you out or to the farmers' market or show you around if you want. My brother is your age and I know he's got a good group of friends." Many of them were fellow coffeeshop employees and they'd all get together at someone's house to play games or even just have pizza and a movie night.

"Thanks, that would be great."

Since I knew their childhood was a sensitive topic, I steered far away from it, but I hoped at some point I could get Lark's perspective on their mother and her *teachings*, if they could be called that. They seemed to have much less effect on Lark than they had on Honor, but maybe because Honor was the oldest and might have shielded Lark from the brunt of it.

Lark talked about college and I reminisced about my college days.

"It was seriously so fun. All my friends were right there, and you could always find someone to hang out with, even in the middle of the night. I don't even think I kept my door closed most of the time," I said. "It was the best."

"That hasn't really been my experience," Lark said. "It's okay, but I'm not having the time of my life."

That was strange to me, because she was so personable

and open and bubbly that you'd think she would have no problem making friends. Maybe her mother's "other girls are out to get you" had affected her more than I'd initially thought.

Now I just wanted to take her under my wing and maybe absorb her into my friend group, or shove her into Liam's.

"Stop it," Honor said under her breath.

"What?" I asked as Lark was distracted by something on her phone.

"Stop trying to figure out how you can fix her problems," Honor said under her breath.

"You know I can hear you since we're sitting at the same table," Lark said in a normal voice. "I don't care if Layne wants to fix my life. It's kind of sucking at the moment."

"Maybe things would be better if you had some direction," Honor said tentatively, and Lark let out a loud sigh.

Fortunately, our appetizer plate arrived and thwarted a potential sister argument.

"You and my brother would get along. You can commiserate about being nagged by your older sisters," I said to Lark as she dipped her boneless buffalo wing in ranch.

Honor had gone right for the spinach artichoke dip and was using a spoon to place it atop a chip. Things had changed so much since that first dinner with the Jewels where I'd seen her do that.

"Sounds fun," Lark said.

"And if you're ever looking for work, he always has openings at the coffeeshop. Even for just part time," I said, and Honor nudged my leg under the table.

"I would love to work, but my sister is weird about it," Lark said, glaring at Honor.

"You're supposed to be focusing on school," Honor said. "That's your job."

"Well, right now I'm not in school, so working would give

me something to do so I don't stab myself in the eyeball from boredom," Lark said.

The banter didn't make me uncomfortable at all because I was so used to doing the same thing with Liam.

"This is really good," I said loudly about the pretzel bites with beer cheese dip.

That seemed to break the tension and I told Lark about the twins and their plan to get their parents back together.

"That is really cute," she said, when I told her about the schooner cruise.

"Honestly, I think they will get back together. Neither of them has had any luck dating, and there's just a chemistry between them. I'd like to see them at least give it a shot and if it doesn't work, it doesn't work, and they can keep being friends and co-parenting," I said, trying not to drip cheese into my lap.

"So you're a romantic?" Lark asked, her eyes flicking to Honor.

"I am, and proud of it," I said.

Lark raised her eyebrows. "Interesting."

"Go ahead, tell us what you're thinking," Honor said.

"No, no, I'm good," Lark said, putting her hands up. "I just think it's interesting."

Our entrées arrived and I got into a conversation about books with Lark, who said she wasn't much of a reader, but was open to suggestions. I had to stop myself from talking too fast at her and getting too excited.

I caught Honor looking at me at one point. "What?" I asked, hoping there wasn't something on my face.

"Nothing," she said, hiding a smile. "Nothing."

∽

THE DINNER WAS PUNCTUATED with laughs, even from Honor, and I was really enjoying Lark. She definitely needed to get out of the house and do something, and I didn't agree with Honor's rule about no working.

Reading between the lines, Honor was footing the bill for Lark's school, because she hadn't gotten much financial aid due to their mother's income. Pretty shitty system if you asked me.

Still, that put a lot of pressure on Honor that she didn't need to take on. Even if Lark got a part-time job during the school year, that might help her feel more in charge of her own education. Or maybe Lark didn't even want to go to college. That was another possibility, and I didn't think Honor would like that at all.

That woman needed to loosen up and not be so rigid about everything and I was going to do what I could to help in that.

Oh, and make her believe in love. That was first and foremost.

∼

HONOR PAID THE BILL, even though I put up a fuss. Lark just rolled her eyes.

"Don't even bother. She won't let you," Lark said. "Trust me. I've been fighting with her almost my whole life."

"I like fighting with her. It's fun," I said, grinning at Honor.

"I think we have different definitions of the word 'fight,'" Lark said.

∼

"YOU SHOULD COME HANG out with us," Lark said as we got in the car.

"You don't have to," Honor said quickly.

"No, I'd love to," I said, reaching over and squeezing Honor's hand. "You always come over to my place. I'd like to see yours."

Honor's other hand clenched on the steering wheel.

"I'd love to see your place," I said in a soft voice. "And visit Lorna's chickens."

Honor nodded once. "Fine."

I bit my tongue so I didn't make a snarky comment about how excited she looked about the prospect of me coming over.

Once it was over with and she saw that I was not going to judge her living situation and run away screaming, her anxiety would go away.

Hopefully.

∼

LARK WAS a little more subdued on the ride back and I could see that her extreme energy was not an all-the-time thing. She'd just been excited to meet me, and I could understand that.

Honor's jaw clenched more and more the closer we got to the house. When we finally pulled into the driveway and she turned the car off, there was complete silence.

"I'm going to go inside," Lark announced, hopping out of the car and slamming the door to give us some privacy.

"I have to tell you something," I said to Honor. "I drove over here once."

She turned to face me. "What?"

"Yeah, I mean, everyone knows where Lorna lives, so I figured out this was your house by process of elimination."

"I couldn't afford much," she said in a small voice, looking down at the keys in her hand.

"Hey, babe," I said, and she looked up at me. "I literally don't care where you live. I mean, as long as it's safe and not completely falling apart or dangerous or something."

Honor shook her head. "No, we got the mold taken care of and fixed the leaky roof before I moved in."

"Mold?" I asked.

"It was taken care of," she said.

"Listen, if you ever need someone to take a look at anything, Mark has a great handyman who adores me, and he'd come over and take a look if your landlord is a jerk about it."

"Lorna is my landlord," Honor said, laughing under her breath.

"Wait, really?" I hadn't known that Lorna owned both places.

"Yeah. She's been really great and gave me a good deal. Is it the house that I imagined myself living in? No, but I'm paying for it all on my own and that's something."

I couldn't miss the pride that shone through her eyes about that. She should be proud. She could have just married some random rich guy. Instead, she got this little place on her own and was putting her sister through college. That was a lot for one person to handle without any support.

A chicken jumped on the hood of Honor's car and glared at us, as if we were trespassing.

"That happens a lot," Honor said. "I go to the car wash a lot."

I wanted to ask her why she put such value in having a fancy car, but I figured Honor was dealing with a lot tonight and I didn't want to push it.

Lark came through the front door and looked at us, her hands on her hips. "Are you coming in?"

"Let's go," I said, opening the door.

Honor followed me as I walked up the creaky porch steps. The porch was teeny tiny and only had room for two chairs and a little table.

"Want a drink?" Lark asked as I walked through the front door.

"Yeah, absolutely," I said, looking around.

The place was definitely shabby, but it was cute. Lorna had obviously had a hand in decorating.

There were chickens everywhere, and the main color scheme was yellow, white, and red.

"It was like this when I moved in," Honor said behind me.

"Yeah, this doesn't seem like your style." I pointed to the row of chicken pictures on one of the walls.

"You get used to it after a while, if you can believe that."

She led me to the red-and-white checked couch to the right of the front door.

Honor opened what looked like a china hutch to reveal a TV.

"This is mine," she said, pointing to it. The screen barely fit in the hutch, even though it was small.

"Here you go," Lark said, bringing glasses of rose over to all of us.

"Thanks," I said, taking one from her.

"Do you want to see my bedroom?" Lark asked.

"Sure," I said.

"You're sitting in it," she said, laughing.

"There's only one bedroom," Honor said.

"I refused to share," Lark said. "So be nice to my bed."

"I will," I said, worried about spilling anything on the couch.

Honor's spine was still rigid, and I wanted to tell her to chill out.

"Does this place have a name? You should absolutely call it The Chicken Coop or The Hen Den or something."

Lark burst out laughing and so did Honor after a second.

"I'm going to tell Lorna that. She'll love it. We could put a little sign on the door."

"I'm not living in a place called The Hen Den," Honor said as she sipped her wine.

"Then we're calling it The Chicken Coop," Lark said,

cackling. "And on that note, I'm going to go sit on the porch and chat with the chickens."

I wanted to tell her that she didn't have to go, but I also wanted to have some time with Honor and check in and see how she was doing.

Lark saluted us with her wine.

"Layne, it was lovely to meet you, please come over again, and I absolutely approve of you dating my sister," she said before she yanked the door open and slammed it.

"We're not dating," Honor said, but Lark was already outside.

I turned to look at Honor. "Wait, we're not dating?"

"I don't know, are we?" she asked.

"If we're not dating, then what are we doing?" I asked.

"Hanging out?" Honor suggested.

"Babe, that's dating."

"I didn't want to presume," she said.

"Go ahead and presume all you want. I have no issue with saying that we're dating," I said.

"Oh, okay," Honor said, taking a gulp of wine.

"You good with that?" I asked, trying to meet her eyes.

She inhaled and then thought for a moment.

"Strangely enough, yes," she said. "That's surprising. I expected to feel trapped, or a creeping sense of dread, but the idea of dating you feels…right."

My heart squeezed a little bit at her words. She turned to me and smiled the most heartbreaking smile.

"Dating you feels right to me, too," I said, setting my wine down and leaning into her.

Just before our lips met, she spoke. "What do you really think of the house?"

"I think that Lorna has a chicken addiction," I said, and she chuckled as I slipped my fingers through her hair.

"But I can live with it."

"I have nightmares about this house. About all the chickens coming alive and pecking me to death," Honor whispered.

"That sounds terrifying," I said, my hand tracking from her hair and down the side of her face to her neck. Her pulse beat against my fingers.

"You might be able to help me forget about the killer chickens," she said.

"I think I'm up for the challenge," I said and then she kissed me, and I didn't think either of us were considering chickens.

Chapter Seventeen

Honor's mouth devoured me hungrily, pushing me back on the obnoxious couch. Briefly, I remembered that this was Lark's bed, but I hoped she wouldn't mind too much. It wasn't like we were going to fuck on her bed and then walk away.

The sounds Honor made were desperate, as if she'd been deprived of kissing me and now she was going to make up for it.

The second her tongue entered my mouth, all rational thought departed from my brain and my world centered on what we were doing together.

She tasted like the wine, but with her own underlying sweetness that made me think of chocolate, strangely enough.

Kissing Honor was decadent and delicious, and I could have spent the rest of my life kissing her if I didn't need to eat and sleep and do other things.

I could quit my job and devote myself to kissing Honor full time.

Unable to resist, my fingers sought her skin, sneaking under her clothes and seeking to touch as much of her as I could.

Her hands weren't idle, either, as they traced my neck and

shoulders and one slid between us, but she couldn't get it under my dress. She let out a frustrated sound and looked down at me.

"I don't like this dress," she said.

"What's wrong with it?" I asked, looking down. From this angle, my boobs were practically straining to break free of both my bra and the dress.

Honor didn't answer and started attacking the buttons.

"They're not real," I said. "They're just for decoration."

"I take it back," she said, sitting up. "I *hate* this dress."

"If you hate it that much, I should probably take it off," I said, pushing myself up so I could pull the straps off my shoulders and yank the top of the dress to my waist.

"Better?" I asked as I revealed my favorite black lace bra to her.

"Oh yes," she said, running her finger down one strap. "I'm trying to remember that my sister is right out on the porch and could walk in at any moment, but I really, really want to see you naked."

This was a change from what she'd said the other day.

"You're ready to see me naked?" I asked and Honor stared at me.

"Yes, I am absolutely ready to see you naked."

"Just to clarify, will you be naked as well?" I didn't want to be the only one.

"I think I could make that happen," she said and then frowned as I pulled my dress back up.

"Then let's go somewhere where your sister can't walk in. Come back to my place with me. There are zero chickens."

Honor looked down at me and smiled slowly. "No chickens is definitely a plus."

∼

HONOR and I somehow got ourselves together and she tossed some stuff in a bag and we headed out. I could barely walk, I was so fucking horny.

"I'm staying at Layne's. Don't burn the house down," Honor said to Lark.

"You got it," she said, raising her wine glass in our direction.

Honor put her bag in the car and then got in the driver's seat.

"You're not worried about Mark seeing your car parked in the driveway?" I asked.

"Fuck it," she said, and I almost gasped at how forceful she sounded. "Fuck it. Fuck everything. I'm tired of not doing the things I want."

"Fuck me, please," I said, and she turned to give me a heated look.

"I plan on it."

∼

THE DRIVE HOME took three thousand times longer than it should have and I literally had my legs squeezed together the whole time and clenched my hands together so I didn't touch myself.

By the time Honor parked the car, I was actually shaking.

"Let's go," I said and threw myself out of the car. Honor grabbed her bag and we rushed into the house. She slammed the door and then pushed me up against it, dropping her bag with a bang on the floor.

"No chickens," I said.

"No chickens," she said and then she kissed me so hard that she might have drawn blood. I didn't care. She could bite me as much as she wanted to. Go vampire, I didn't care. As long as she didn't stop.

Honor's hands yanked at my dress and I decided it was time to finally lose it.

I kicked off my shoes and then reached down to pull the dress over my head.

"I like this," Honor said, fingering the edge of my skintight shorts that matched the bra.

"I was hoping you would," I said, trying not to sound too breathless.

Of course, I had my own body insecurities like everyone but, right now, I felt sexy as hell as Honor looked at me.

"Has anyone ever told you that you have an incredible chest?" Honor said, her eyes completely focused on said chest.

"Yes, but it doesn't hurt to hear you've got a killer rack," I said. It really was one of my best features. "But it wouldn't hurt to compare."

Hers definitely weren't bad either. Not as big as mine, but they were perfectly shaped.

"I'm sure yours are real," Honor said, meeting my eyes, almost daring me to say something.

"If you mean by 'real' I didn't go to a doctor for them, then yes. Unless yours are literally not attached to you and they're actually just balloons filled with pudding, I think they're real, Honor."

Now I was even more interested in seeing them.

"A lot of people would say that they aren't real," Honor said, tension between her brows.

"Well, those people can go fuck themselves. Just take your clothes off, I'm dying here," I said.

"I'd rather stare at you," she said.

"Honor," I said, taking her hands. "I have been getting myself off at the thought of your naked body for weeks. So don't think that there's anything that you have that I don't want to see."

She blinked twice at me. "What?"

"You heard me," I said, squeezing her hands. "Do you need some help? Because I'm more than willing to undress you and find out that my fantasy was nothing compared to reality."

My imagination was good, but it wasn't that good. In this case, reality was better already.

Honor laughed a little bit. "You always have the most interesting way of putting things. I like the way your mind works."

"You're not thinking about my mind right now are you, though?" I asked, stroking her arms.

"No, I have other parts of your anatomy at the forefront," she said and then turned to the side and raised one arm to reveal the side zipper of her dress.

"I was surprised you didn't go casual tonight," I said as I pulled the zipper down and helped her step out of the dress.

"I like the way you look at me when I wear something like this," Honor said as the dress pooled on the floor. She leaned down to pick it up and then folded it over a chair.

I didn't really hear what she said, because I was too busy staring at Honor in a matching nude bra and boy shorts. Her bottoms were unexpected. I'd imagined her more of a thong girl, but I guess I'd been wrong.

"Fuck," I said as I stared at her. "Babe, you are…what's that?"

Something peeked at me from the corner of her hip that was partially covered by her underwear. I reached out and pulled that side down just a little bit to reveal a small tattoo.

It was the outline of a single long-stemmed rose.

"This is unexpected."

Honor put her finger under my chin and lifted my head. "I'll tell you about it later."

Later was a good plan. Right now, I wanted to touch and taste as much of her as possible.

I took her hand and led her to my bedroom, patting myself on the back for making my bed this morning. I didn't always, but something had told me to make it today, just in case.

My vibrators were all charged, and I had a fresh bottle of lube in my bedside table.

Honor closed the door and pushed me toward the bed until my legs hit the edge and I squealed.

"You taking charge?" I asked and she put a hand on my chest to get me to climb up on the bed.

"You like it," she said. "Aren't you tired of taking care of everyone else? Don't you want someone to take care of you?"

I closed my eyes for a second, because she'd gotten me exactly right.

"Yes," I said, and she smiled.

"That's what I thought."

Honor followed me up on the bed and I tossed some of the pillows aside to make room for both of us.

"Can I take this off?" Honor asked, tugging at my bra strap.

"If you insist," I said.

"I do," she said, and I reached behind the bra and flicked the hooks so she could pull the rest of it off me before setting it on the chair beside my bed. Honor wasn't the kind of woman who flung a bra across the room. No, she set it on a chair so you could find it later.

"Layne," she said in a reverent voice as she cupped my breasts in her hands. They spilled out, as they were wont to do.

"Hey, my face is up here," I joked, and she propped herself on one hand and kissed me as she stroked my breast. She quickly focused her touch on one of my nipples which were both so hard they could cut glass. I whimpered into her mouth and she smiled.

"Tell me what you want, Layne," she said, and I tried to answer her, but it came out completely garbled as she pinched my nipple.

"What was that?" Honor asked, chuckling a little bit.

"Mouth," I managed to get out.

"You want me to put my mouth on you?" she asked, even though she knew perfectly well that was what I meant. My communication skills had deteriorated again. Maybe I should just start pointing.

"Here," I said, doing just that and pointing at my nipple. Honor laughed, but the sound changed a moment later when she did what I asked and took my nipple into her mouth, giving it a nice long lick.

For someone who had never been with a woman before, Honor was doing an incredible job.

"Wait," I gasped out, and she immediately stopped and looked up at me for direction.

"You can stop anytime you want. Just tell me. And if there's anything you don't want to do, tell me," I said, struggling to make my thoughts coherent.

"I don't want to stop," Honor said. "I want to find out what I've been missing. A lot, apparently." She licked my nipple again and I arched my back, pushing myself against her.

Honor lavished her attention on one nipple with her mouth while her hand worked on the other, rolling it between her fingers and then she pinched me at the same time she nipped the other and I let out a sound I'd never heard myself make before. I was so fucking wet already, I was probably dripping on the bed. Whatever, I'd just change the comforter after we were done.

Honor pulled back and looked down at my breasts again, pushing them together to create cleavage.

"Yours are definitely better," she said.

"I'd have to see yours to compare," I said, cupping one of them through her bra.

I wanted to ask her if the surgery hurt, and how long ago she'd gotten them done, but this wasn't the time. I filed that away to ask about later, along with the tattoo. So many surprising things about Honor Conroy.

Honor removed her bra without another word and I almost gasped at how perfect she was.

"Can I touch you?" I asked. Honor took my hand and put it on one of her breasts.

I couldn't stop the moan that escaped my mouth. Perfect. She was perfect.

I brushed my thumb across her nipple, and she pulled her bottom lip between her teeth.

"What do you want?" I asked her, and her eyes opened.

"Open your mouth," she said, and I did exactly that as she leaned down and set her nipple in my mouth.

It was unexpected and so fucking hot that my brain stopped for a moment before I realized I had Honor's nipple in my mouth and all my wildest dreams were coming true.

I flicked my tongue against her nipple and then sucked gently.

"More," Honor said. I couldn't see her face, so I had to go off what I could hear.

I sucked harder and used my teeth on her nipple and was rewarded by her nails digging into my scalp and a sound of pleasure coming from her lips.

I alternated between soft touches, licks, and bites until I moved on to the other breast, giving it equal attention.

Honor held herself above me, but I could feel her trembling, taste her heartbeat against her skin.

If she decided to suffocate me with her magnificent chest, I would die happy in this moment.

Honor let out a gasping breath and sat up. Her nipples were darker and wet from my mouth. I definitely liked that.

I cupped them in my hands.

"I could spend all day with these," I said.

"Maybe I'll let you someday. Right now, I have other parts of your body in mind to give some attention."

"Oh, you do?" I asked. "Are you talking about my elbows? My knees? My heels?"

Honor laughed under her breath and shook her head.

"None of those, although they've very nice, and I intend to touch and taste them, but there are different areas that I'd like to focus on now, and you know it, Layne."

I felt like I was being scolded by a sexy teacher and I wasn't mad about it.

Honor might be younger than me, but right now, she had the upper hand and I was content to let her keep it. I'd always been comfortable to let my partners be more aggressive in the bedroom. Honor had been right about me loving it when other people took care of me in this way.

"Is it the back of my neck, because I can turn over," I said, wiggling my hips.

Honor squeezed her legs on the outside of mine.

"I'm not talking about the back of your neck."

"Where then?" I asked, making my eyes wide and innocent.

She slid her hand down between my breasts, stopped briefly to circle my belly button, and then cupped me over my lacy underwear.

The warmth of her hand and the sudden pressure made me writhe.

"Right there," she said as I pushed myself into her hand, seeking more contact. The lace was an irritating barrier that I wanted gone.

"Touch me, Honor," I said. "Please."

Moving down the bed, she hooked her fingers on the sides of my underwear and shimmied them down my hips and then set them carefully with my bra on the chair.

Here I was, in all my naked glory, laid out for her.

Honor looked down at me with fire in her eyes and it burned inside me, making me bold.

"Are you going to touch me, or am I going to have to take care of myself?" I said, stroking my center with my hand. I was already so slick that my fingers slid easily.

Honor arched one eyebrow. "If you're going to just get yourself off, I guess you don't need me. I've got some laundry I should fold," she said, pretending like she was going to get off the bed. I reached out and grabbed her wrist to stop her with the hand that I'd just been using on myself. Now her skin was wet with my desire, and I definitely liked that.

"Get back here and get me off," I said, and she let out a startled laugh.

"You're always surprising me, Layne Gray."

"You like it," I said, sliding my grip from her wrist to her hand and guiding that hand where I wanted her to touch me.

When her fingers brushed my clit, I moaned and arched myself toward her.

"More," I said.

"I'll give you more, babe," she said, and I barely even registered that this was the first time she'd called me "babe."

Honor moved her body between my legs and spread my hips wider, ending up putting one of my legs over her shoulder.

This woman didn't waste any fucking time and I couldn't be luckier.

"Tell me if anything is too much," she said, and I remembered, belatedly, that this was her first time with a woman. There was no hesitation with her, no nervousness. No asking for a road map. I would have given her one, had she asked, but the fact that she was barreling ahead on pure confidence?

Hot as fuck.

I propped myself up on my elbows to watch her as she studied me for a moment before leaning forward and licking a circle around my clit.

It was like being hit by lightning.

"Holy fuck," I said, collapsing on the bed. Honor let out a little chuckle before licking me again, trying out different patterns.

I tried to give her as much direction as I could in my garbled whimpers and moans. She got the idea.

Once Honor had discovered exactly what to do with her tongue to make me scream and curse, she slid one finger inside me as she continued to work at my clit.

I was already so close. "More. Two fingers. Or three," I managed to gasp out.

Honor made a satisfied sound and didn't lift her mouth from my clit as she added a second finger as she pumped her hand in and out of me. Before I could even tell her to curl her fingers, she did so and found my g-spot, sending me rocketing off the bed, and a rush of wetness soaking the blankets.

Really should have put down a towel, but how did I know Honor was going to be so good at this?

I never should have doubted her.

"Are you ready to come?" Honor asked, lifting her head. Her hair was a mess and so was her face. Knowing that I was the reason for the dishevelment was satisfying.

"Yes," I said. "Please make me come, Honor," I said, putting my hand in her hair and then pushing just a little so she'd put her mouth on me again.

Honor chuckled in her throat before sucking my clit into her mouth again and turning up the tempo on her thrusting fingers.

She did something magical with her tongue at the exact same time she pressed against my inner walls and I completely shattered into little bits of starlight. The climax consumed me and wouldn't let go, taking hold of my entire body from head to toe.

Someone was making some very weird sounds and it took forever to realize it was me.

I floated down from the orgasm and still saw little stars when I opened my eyes and took a shuddering breath.

"Am I alive?" I asked, my words coming out like mush.

Honor entered my line of vision. I didn't think I could move my head or anything else right now.

My body was heavy, my skin tingling. Everything was perfect and right, and I was looking into Honor's face.

"Still breathing?" Honor asked, stroking my cheek with damp fingers.

"Think so," I said. "For someone who's never done that, you were extremely good at it."

Honor wiped her mouth and then tucked some of her damp hair behind her ear.

"I watched a lot of porn," she said, and I almost choked.

"Like, more porn than usual?" I asked.

"Little bit. Once I thought about being with you the first time, I couldn't stop thinking about it. I wanted to make sure it was good for you."

"I wouldn't say it was good. I'd use words like 'mind-blowing' and 'life-altering' instead," I said. "You could teach a class."

I patted her shoulder with a floppy hand.

"That's nice to hear," she said. "Being complimented on your oral skills is always a nice ego stroke."

I put my hand in the center of her chest. I'd finally gotten back some of my energy and I was ready to give her everything she'd given me.

"And now it's time for you to experience my skills," I said. Honor moved back so I could sit up and we could trade places.

I cringed at the wet spot and reached under my bed to pull out one of the spare towels I kept down there for sex purposes.

"Should have put this down earlier," I said, and she moved to the side so I could lay out the towel.

"How do you want me?" Honor asked in a low voice, running her hand up her hip.

"Mmm, there are so many options," I said, tapping my finger on my chin. "How do you feel about getting on your knees?"

"In other circumstances, I hate it, but in this context, I love it."

Honor got on her hands and knees and pressed her head to the pillows and put her ass in the air right in front of me, and I didn't know what I'd done to be blessed with this moment, but I was going to enjoy the hell out of it. She still wore the nude-colored underwear and it was time for them to go.

"These are coming off. They're hiding your perfect ass," I said, and she wiggled her hips just a little.

I pulled them down and it took a little maneuvering before I could get them over her feet and off her body.

Once she was fully naked, I got to appreciate her ass.

It was glorious. I wasn't a writer or a poet, but I definitely could have come up with a sonnet about Honor's derriere, if given enough time.

There were a few freckles sprinkled here and there, like pinches of cinnamon on her skin.

I couldn't stop myself from kissing one of them. Honor made a startled sound and then pushed back against me.

"Such a great butt," I said, stroking the spot I'd just kissed.

"I can take credit for that," she said, her entire body trembling.

"Don't worry, I'll take care of you later," I whispered to her butt, and she laughed.

"Who are you talking to?" she asked.

"Can you spread your legs a little bit more for me, babe?" I asked. She did, and I realized that she wasn't at the right angle for me to devour her the way I wanted to, so I pulled one of the pillows off the floor.

"Let me just slide this here," I said, pushing the pillow until she got up on it.

"Much better," I said, stroking up the insides of her thighs. She was already glistening for me and my mouth watered at the thought of tasting her.

I fucking loved oral. Loved it. Would do it every single day if I could. In my opinion, sex was sloppy and messy and weird and that was how it should be. Let me get totally wrecked by sex. Let me ruin a mattress or a couch, I didn't care. It was worth it.

I leaned closer to Honor and kissed her ass again on my way to other destinations. One hand reached and stroked her belly, moving toward her center. Her legs were already shaking, and I loved seeing her so excited and out of control already.

With one hand, I parted her folds in search of her clit. Everything about her here was pink and perfect.

"Of course, you would get a full wax," I said.

"Does that bother you?" she panted.

"Full bush, no hair, and everything in between is fine by me. I don't discriminate."

All of it was good.

"Ready, babe?" I asked.

"Yes, please, fuck," she said and that was all the encouragement I needed to lean in further and completely bury myself in her.

One hand kept me propped up and the other slid two fingers into her slickness. She was practically dripping, and nothing could be better. I listened to every gasp and noise and command as I learned her body, learned what she needed. Honor demanded more fingers, more suction on her clit, and alternating flutters with my tongue.

I didn't care if it took all night and gave me lockjaw, I was going to satisfy this woman. She deserved it. She deserved everything.

"Oh fuck, Layne, I'm so close," she said, reaching back and driving my face even further into her body. I couldn't breathe, but who cared? I slammed my fingers into her and fluttered my tongue and then I felt the orgasm ripple against my fingers as her legs clenched me and her body jerked repeatedly.

I had to come up for air, but I kept fucking her with my fingers until she pushed my hand away and rolled onto her back, her cheeks flushed.

"Your mouth is good at something other than talking," she said, reaching out and tracing her fingers along my lips. I grabbed her fingers and licked them clean.

"That was filthy," she said.

"You liked it," I said, grinning against her fingers.

"I did," she said.

I flopped down on my back next to her.

"Your bed is a mess," Honor said, pulling the pillow out from under her and showing it to me.

"That's what washing machines are for," I said. "You can help me make the bed after round two."

I patted her arm.

"Round two?" she asked, turning to face me.

"Oh, are you not ready to go again?" I asked.

"I didn't know if you'd want to," she said, and I rolled onto my side and stroked her cheek.

"Honor. If I could spend the next week with my face between your legs, I would say that was the best week of my life. I've gotten a taste of you now. I'm officially addicted."

She digested those words and then smiled.

"I like fucking you, too."

WE DID GO for round two, this time using our hands so we could kiss as we finger fucked each other on my bed. After that, we hit the shower and Honor helped me cram the sheets into the washer and put new linens on the bed.

"What does your tattoo mean?" I asked as we tangled our bodies together.

Honor rolled her eyes. "It doesn't mean anything. It means that my mom hates tattoos and I went out when I was sixteen and got it done by a shady dude who didn't flinch when I forged my mother's signature on the form. I flipped through the book and this was the first one I didn't hate."

She looked down at the tattoo, which was a little fuzzy around the edges, I had to admit.

"I like it," I said, wiggling down and putting a kiss right on the tattoo. "Was your mom mad?"

"She went nuclear. It was worth it," she said with a grin.

Her stomach rumbled and her face went red.

"Snack time?" I asked. "It's never too late for snacks."

"Got any brownies?" she asked as she followed me into the kitchen.

"Are we allowed to eat brownies without an apology attached to them?" I asked.

"We can do whatever the fuck we want, babe," I said, opening one of my cabinets and pulling out a box of brownie mix. "They won't be slutty, but we can eat them fresh out of the oven."

Eating warm brownies in bed after amazing sex? Life didn't get better than that.

Honor asked if she could help me, so I had her line the baking dish with parchment and hold it while I poured the batter in and smoothed it out.

It went into the oven and I licked the spoon I'd used to mix.

"Don't tell the twins that I'm doing this. I've put the fear in them about eating raw batter and I don't want to undo that," I said.

"I don't really foresee a situation where it's going to come up, but I promise," she said.

"Speaking of the twins, do you hate them?" I asked. Honor pushed her still-damp hair back from her face.

"No, I don't hate them. I know why you think that. I just don't really know what to do with children. I don't know what to talk about with them. What's appropriate? They're strangers to me," she said.

"We can work with that. They just started getting into comics, and if you talk about movies, you'll probably be a hit. I know they pranked you a bunch of times, but they really are good kids. Mostly."

I had to add that last little bit.

"I suppose," Honor said.

"They're just kids. Until two years ago they both believed in Santa. They're relatively harmless, and once you get to know them, they're great."

I had to stop myself from gushing too much about them.

"Since my mother didn't like me to play with other kids, I only really played and hung out with Lark, and she was…Lark."

I nodded. Lark wasn't like anyone I'd ever met and that was saying something.

"We'll take it small doses. Before you know it, they'll be begging to steal your clothes."

Honor gave me a horrified look. "They can't have any of my clothes."

"They wouldn't fit into them for a few years anyway, calm down," I said, pulling out two glasses for water.

"Do you want some tea or something?" I asked.

"I'd love some tea," she said, so I filled up the kettle and got out cups for us.

"I'm not scared of them," Honor said about the twins.

"I know," I said, trying to reassure her. She was absolutely scared of them, but that was okay.

I'd have a talk with them and tell them to be nice to her.

"So now that your car is in the driveway overnight and everyone in the house is going to see it tomorrow, does this mean that you're okay with telling people? I don't mean driving through town and yelling through a bullhorn, but telling Mark and the kids, and Sadie and my friends?"

Honor gripped the edge of the counter and took a breath before she met my eyes.

"Yes, you can tell people."

"You sure?" I asked. Her white-knuckle grip on my counter was at odds with her words.

Honor stood up and came over to me, cupping my face in both her hands.

"Yes, you can tell people," she said, kissing my lips. "You're going to have to be patient with me. I'm still undoing years of bullshit."

"It's okay," I said, pulling her into a hug, running my hands up and down her back. This woman needed more orgasms, more hugs, and more reassurance in her life. And fun. And brownies.

Definitely less chicken decor.

Honor melted into my hug, sighing softly as I held her.

"You're a really good hugger."

"I'm really good at a lot of things," I said, and she laughed.

The teakettle went off and I had to go deal with it. Honor chose a tea that helped with sleep and I did the same.

"It's nice here," Honor said.

"Well yeah, there's no chickens. And you don't have your sister sleeping in the living room."

She cringed as she added some honey to her tea.

"I'm not insulting your house," I said hurriedly. "Just

maybe that Lark could get a job or something to help you out with the bills and then you might be able to rent somewhere with two bedrooms."

Honor looked down into her cup. "I didn't want her life to be like mine. I wanted something better for her."

I understood where she was coming from. Did I ever.

"She's an adult, though, Honor. She's not a child that you need to protect from the world. You can help her with school, sure, but taking that all on yourself while you're trying to deal with your own shit is going to run you into the ground." Something would have to give.

Honor sighed. "I know you're right, but it pisses me off. Why can't I do it all? Why can't I just win the lottery or something and pay for Lark's college?"

"Does Lark even want to be in college?" From the way she'd talked today, I didn't really get the vibe that she did. That she might have been doing it out of obligation to Honor, which was not a good reason to get into thousands of dollars of debt.

Honor blinked at me. "I guess I never really asked."

"Hold on," I said, putting my hand up. "You didn't ask her if she wanted to go to college?"

"I always told her that I'd pay for it. And that she was going. And I know she used to want to, because she knew it would make our mother angry. She also used to threaten to be a teenage mother, but I guess she didn't follow through on that one."

The timer went off on the oven and I went to check the brownies with a toothpick before deciding they were done and pulling them out to cool on a rack.

"I'm not saying that the only reason she's in college is because she wants to make you happy, but I really think you should talk to her about it," I said.

Honor set her tea down and gave me a smile. "You're just

fucking up absolutely everything, aren't you? Just blowing up my life like a hurricane."

"I'm sorry?" I said, even though I wasn't.

Honor grabbed my chin and pulled me toward her for a kiss.

"Don't be."

∼

I OFFICIALLY DISCOVERED my favorite way to spend time was to have sex, eat brownies, and then have sex again.

Honor and I both needed to work the next day, but that was of little importance. Technically, we had the same boss.

"It's not fair how pretty you are," I said as I stroked her hair. Somehow, it was still perfect. Apparently, Honor was just one of those people who was blessed in the looks department.

"I'm not that pretty," she said, rolling her eyes. "And it's a lot of work."

"You look perfect right now, what are you talking about?"

"Layne. I have breast implants and eyelash extensions and if my mother was still in charge of me, I'd be getting filler and Botox."

"Botox? What the fuck do you need Botox for? You're a baby," I said.

Honor made a face. "I don't think it's appropriate for you to refer to me as a baby in that context when we're naked together. Doesn't seem right."

"Yeah, it felt bad saying it, sorry about that. You need another brownie?" I asked.

"No, I couldn't possibly eat another one," she said, touching her stomach.

"My point is, that it takes effort to look the way I do every day. I'm going to have to get up in," she said, looking at the clock, "two hours and fifteen minutes and start getting ready. I brought everything I'd need."

I wasn't going to lie, the prospect of watching Honor get ready was like being invited into her inner sanctum. I mean, her other inner sanctum.

"Can I watch?" I asked.

"I guess so?" Honor said. "It's not that interesting, I promise you."

"Oh, I think it's going to be very interesting."

Honor laughed. "You are a strange creature, Layne."

"You wouldn't have me any other way," I said.

"Correct," Honor said.

Chapter Eighteen

I KNEW how apply makeup for the rare occasions when I wore it, but there was little else involved in my morning routine. I had a concept of other people taking an hour or more to get ready, but I would always rather sleep or spend that energy on making a big breakfast. Or masturbating.

At first, as Honor started getting ready, she ignored me, but then I asked a few questions and she started narrating what she was doing.

"I feel like I'm filming a tutorial video," Honor said.

"You should. I'd watch it."

"Not my thing," she said, picking up a brush and adding highlighter to her cheekbones.

"I'm afraid one of these days the twins are going to ask me to start a video channel or something and then I'll be roped into saying things like 'like and subscribe!' and then I'll have to quit," I said.

I'd brought a chair into my bathroom so I could observe as she leaned over the counter and studied her reflection in the mirror as she added another layer to her face.

Honor used the fanciest contraption I'd ever seen to give

herself those perfect waves and then it was time for her to dress.

"Zip me up?" she asked, turning her back so I could help her with the gold zipper on her black dress.

I reached the top of the zipper and placed a little kiss on her back.

"All done," I said, and she turned and struck a pose.

"What do you think?" she asked.

I clapped. "Outstanding. Incredible performance. Five stars! Two thumbs up!"

"Shut up," she said, pretending to throw a shoe at me.

I ducked and then gave her a kiss on the cheek. "Now it's my turn." I still had my pajamas on from the night before and my hair was hopelessly tangled.

"Go get dressed," Honor said, smacking me on the ass.

"Oh, do that again," I said, and she did.

"If you don't hurry, we're going to be late," she said as I was about to ask her to smack me a third time and then take me back to bed.

"Ugh, fine. We'll be responsible adults and shit."

I threw on some clothes and brushed my teeth before Honor came to hurry me along by helping with my hair. She brushed and braided it for me while I chugged some coffee and ate the last brownie.

"Don't you judge my choices," I said to her. "What are you going to eat?"

Honor pulled a shaker bottle out of her bag that had a few different colored powders in the bottom.

"What is that?" I asked.

"Breakfast?" she said, going to the fridge and grabbing my almond milk.

She poured it into the bottle and then shook it up in front of me. "Emergency breakfast."

"I could have made you something. Or I can make you something over at the house. You can eat with the twins."

Honor chugged her drink and then shook her head.

"I'll pass," she said. "I don't think I'm ready for that yet."

"They're really not that bad, I promise."

Honor finished her drink and we set off on the "commute" to work that took all of one minute.

We walked into the house together and it was anticlimactic because no one was around.

"Should we call everyone downstairs and make an announcement?" I asked Honor, mostly to see the look of horror on her face.

"Absolutely not," she said.

"Okay. Well, if you change your mind about breakfast, let me know. I have to go wake the twins." I gave her a quick peck before heading up the stairs. I stopped halfway and looked over my shoulder at her.

"You look hot as fuck today," I whispered.

She couldn't hide her smile as she headed to Mark's office.

The twins were hard to get out of bed, and I suspected they'd stayed up late to read again. There were worse reasons for them to lose sleep, so I never snitched on them to Mark.

"Come on, chickens, we need to get ready to go to your mom's," I said.

"Chickens?" Riley said, squinting at me as I pushed her toward the bathroom.

"Sorry, I've had chickens on the brain," I said.

They finally got ready and I pushed them downstairs so I could start breakfast.

Today was cinnamon French toast with cream cheese drizzle, sausage, and fruit salad, and I was pulling out some berries when two people entered the kitchen that I didn't expect.

"Good morning," Sadie said, and I dropped both boxes.

"Mom?!" Riley and Zoey both shrieked at the same time,

leaping up from the couch and running to hug their mother, who wore one of their dad's robes that was too long and dragged along the ground. Her hair was disheveled, and it was obvious that she had spent the night. I gaped at her as Mark rounded the corner, but he wore his regular work clothes.

Riley and Zoey jumped up and down even as Sadie blushed and even Mark was red.

I leaned down to pick up the berries to give them some privacy. I tossed them into a colander to wash and stood up.

"Good morning," I said, my voice squeaking.

"Nice to see you, Layne," Sadie said, running her hand through her tangled hair.

"Nice to see you," I said, pretending this was a thing we did all the time.

I hummed to myself as I washed the berries and the twins chattered away to Sadie before she said she had to go get dressed.

I had the distinct feeling that Honor was hiding, so I excused myself and went to search for her, finding her in Mark's office staring at her computer, but not doing anything.

"Oh my god," I said, closing the door behind me. "Did you see Sadie?"

"Yes," Honor said. "I can't believe their plan worked."

"I can't believe it either," I said. "I don't know if I've ever been this shocked in my life. Except for maybe when you kissed me that first time."

"I shocked myself with that one," she said.

"My mind is officially blown," I said. "I'm supposed to be making breakfast, but I don't know how to deal with this situation." I looked at her and begged with my eyes.

"You want me to come with you," Honor said. It wasn't a question.

"Yes?" I said. "Please?"

Honor leaned back in her chair. "You're lucky you're so cute when you beg."

She stood from her chair and followed me back out to the kitchen.

Riley and Zoey were still excitedly talking to Mark, and I guess Sadie must have gone to get dressed.

"Are we ready for breakfast?" I asked, hating how fake my voice sounded.

"You haven't cooked anything," Riley said, and Mark gave her a look. "What? She hasn't."

"Why don't you go and help her, then?" Mark said, shoving both of them.

I pulled the rest of the ingredients out and started whipping the eggs and half-and-half and spices for the batter.

"Which bread did you need?" Honor asked, and I almost knocked the bowl off the counter. Everything was upside down today.

"Uh, that one," I said, pointing to the loaf she held in her right hand.

Riley and Zoey stared at Honor as if she was an alien. I mean, I guess she was.

"Thanks," I said to Honor as she handed me the bread and then washed her hands in the sink.

"Did you have a sleepover, too?" Riley asked Honor. She flicked her panicked gaze at me.

"Yes," she said. "I had a sleepover at Layne's."

I guess we were telling people now.

"Like Mom's sleepover with Dad?" Zoey asked, and they might be young, but they knew exactly what was going on.

I glanced at Honor and nodded. "Yup. A lot like that."

Riley and Zoey shared a twin look.

"Okay," they said in unison.

∽

HONOR DIDN'T HELP MUCH in the kitchen, but the twins were nice to her, which I appreciated. I guess the pranks were over now.

Mark and Sadie reemerged when I was flipping toast in the pan and the twins were telling Honor about the comic they'd stayed up late last night reading.

She was doing her best to pay attention, but they kept talking over each other and it was a little confusing.

Still, Honor was doing her best and it was really sweet.

"I wish I could stay, but I have to go and open the shop," Sadie said as I handed her a cup of coffee.

"And I need to take you to get your car," Mark said.

"Yes, you do," Sadie said, looking up at him with a smile.

There it was. That fire that they'd always had between them.

"You could just move back in," Riley said.

Sadie almost choked on her coffee. "I think it's a little too early for that, and we are going to need to sit down and talk as a family about how things are going to look going forward. Just because I stayed over doesn't mean we're getting back together."

"We know," the twins said.

"Okay. Then we need to get going. I'll see you both tonight, my loves. Give me hugs." She hugged both of the kids and Mark said he'd be back once he dropped Sadie off.

Then it was just me, and Honor, and Riley, and Zoey.

"I can't live with myself if you end up just having that powdered smoothie thing," I said, adding some food to a plate for Honor.

"You can eat with us," Riley said, pointing at one of the empty chairs that pulled up to the kitchen island.

"Are you going to talk about anything gross or throw a fake bug into my food?" Honor asked.

"No," they both said.

"We're not doing that anymore. We're much more mature," Riley said, and I couldn't look at Honor or else I would have burst out laughing.

"That's good to hear," she said, staring down at her plate, her shoulders shaking subtly.

She was absolutely laughing.

"How's your French toast?" I asked loudly.

"Good," they both said.

Honor finally looked up and she was smiling. I smiled back at her and then she winked.

Yeah, things were going to be fine.

∼

IT SUCKED when I had to take the twins to Sadie's house, but if things worked out, Sadie might end up moving back in and then I wouldn't have to bounce the kids back and forth and I could make Honor take make-out breaks with me in the guest room all the time. And on her lunch breaks, we could sneak over to the guest house for a quickie.

After they talked and speculated about their parents, they wanted to know what had happened with Honor.

"Well, I met her sister and we went out to dinner and then back to her house and I asked her if she wanted to sleep over and she did." That was the tamest version appropriate for younger ears. Sure, the twins had had "the talk" with their parents and several of their friends and classmates were dating, or had their periods, so they weren't complete strangers to the things that adults did with each other.

"Did you have a pillow fight?" Riley asked me as we put together our antipasto plate for lunch with what we had in the fridge. It wasn't authentic, but that didn't really matter. It was the spirit of the thing.

"Sort of," I said. Putting a pillow under Honor to make a better angle for me to tongue fuck her counted, right?

"We had brownies," I said, changing the topic to something more innocent.

"Can we have brownies?" Riley said, her eyes lighting up.

"I want brownies!" Zoey said. "Please?"

There just happened to be two boxes of different brands of mix in the cabinet that I must have bought at some point, so I agreed that could be our afternoon activity. We'd bake two batches and do a taste test to see which brand was better. The twins loved doing things like that.

"Are you going to marry Honor?" Riley asked as I rolled up little slivers of turkey to set them on the tray.

"We just started dating. It's a little too early to think about that," I said, even though an image of Honor in a white dress flitted through my brain.

"But you love her, right?" Zoey asked, her face a mask of concentration as she arranged little balls of mozzarella that kept rolling on the plate we were using.

"I…" I said, trailing off and staring. "I think I do."

"You either love someone or you don't. There's no half-way," Zoey said, with all the wisdom of her eleven years.

Honor. The beautiful, difficult, frustrating, funny, adorable woman that I couldn't stop thinking about. The woman that had infiltrated my book club and my life and then my bed and my heart.

I wouldn't make slutty apology brownies for just anyone. I'd only make them for her.

There had been times last night, when one or both of us had dozed off. Sometimes I'd wake up and see her in my bed and sink into the feeling of how right it was. How wonderful it felt to have her there. I let myself entertain little fantasies about me making her coffee before we walked over to the house together.

We'd hang by the pool on the weekends and join Joy and Sydney for dinner out and book club every month. She'd go to the farmers' market if I was busy with the twins and I'd set out an extra plate for her to eat with the family when she worked late. We'd eat brownies in bed and argue about what to watch and I'd miss her when she went on business trips with Mark.

And someday, if I stopped being a nanny, she and I could get a place of our own. A nice place that didn't have anything to do with chickens. I'd find a new job and kiss her before she left each morning and welcome her home when she came back. Lark might stay with us on her summer breaks, and Liam would come over when he didn't want to cook, hopefully bringing Gwen.

Honor was what I wanted. Having her in my life in every way was what I wanted.

"You're right," I said to Zoey, putting my arm around her. "I do love her. But she doesn't know yet, so I need you to keep it a secret for right now. I'll let you know when I tell her, but she should hear it from me, right?" I asked.

"Right," Zoey said, and Riley nodded.

"If you get married, can we be in the wedding?" Riley asked.

"Of course. I have to have my best girls in my wedding," I said. "But don't start planning it yet."

"It's okay. We're planning Mom and Dad's wedding first," Riley said.

I sighed and lectured them, again, that they shouldn't count their chickens before they'd hatched.

⁓

I FOUND a surprise when I got home from Sadie's and went over to the main house to work on dinner. There was a note from Mark that he had gone out to have dinner with Sadie and that I was off the hook.

I did some cleaning and then wandered back over to the guest house. I almost screamed when I realized someone was already there.

"Jesus Christ, you scared me," I said, one hand on my pounding heart as I turned to see Honor in my kitchen.

"Sorry. I wanted to surprise you," she said, stirring something on my stove.

"Aw, babe, are you making dinner?" I asked.

"I can make one thing, and it's spaghetti. Lark is the cook in our family," she said, pointing with the wooden spoon in her hand.

I walked over and gave her a kiss.

"How was your day?" I asked, snuggling up against her as she stirred the meat sauce. The pasta water was bubbling away, and she tossed in a box of spaghetti noodles.

"It was good. If I said I didn't miss you or spend a lot of time thinking about you, I would be lying."

She kissed me again.

"Same," I said. She smiled at me and my heart skipped a beat.

Fuck, I loved her. I really, truly did.

"Thanks for making dinner. This is a great surprise. I mean, much better than being bludgeoned to death by a traveling serial killer."

She stared at me.

"Sorry, I watched a documentary last week," I said.

She laughed and I told her how the twins had been, and she told me about some of the funny emails she'd answered and then the pasta was done, and she drained it into the sink.

"Lark is thrilled that I'm staying over. She likes having the house to herself," she said as she leaned back to avoid getting blasted in the face with steam.

"So this is all working well for everyone," I said as she shook the colander and then dumped the pasta in with the sauce.

"Yeah, she is basically campaigning for me to move in here so she can take over my bedroom, but I said it was too soon. Right?"

I'd gotten too distracted by her body in that dress and hadn't heard the last few words she'd said.

"Right," I said.

"What did I just say?" Honor asked, putting one hand on her hip.

"Something about Lark and you moving in here," I said. "Sorry, I was too busy looking at your butt. You look too hot in that dress."

I shrugged and Honor snorted. "You're shameless."

"Oh, absolutely. Shame is not something I suffer from."

Honor hadn't been lying about only being able to cook spaghetti, because she'd forgotten completely about sides, so I dumped a salad from a bag into a bowl and added some shredded carrots and quickly toasted some bread with cheese for a side.

"I'm going to talk to Lark about college," Honor said as she used a spoon to twirl a perfect amount of pasta onto her fork.

I'd already splattered sauce onto my shirt about five minutes after we sat down.

"Great, I think it'll be good to sit down and figure out what she really wants. It might be college, and it might not be. She might not know, but giving her space to figure it out is what she needs."

Honor nodded. "I know. I would rather have her be happy than force her into doing something she doesn't want to do just to get revenge on our mother. I need to let that go. I'm also going to think about talking to someone about everything. You helped me see how toxic some of my thoughts were. I knew they were hurting me, but I didn't know how to get out of the cycle of those thoughts and lessons repeating over and over in my head."

I reached across the table and squeezed her hand.

"You don't have to work through everything and figure out everything at once. We're all works in progress."

"I like that way of looking at life," she said. "You know, you're pretty wise for your age."

"Is that a crack about me being older than you?" I asked.

Honor winked. "I've always had a thing for older women."

"Is that so?"

She told me about all the woman crushes she'd had and yep, she had a type.

"You wanna hear my type?" I asked her.

"Tell me," she said.

"Hot and mean," I said and she smacked me on the arm.

"Is that what you think of me?" she said, but she was laughing.

"I mean, you literally wanted me to, so it's just a tribute to your acting skills."

She laughed again. "You're lucky you're hot and good in bed."

I pretended to toss my hair over my shoulder dramatically. "Thank you, thank you very much."

∼

"YOU KNOW, for someone who isn't moving in, you did bring a lot of your stuff," I said as she put some of her things in the bathroom that she'd need the next morning to get ready. We'd just finished dinner and we were both exhausted from barely sleeping the previous night. I definitely had plans for fucking tonight, but sleep was also on the menu.

"I just like having my supplies with me," she said.

I came up behind her and put my arms around her waist, pressing my face into her back.

I loved that I could smell her perfume all over my house.

Honor leaned back against me and sighed, but it was a happy sigh.

"I have to admit, the incredible sex and not having to look at chickens have their appeal," she said, turning and putting her arm around me.

"And the brownies. And the shortened commute," I said. "All definite bonuses."

Honor kissed my temple. "I want to go back and kick myself for holding back for so long. We could have been doing this weeks ago. What a fool."

"You can't be smart about everything," I said, looking into her eyes.

"I'm smart about most things. Not you, though." She ran her fingers through my hair. I'd taken out the braid she'd done for me earlier.

"It's okay. You got there in the end," I said.

"You definitely helped. I was so scared of being with you. I was scared the sex would be bad and then I'd have to see you every day and all you'd think about me was that I was bad at sex." She cringed.

"It's good that didn't happen, so we don't need to worry about it," I said. "Instead of worrying about what if we'd had bad sex, we could be having great sex." I wiggled my eyebrows to make her chuckle and she did.

"You're right."

"I seem to be right a lot lately. Must be those extra years of wisdom I have on you," I said.

"Is that a crack about me being younger?"

I kissed her instead of answering.

∼

HONOR and I ended up in bed a short time later, and we fucked slowly and deeply and the orgasm that hit me was a slow build, like thunder in the distance, but when it struck me, it was all-consuming.

Afterward, we snuggled together, talking about this and that.

"Can you help me come up with some ideas of what I could do for work? I feel like I need a backup plan. Just in case." I'd never really had one before. I'd just been so sure that this nanny job was going to work out, and for the past ten years, it had.

"You could always work at a daycare or a preschool. Or be a substitute teacher, if you wanted to keep working with kids."

I thought about that. "I don't know if I want to work with a bunch of kids, though. They might drive me nuts."

"What about being an aide? You'd be in charge of one kid."

That was an idea.

"Okay, how about jobs that aren't kid-related?"

"There're all kinds of things. You could even work for Mark. There's plenty of things he needs done. I could help you look for personal assistant jobs."

I could also work at the boutique, and Liam would give me a job at the coffeeshop in a heartbeat. There were options, and I felt good about having so many. Just in case.

"You're so casual about it," she said. "I stress out about the future constantly."

"Babe, I pretend that the future isn't happening so it doesn't freak me out. That's not the same thing."

I told her how I'd ignore my own loneliness and fears about the future of my job by reading or heading to the beach or doing anything else.

"We both have our ways of coping with negative shit, and I don't think either of us is great at it," I said.

"You're better, I think," she said. My head was snuggled right on top of her breast, using it as a pillow. Her heartbeat bumped in my ear.

"Does thinking about our future stress you out?" I asked.

"What do you mean?"

I moved so I could see her face. "I know we just started dating, but I want to know what you see. For you and me."

If I was going to tell her I loved her, I at least needed to be somewhat sure she was going to say it back. The worst thing imaginable would be if she didn't say it back or said something like "thank you" and then got up and left and I never saw her again.

"I see," she said, taking a breath and then smiling softly. "I see us going on vacation and arguing about what to pack. I see us having more beach days and snow days. I see us having breakfast together and hanging out with your friends and picking out paint colors and filling our bookshelves. It's as if the minute I let myself, I could imagine so many things with you," she said, almost in awe. "It's like I flipped a switch and opened a whole new world when I let myself think of it with you."

I couldn't stop from kissing her.

"That's exactly what I see," I said, once I could breathe again. "I have something to tell you."

Her eyes went wide with panic. "What?"

"I love you," I said, my voice only shaking a little bit. "I know it's soon and I know it's probably too much, but I wanted you to know."

Honor closed her eyes and then she started laughing.

This was not a reaction I was expecting, and I didn't really know what to do with it.

"Fuck, you can't scare me like that, babe," she said, opening her eyes. "I thought you were going to tell me something terrible."

"I mean, I hope it's not terrible?" I said, starting to panic.

She pulled me down to kiss me again.

"It's not terrible at all, because I love you, too," she said, placing a kiss on the tip of my nose.

"You do?" I asked.

"I do, you maddening, ridiculous, glorious woman. I do."

Those were all nice things to hear. I smiled at her and wanted to do a victory dance, so I jumped up on the bed and started shaking my hips.

"What the hell are you doing?" Honor said, busting out laughing.

"Victory dance!" I said. "Join me."

I held my hand out and she got up on the bed and we danced naked together before she pulled me in and back down to the bed for something much sexier.

Epilogue

"Don't speed," Honor said as she handed Lark the keys to her new car. Technically it was a used car, but it was new to Honor. She'd sold her fancy car and got something cheaper so she could save some more money.

"I know, I know," Lark said, rolling her eyes. "If you don't let me go, I'm going to be late."

"Good luck!" I called.

"Don't need it," Lark said, waving at me as she got in the car and headed out for her job interview at the café with Liam. She was a shoo-in, but still needed to go through the process.

"She's going to be fine," I said, kissing Honor on the cheek. We went inside the house just to check on things. Honor had been staying with me for the past few weeks, so The Chicken Coop was basically Lark's now, and she'd be living here through the rest of the fall and winter since she wasn't going back to school. At least not for the next year until she got some more experience and life under her belt.

Honor had been completely supportive of her wanting to take a break, and the fact that she didn't have to foot the bill for another year of school meant that we had booked our first tropical vacation together in the middle of January and I was counting down the days.

"Shall we?" I asked, and we left The Chicken Coop and got into my car. The bookstore was doing an event with Jack Hill, the famous Maine horror writer, and everyone was going to be there.

Honor was completely integrated into our book club now, and she got along great with Joy and Sydney, once they'd warmed up to her.

I'd seen so many changes in Honor in the past few months, it was astonishing.

She didn't wear her hard shell as much anymore. Her smile was more open and frequent, and she laughed a whole lot more. The twins had even decided she was completely cool, and now begged her to do their makeup and hair and teach them how to dress. They'd even made her a matching friendship bracelet like mine. Honor had grown close with them as well, once she figured out they were just people.

My phone went off with a new notification as I drove, and I asked Honor to check it.

"Your dress shipped," she said.

"Finally. I was starting to panic," I said. Sadie and Mark were officially back together and this Christmas, they would be re-marrying in a beautiful and intimate ceremony at the house, and I was one of the bridesmaids.

The twin's plan to get them alone together had finally broken the ice that had built up between them for years and they realized all the things between them weren't so big after all. They were different people than they were when they first got together, and they'd grown into two people who wanted to share a life and dreams together.

I had to do an intervention with Riley and Zoey when I found them trying to give advice to their other friends who had divorced parents. They didn't seem to understand why their plan couldn't work for everyone and we'd had a long, long talk.

I finally found a parking spot and pulled in.

"Hey," I said turning to face her.

"Hey, what?" she said, not looking up from her phone. "Hurry, we don't want to miss the beginning."

"I just have a question to ask you first," I said.

"What's that?" Honor looked up, and she was so stunning she took my breath away. You'd think I would have gotten used to her beauty by now, but it hit me like a truck every single day.

I leaned toward her.

"Now do you believe?" I asked.

"Believe in what?"

"Do you believe in love?" I asked. That had been my goal, along with getting her to make friends and create a life that was hers and wasn't dictated by the twisted teachings of her mother.

"Oh, Layne," Honor said, reaching for me. Our lips met and she pressed her forehead to mine. "I didn't believe in love until you."

"Mission accomplished," I said, and she laughed.

∼

THANKS SO FOR READING! **Reviews are SO appreciated!** They can be long or short, or even just a star rating.

∼

READ ENCHANTED BY HER, where Joy agrees to pay newcomer to Arrowbridge, Ezra, to be her date to her sister's wedding. Falling for her new fake girlfriend was definitely not in the plan…

Turn the page to read the first chapter!

About Enchanted By Her

I was NOT looking forward to my sister's wedding in the fall. It's just another reminder of how single I am and how much pressure my family is putting on me to "find the one." Don't get me wrong, I'm a hopeless romantic, but all their meddling is making me feel a little murderous.

Then one day a woman walks into the bookshop where I work. She's got a sleeve of tattoos, an undercut, and a smile that makes me want to swoon. Overcome by her hotness, I blurt out a proposal: how would she like to come with me to a wedding and pretend to be my girlfriend?

Turns out Ezra Evans is new to Arrowbridge and she'll do it, but not for free. We shake on it and then I have my very own fake girlfriend and no idea what to do with her. Ezra seems to have plenty of suggestions, many of which make me blush. Things between us heat up even more during the wedding, and I can't stop wondering if this relationship might be something real after all.

"Mom, I'm at work," I said as I answered the phone. I had told her one thousand times to just send me a text message if she needed something, but she always ignored me, as usual. As her youngest, I might be a legal adult, but I was still her baby.

"I know, Joy, but Anna really needs to know if you're bringing a date. She's doing the seating chart on her lunch break," Mom said.

I leaned my forehead against the bookshelf in front of me. I was supposed to be tidying up the shelves, but instead I was fighting with my family again. This argument had been going for weeks, months, even.

Ever since my sister Anna had gotten engaged to her fiancé, Robert, she, my other two older sisters, and my mom, had been breathing down my neck to bring a date.

In their minds, I was poor, single Joy, and if only I was in a committed relationship, I would be happy, and they could stop worrying about me dying alone. It didn't matter if I pointed out that I had two incredible best friends and a job that I loved and a book club I helped run.

Nope, none of that mattered because I didn't have a ring on my finger or a woman on my arm. They were all happily married and they wanted me to have that, too. It wasn't that I didn't want to be in a relationship. I wanted it more than anything. My romance-novel habit had definitely affected my views on romance, and I would love nothing more than to be with someone.

Anytime she wanted to show up, I was ready for her.

"Yes, I have a date," I blurted out, because I was out of patience. If it would get them off my back, I'd say I had a date and worry about the details later.

"You do?" Mom said so loudly that I'm sure everyone in the bookshop, Mainely Books, could hear her.

"Yes," I said, trying to inject my voice with confidence. I

didn't lie to my family. Ever. I just wasn't good at it. I felt too guilty.

This was going to be a challenge.

"Oh Joy, that's wonderful. Well, I can't wait to meet her. I have to go because my break is over, but you call me later and tell me all about it." She hung up before I could say goodbye.

"Fuck," I breathed as I leaned against the shelf again. I should call my mother back and tell her that I'd lied. The guilt was already churning in my stomach like a bad burrito.

Someone tapped me on the shoulder and I looked up to find my boss, Kendra, standing next to me.

"Sorry, sorry. If I didn't answer, she would have blown up my phone," I said, and she just shook her head as she smiled.

"Don't even worry about it. You know how my mom is," she said. Kendra's parents lived in Boston, but she talked to her mom at least once a day and they came up and visited often, so she understood what it was like to be close with your parents.

"I'm not busting you. I just wanted to let you know I'm doing a coffee run and see if you wanted a latte," she said. Kendra and I were the same age and it was nice having a boss that you could also be friends with.

"Yes, please," I said.

"Caramel?" she asked, and I nodded.

"Be right back."

Kendra left and I finished the shelves I was working on as the bell over the door dinged again, announcing a new customer. I turned to offer whomever it was a bright smile and had the breath knocked out of me instead.

The newcomer hadn't seen me yet. She had light-brown hair that was kept half long, and the bottom half was shaved into an undercut. My eyes traveled across her face, which was somewhat obscured by a pair of sunglasses, and flicked next to her right arm, which was almost entirely covered in colorful tattoos. She raised one hand to take her glasses off and I caught a glimpse of knuckle tattoos, but I couldn't make out what they were.

"Can I help you?" I asked, my voice loud in the shop. The hot customer swiveled toward my voice and smiled.

"Not right now, but I'll let you know," she said, her voice deep and slightly rusty. She hooked her sunglasses on the collar of her T-shirt and walked further into the space as I tried to remember how to get oxygen in and out of my lungs.

I pretended to be working on the shelf that I'd just fixed so I could calm myself down. You'd think with plenty of queer people living in Arrowbridge that I would be used to seeing beautiful women all the time, but this one hit me like a truck.

My friend Layne's type, we'd discovered, was "hot and mean," exemplified by her girlfriend Honor that she was completely in love with. My other best friend, Sydney's type was "big tits, low inhibitions."

My type? Tattoos, a hint of danger, an edge of excitement.

Everyone called me the sweet girl, the nice girl. The little sister, the friend, the safe one.

Sometimes I got tired of it.

Finally, I peeled myself away from the shelf and walked around, pretending I was doing something booksellery, but I was really just tracking the hot customer. The door opened and the family that had been in the shop with us left without buying anything, so it was just me and the hot customer. I went back to the counter and fiddled on the computer as she browsed. I'd told her she could ask me if she needed any help, and I didn't want to annoy her out of the shop, so I kept my mouth shut and pretended to be busy.

She disappeared into our romance section and I cheered internally. If she wanted any recommendations, I was ready to pile her arms with books.

As I pretended I wasn't watching her every move, she pulled out three titles and then approached me.

"I'll take these," she said, setting the books down.

"Great," I said. "Did you find what you were looking for?"

My fingers trembled as I turned the books over to scan them.

"I'm not sure. I'll find out when I read them," she said, pulling a card out of the back pocket of her jeans.

"You didn't read the blurbs on the back?" I asked, knowing that she hadn't because I'd been watching her.

"Sometimes I like to be surprised. Life can be too predictable sometimes, don't you think?" she asked, turning her head slightly to the side. She tapped her card to pay and I read the letters inked on her knuckles. LOVE, with the O as a heart instead of a circle.

"I do," I said. "Are you just visiting Arrowbridge?" It took a few tries for me to get the three books into the paper bag with the Mainely Books bookmark and the receipt.

"No, I just moved here, actually. A whole new adventure," she said, taking the bag from me.

Before I could lose my nerve, I had one more question for her.

"How would you like to go to a wedding?"

Find out what happens next…

Afterword

Like this book? Read Just One Night and meet the Castleton Crew where the beach days are hot and the romance is hotter!

Want more Layne and Honor? Sign up for my newsletter and see what happens when Honor plans a surprise getaway for Layne, gain access to free books, bonus chapters, short stories, news, and more!

Reading List

The Headmistress by Milena McKay (Chapter Two)

The Lady's Guide to Celestial Mechanics by Olivia Waite (Chapter Four)

The Seven Husbands of Evelyn Hugo (Chapter Four)

Back in Your Arms by Monica McCallan (Chapter Seven)

About the Author

Chelsea M. Cameron is a New York Times/USA Today/Internationally Best Selling author from Maine who now lives and works in Boston. She's a red velvet cake enthusiast, obsessive tea drinker, former cheerleader, and world's worst video gamer. When not writing, she enjoys watching infomercials, eating brunch in bed, tweeting, and playing fetch with her cat, Sassenach. She has a degree in journalism from the University of Maine, Orono that she promptly abandoned to write about the people in her own head. More often than not, these people turn out to be just as weird as she is.

Connect with her on Twitter, Facebook, Instagram, Bookbub, Goodreads, and her Website.

If you liked this book, please take a few moments to **leave a review**. Authors really appreciate this and it helps new readers find books they might enjoy. Thank you!

Also by Chelsea M. Cameron

The Noctalis Chronicles
Fall and Rise Series
My Favorite Mistake Series
The Surrender Saga
Rules of Love Series
UnWritten
Behind Your Back Series
OTP Series
Brooks (The Benson Brothers)
The Violet Hill Series
Unveiled Attraction
Anyone but You
Didn't Stay in Vegas
Wicked Sweet
Christmas Inn Maine
Bring Her On
The Girl Next Door
Who We Could Be
Castleton Hearts

Kissed By Her is a work of fiction. Names, characters, places and incidents are either the product of the author's imagination or are use fictitiously. Any resemblance to actual persons, living or dead, events, business establishments or locales is entirely coincidental.
No part of this book may be reproduced, scanned or distributed in any printed or electronic form without permission. All rights reserved.
Copyright © 2022 Chelsea M. Cameron
Editing by Laura Helseth
Cover by Chelsea M. Cameron

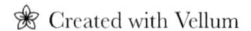

Created with Vellum

Printed in Great Britain
by Amazon